J R Z D V L Z

A Novel

LEE KLEIN

Sagging
Meniscus

Printed in the United States of America.
Set in LTC Garamont with LaTeX.

ISBN: 978-1-944697-32-7 (paperback)
ISBN: 978-1-944697-33-4 (ebook)
Library of Congress Control Number: 2017943620

Sagging Meniscus Press
web: http://www.saggingmeniscus.com/
email: info@saggingmeniscus.com

"A Mob's a Monster; Heads enough, but no Brains"

—*Benjamin Franklin, Poor Richard's Almanack, 1747*

J

R

Z

D

V

L

Z

CONTENTS

Note to the Reader

Streaks of phosphorus, a reptilian chicken, a hybrid of man, rat, and heron with the horns of a ram and the sculpted physique of a dumbbell enthusiast … an unkempt crowd paid a dime to see something along these lines, a weird and horrific beast sure to force squeals from deep inside them, but when the threadbare curtain rose, they laughed. My story could begin with a curtain rising on a pathetic rendition of me in February 1909, and then I could describe what happened to the animal onstage, slathered in green paint, a pair of antlers atop its head, makeshift wings across its back, heavy-buckled shoes on its paws. Or I could begin in mid-January 1909 when headlines in New York and Chicago proclaimed "New Jersey on alert! Mass hysteria!" after a snowy week yielded hundreds of sightings of a retriever-sized rat with wings and a chirping bark, a Jabberwock with eyes like blazing coal, a beast of fur and feathers with the face of a German Shepherd. My story could begin with reports filed for every supernatural encounter just five days after the largest New Jersey Pine Barrens landowner died on January 11, 1909, a man who dreamed of channeling freshwater from an enormous aquifer beneath his land to every faucet in his choleric hometown of Philadelphia. Or I could begin my story nearly a hundred years later, with my final appearance in beast form—an eyewitness account of which a prestigious national magazine published a few years ago, inspiring me to set the record straight. Or I could begin, quite naturally, on the day of my most unnatural birth, when I, the thirteenth child of Mowas Leeds, de-

1

voured my family (save one sibling) moments after my arrival into this
world on the night of a raging nor' easter toward the end of October, 1735.

A composite of thirteen beasts in a single body, a chimerical advance on the ancient Chimera, or perhaps no more than a prank of a famous early American, I've arranged this story as I am. Yet even after
compressing some two hundred and seventy-five years into something re-
sembling a straightforward progression, I feel the need to apologize for its
form. Maybe my unusual shape and the persistent repercussions of unfortunate early experience make me yearn for start-at-the-start/end-at-
the-end convention? Stiff and flightless, my wings like pungent drapes,
my tail an ancient and inanimate cable of flesh, at this point I believe
an unassuming storyline accurately portrays the convolutions of truth.
You may prefer a more monstrous monster, of course, a gargantuan brute
who stalks with Cyclopean single-mindedness scrumptious human beings like yourself. If so, please realize that what follows relates a tender creature's quest for a semblance of acceptance. As such, instead of
introducing myself as some apoplectic fiend, I hope these apologies prepare you for the storms and silences to come. A unique creature, or so I
once thought, I've stitched together this undulating composite of memory,
conjecture, speculation, projection, hearsay, fantasy, and fact. Whenever
encountered in beast form, like the brightest stars of a constellation, my
parts were recognized before the whole: similarly, as elements of this story
accrue and come alive in your imagination, if you sense a reasonably co-
herent human spirit rise from the words, I'll have successfully reclaimed
the complexities of my life from the simplifications of legend.

Adam Merriweather
2017

Accursed Birth

SOLDIER EMERGED from the cave of night. He stood at my mother's door and gasped with dehydration and hunger, though his stomach did not seem hollow.

"Please keep me till dawn," he said. "I've lost my fellow sentries. A strange cry in these pines, as though legions of abysmal phantasms formed a choir and merged their voices into a single sound."

"My husband lately crossed the bogs to the west never to return," my mother said. "Maybe this cry felled him?"

"Such coincidence must be linked to the beast we pursue."

"A beast?" she said.

"An unseen threat against which the Crown cannot defend. We shake as though from cold despite warmth in the air."

"Wandering in the dark only improves thy state by chance. Settle in as we heat soup for comfort."

"I extend the security of my presence on such a horrid night."

"It was peaceful before you appeared," my mother said.

"Until I heard the beast's wounded, diabolic howl. Without a notion of its presence I would conclude myself mad to perceive such clamor."

How fantastic for my mother Mowas to entertain a man offering security and intimations of what might have happened to her husband: not face down in the tide but fated to encounter this

3

scream, perhaps no more than a transparent shimmer that sliced the air and enveloped man and beast in unknown and inescapable space.

The soldier described subterranean expanses beneath the pines. In these endless lairs in limestone rock, a beast that roamed long ago may endure. Perhaps now, with so many arrived from across the ocean, some unseen enemy defended its home.

"Could this beast be related to those impressions they found last summer after the floods?" said Mowas. "Those colossal prints of claws?"

"They have dug around those sites and there found evidence of an unfathomable behemoth, its snout like that of a mallard, but wingless, with a backbone and tail as long as from here to the path out front."

"A relative of this monster could still be alive?" she said.

"If it exists, like so many monsters it may only wish to inhabit a paradise beyond the incursions of man, and so when threatened it strikes to restore its isolation."

My mother's eldest son asked to spend the night on guard. His hands held axes. But Mowas sent him to sleep, saying the soldier would keep the peace.

Her eldest daughter delivered a warm bowl to my mother, who thanked her and handed it to the soldier, who blew at its steaming surface. Relief entered his eyes as the broth calmed his blood.

"Care for your sisters and brothers," Mowas said to my doomed half-sister, "and once they're asleep put yourself to bed and forget all you have heard. The morning shall restore our safety, and this good soldier shall protect us tonight."

They whispered once alone. The night was cool and quiet. They sat side by side, uncommonly alert. She said she felt not much grief for her lost husband. Life on the salt marsh with a dozen children had turned her into an impression in stone herself.

"And might you ever return to life?" the soldier said.

"Doubtful."

"It is a time for the improbable, perhaps."

He seemed restored, and considering the threat at large, my mother was not wary. She welcomed this man. His unleveled accent soothed her.

The soldier held her, an arm around her shoulders. He pressed his side to hers.

"We must be strong and alive," he said, "and not yield to temptation that does not make us stronger and more vital. Your strength is clear, so let's bring life to your blood." He kissed her cheek. She froze. He turned her, found her mouth, warmed and wet it, and made her smile.

She was no longer in control. He led her into the pines. She wanted his weight on her, and then she had it.

Another child was soon inside her. She told her husband's brother about the soldier and what he had said. Daniel Leeds told others and soon word passed through Estellville and beyond. She was jeered for falling for this soldier's tale, succumbing to a loyal militiaman.

A pale pastor appeared who threatened her, who could not make her dispel her belief in the unseen, who scoffed at the idea of an enormous beast, who when cursed by Mowas informed her that the child she carried would be born a devil. The beast the soldier mentioned, his words would manifest inside her as artful manipulation transformed into terrible fact.

"End the life of this child now," the pastor said, "and your own life, too, before we do it ourselves."

My mother's eldest son, Japhet, was armed with an ax. At her brother-in-law's house, they related the pastor's threats. Titan, Daniel's son, composed a tract against this righteous man who sought to replicate the witch hunts of Salem, who blurred the distinction between church and occult, his belief in both too strong to champion integrity or strength of mind, a purveyor of impossibilities all honest insight must reject.

What mattered most was protection of Mowas, abandoned by Daniel's brother, manipulated by a crafty soldier of the Crown. Fears he instilled in her mind as he discerned her weaknesses and worked on them, as wicked as any devil. They agreed to unite against iniquities perpetrated by representatives of colonial oppression.

A squadron of the humblest sort guarded Mowas's home. They surrounded it in a brambly obstruction so any evil seeking entry had to breach what now seemed a fortress. Those who supported the extraction of Mowas Leeds and her unborn child, those loyal to no force beyond their fear, heard of this armed formation and decided to wait and see. Perhaps those around her compound would beat back the devil she delivered, the militia protecting the colony from Mowas Leeds herself.

All remained stable until an October night when a cruel nor'easter forced the men guarding the house to seek shelter, abandoning their post despite imminent entry into the world of the cursed child Mowas carried.

II

The midwives saw in the candlelight my mother suffering as never before, shrieking so each in attendance remembered the tale of that beast in the pines. They thought the soldier perhaps had only heard a woman giving birth, cursing, even forming sounds that seemed to say *Let this thirteenth child be born a devil if I am released from this pain.*

Her last newborn had slipped from her with no more than squinted eyes. But now poor Mowas would not survive if this continued. So much breath escaped with each scream it must have emptied her, the atmosphere charged with passion, expressions so contorted they sent currents of cruel air bursting off the walls as the gale hammered the shutters and daggers of rain pierced the roof.

My mother pushed and prayed and cursed and bartered for release from the force inside her. Midwives squeezed her soaking hands as I breeched. My voice joined my mother's cries. The midwives cleaned me and placed me on my mother's chest.

Nothing is more traumatic than the first moments of life. Everything ahead. The shock of first light. Pushing, pulling, no control. Heartbeat quickens, hysterical birthing body, wailing far off, muted. Snip of the cord, blurry vision, senses opening, first breaths.

My mother's expression transformed from relief to horror as my shape shifted: softest skin turned scaly, long leathery wings burst from my shoulders, a tail extended as long and as hairless as a rat's, my cute little newborn face elongated and nostrils flared as gummy black jowls like a retriever's formed to imperfectly conceal the sharpest teeth.

My wings spread to shade the room from candlelight. My claws entered the midwife who first touched me. I consumed her, as well as her colleagues, before I feasted on the body that had made me. As sentimental as a rampaging warrior, I flew down the steps toward my brothers and sisters. I devoured every last one until carnage was all there was.

I eyed the chimney and shot into the storm.

Need for comfort insulted by a howl into my newborn face. Reasonable post-partum terror, I now suppose. What was there to do but use claws and consume the entirety of their insides? These Leeds so liquidy fresh. Each heart a still-beating delicacy surrounded by lungs so light on the tongue. My first tastes.

One, two, three, four, I lost count, so many, each smaller than the last, easier to open and devour, and then into the open air, rainwashed clean, leathery wings responding to winds, firing me away, but where?

I soared to see how my body responded, above the clouds, a universe of stars, unbridgeable distance, breathing difficult, flying upward, up. I descended under intermittent flashing to make a life in cool rain and mist. Disordered, seething terrain. Where to stop, if ever, and retreat, away from those I had bloodied, who overburdened my light body in flight. Down to the river, an overhang of rock, a safe place to recover before the first day of a life of sorrow.

Oh why, I wondered. Sense formed as swiftly as my body transformed. The first woman who touched me did not deserve what I did. Those other women, children, brothers, sisters: mistakes I made. Mountainous debt. Regret, regret, my first sensible thought. All I wanted was to make amends for lost control.

But what if mother and midwives had cooed? What if they had placed my snout to a breast while humming a soothing song, caressing the stripe between my curling ram horns? Would I have acted differently if they had acted differently?

I was all reaction: surging blood, primal disorder, unable to compose myself until all else calmed. Beneath an overhang of rock, salty tears from glowing red eyes, the sun risen, I tucked my snout into wings to sleep, but I could not sleep.

In the red-tea river water I saw a reflection—in the center of those glowing eyes, pools of blue, solitary, repentant, sorrowful, the most human part of this animal composite that originated the language I heard in my head, this inaudible internal speech.

I tried to speak but only snorted. A wail muffled by shame. Like an automatic apology, endless lament streamed at once, an unintelligible expression of pain, regret, apology, a narrow blast of hope that penance might restore original innocence.

Two weeks of regret in the wilderness beneath an overhang of rock, subsisting on rabbits and birds, lonely, curious, I elevated over parcels tended by farmers. Easy meals of livestock. In and around Estellville, all forms of humanity tempted me to see if they were brothers and sisters too.

The house where I was born had boards on windows and doors. Limbs had fallen across the entrance in the brambly obstruction, blocking the entry of anyone on foot.

I returned down the chimney. The carnage had been cleared but the floors were still streaked. This would have been my home, the youngest of thirteen, or so I later learned.

Nostrils as sensitive as a bloodhound's, I took up the scent of those who cleaned the house, sniffed along the path, followed tracks these men had made.

I soared atop an extraordinary oak. Its limbs were thick, each fanning to create a space beneath suited for meditation, the way air hangs in a cathedral. They would reduce it to timber no sooner than Winchester Abbey might be quarried for stones.

In nearby printing quarters, two young men labored, bound by blood and duty, to announce what had happened on the day of the birth of Mowas Leeds's thirteenth son. They planned to present the impossible as absolute fact. They worked as though all lives depended upon it.

"I cannot see returning to calendars and trifling practicalities after pushing this account into the world," said Titan.

The cousins, each on either side of the press's bed, lay type, watching an account stabilize in letters. Disordered reality, shock, impassioned attempts at articulation of an impossible scene retold and transcribed into flowing pen strokes on parchment, as ordered and unassuming as any affectionate expression if standing above it. But closer to the page, each word came into focus and revealed such horrors.

"It becomes easier to believe when set in type," said Japhet. "These words put our family to rest."

"Yet gashes of fear shall open in readers. How I envy their current state."

"But better to recognize the threat."

"Reports arrive of slaughtered livestock, unfamiliar prints. Something is present, I am sure of it."

"We are devoted," Titan said. "For my cousins I dedicate these pages before we join the hunt to avenge them."

They would not see me if they stepped from their printing quarters and considered the crown of the royal oak. But a hundred yards away, perhaps. So much made so little sense but I comprehended their words. In exchange for my strange shape, I had received such comprehension, as well as extraordinary endowments of hearing, smell, sight, and access to the thoughts and feelings of certain humans for whom I had an affinity. Streaming thoughts and feelings resonated as though they were my own. But an uncommon swerve indicated they were not my own. My mind on free wander, shades of sense and images arrived that had no place in my memory, and yet I could ignore them no more than that which I saw and heard.

"If you read this account in Poor Richard's, would you think it a hoax, akin to the account of witch trials in Mount Holly? We must make it clear that we are honest."

"We present this account with no more sensation than we find in it," said Titan.

"I would disbelieve myself but dare not. I now perceive a world charged with the potential for inordinate violence."

"But do you believe what Dr. Thorpe and I say about the fleeing beast? The midwives sent me through the worst moments of the storm to run for him and as we galloped in return we saw it shoot from the chimney into the night."

"I believe it if you saw it."

"And I was not alone."

"No, Japhet, you were not alone. Farmers also attest to glowing eyes at the edge of the wilderness."

"Our work may bring this devil some peace."

I was a man whose form was unfortunate, disordered, a deformed composite. But not a devil, even if my actions were devilish. Perhaps if I spoke to them?

III

Silently I swooped, landing on hooves, my heron-like legs springy, my leathery wings spread wider than the printing quarters' breadth. My eldest brother and cousin laid out letters that recounted my tragic arrival. Perhaps these men might understand that I would never again open another chest and suck the organs out.

I tried to introduce myself in a calming, diplomatic tone: "Dear brother Japhet and cousin Titan, please realize there is no need to hunt me, for I am not a threat, I should not be held accountable for regrettable actions, for what I did to our family, I am repentant, and would like to atone and do good, so please help me perhaps achieve that goal, my brother, my cousin, having no father and now, unfortunately, no mother, I ask you to shelter me and raise me as an odd sibling."

All these words traveled from mind to mouth at once. A horrifying screech forced their arms to disrupt the bed of type. They careened against the far wall and, lacking a more perfect articulation for their fright, screamed as well.

"No, no, hush, no," I said—or tried to say—"I only mean to make amends."

I screeched in a way I hoped might indicate a complicated soul, though such comprehension seemed overshadowed by what stood before them.

Japhet recovered first. He grabbed a musket and prayed aloud that it was packed. It clicked. He searched for powder and ball.

Titan fell to the floor. He stared dumbstruck. By the time either man regained speech, I had flapped my horrid wings and disappeared.

Armed with an axe and a musket loaded with ammunition, they stepped from the printing quarters, savoring this step as the last of their lives, expecting me to secure them to my soft furry underbelly with my long tail like a constricting snake, fly them over the ocean, and drop them among the white caps. But they survived that first step, meeting only morning silence and a stillness charged with terror.

"A new Man of Signs," said Titan.

"A what?" Japhet whispered.

"We must undertake a new Man of Signs," said Titan. "Every aspect of the beast seems like some distortion of the astrological visages of bull, ram, crab, fish, scorpion—bat, rat, dog, horse, crane, even what they call *the kangaroo*."

"A horrid joke of a beast, a hideous yet almost humorous assemblage."

"Yes," said Titan, "we must repair the text and describe this weird fiend in detail."

Titan's father, Daniel, made his way to them. His hair was steely. A taste for cranberry wine had made him heavy. Youth had been lost in all respects except in eyes capable of sympathy and sorrow.

"Who screamed?" he said as he rambled into the quarters, ready to mete out blows.

"We both," replied his son, "but you also heard the beast."

"You did not destroy it?"

"We must keep the musket loaded," said Japhet.

"We need guards day and night," said Titan, "as we describe the vision seared in our memories. We will depict it, print it, and disperse this knowledge as soon as possible. It will be our final publication, freely distributed, and then we will commit ourselves to defense against this beast."

"Better to wield words as weapon and warning," said Daniel.

"We will warn and then hunt, and perhaps when the threat is ended return to what once was, if serenity may ever again exist."

When Pastor Dade heard that Mowas Leeds's newborn had not been found, he claimed it had been born a devil, as prophesied—bastard spawn of a British soldier, spurred by the mother's insolence, cursed by the community entire. Yet all remaining Leeds believed that the newborn, like its mother, siblings, and the midwives, had all been victims—otherwise they were related to a monster on the loose.

The printing quarters were guarded by a dozen armed men, the perimeter of the Leeds's home surrounded. If the Leeds sought to profit from their encounter, to capitalize on horror, skepticism may have halved the militia. But with no mind for profit, belief in their words and actions spread, as did alarm.

The fear had once been of witches, although most now believed those unfortunate women were victims of injustice and that simple eccentricities did not merit such a fate. But my appearance outside the printing quarters, the sight they saw was real. They focused on my legs. All else may have been elaborate costume, but those spindly, springy legs, appropriate on some avian marsh predator, coated in the rubbery hide of a littleneck clam, each limb was far too thin to hide a human leg, whereas the torso was too short to conceal even a teenager on peculiarly pliable stilts. The screech belonged to an unidentifiable animal, as well, a sound with direct access to bones and blood.

An impossible fact before their eyes, indubitable, unbelievable. Perhaps the water of this New World caused collective psychosis. That was the only sane possibility: everyone was mad.

Pastor Dade of Estellville appeared grim, prideful, straight-backed. Crossing the clearing in front of Daniel Leeds's home, he was armed with an aura of righteousness, a rectitude that might compel even the most industrious and upright, such as Titan, to relinquish benevolence in pursuit of sin.

"He comes," Titan said as he rested in the shadow of an oak.

Japhet emerged from the printing quarters as though he had sensed Dade's appearance from far off. "Dade," he said. The surname alone carried the sting of an epithet.

"Dade," Titan said, and he spat.

With each step, Dade seemed to need to pull each foot from some deep penetration in the ground. Titan would not sit in shadowed grass if Dade occupied the same yard. He stood to meet this intruder, and with each step he became stronger, confronted by this moral leader who cursed his family for sheltering the enemy.

"Dade," said Titan. "An honor."

"Titan Leeds, a pleasure, as always, to greet one of the country's most renowned printers of almanacs. I see you still haven't fallen dead per Poor Richard's predictions."

"Alive, if not well, as you are here now, but not welcome."

"Very good, very good. As fluent as ever when it comes to wasteful words. A master articulator of insult," said Dade with exaggerated smugness.

"Let's be done with you," said Titan.

I had been napping in my new home, cradled in the crown of the royal oak, after a night flight in search of sustenance to the barrier islands, unpopulated dunes along the coast where gulls and the occasional pelican succumbed to the velocity of my hunger. The batting white eyelash of the surf reflected the moon, and this calmed me, made me believe that life was possible alone, but then curiosity surged and before dawn I returned to visit those who hunted me.

Usually the tree rang with hundreds of birds, but now it was silent thanks to my presence. From my vantage, I saw my cousin Titan confront a man dressed all in black.

"You have amassed men and arms, I see," said Dade, "but such force cannot contain supernatural energies."

"Do you come with another curse? Your last was a success."

"Blame the beast, not me."

"Did you not curse poor Mowas?"

"I cursed her actions, not the woman."

"Leave this land before I turn the men against you."

"I am a man of peace."

"Wielding terror."

Japhet joined Titan and stared as though his eyes alone might end Dade's life.

"A terrible thing you witnessed," Dade said, "the most terrible tragedy I have lived through in this country."

"I don't remember your presence that night," said Japhet. "It is a shame you could not replace any of my brothers and sisters. Even Odd William."

"Such tongues in this family," said Dade. "Worthy allies, if only you might direct your scorn at the beast, the devil child, the monster."

"What then do you offer us?" said Titan. "It seems neither arms nor comfort."

"I wield a power uncommon among men."

"We are familiar with it."

"If you let me, perhaps I can help in some small measure."

Securing Dade's promise that he would not disturb them, Titan and Japhet returned to work while Dade stood like a bulwark against the imperfections of arms.

Dade appeared each morning, standing among them and yet apart. He was as regular a presence as the sun that daily lost strength. Winds swept trees clean as the pages of Titan Leeds's final publication were blown by messengers across the territory. An image of me appeared on one page with arrows leading from descriptions of my disparate features. A complete transcript of Japhet's account followed, supported by Dr. Thorpe, that recounted the horrors they'd encountered, news much of the territory had heard by word of mouth and thereafter used to explain the disappearance of livestock, strange sights, eccentric behavior, sickness, fires.

Once upon a dark time, if lightning struck a house it burned freely as those with water watched. Such were the Lord's wishes: the owners of the house deserved punishment. But now they blamed this devil of Leeds Point, which they believed controlled the land before even the Indians settled it, this beast that sought to reclaim its territories from indulgent Englishmen. Atop the oak, I heard that some were calling for all settlers to return to the Crown, to leave this land to its dragon. Others hoped to slay the beast and savor a hero's spoils (hoarded maidens and piles of gold). The two months of sea travel that separated the colonies from Europe had sent these men thousands of years back in time. Thanks to my birth, they now seemed to live in a legendary era.

Every word I heard referred to me and separated me from my fellow men. The supernatural presence of horns and wings, tail and hooves, disrupted commonalities of feeling and thought. But now, as its leaves fell, the oak was less able to shield me from view. I saw my breath as though it streamed with smoke. Scales and wings kept me warm, but when it rained I longed for warmth. I hid in outhouses most nights as the weather turned, sleeping with an ear out for sleep-dazed wanderers in need of relief. Accentuation of scent seemed an essential aspect of my penance.

Leaves all down, spending nights in outhouses, I wished to prove my worth and redeem myself to those who met at my family's home, armed themselves there, and then investigated claims, footprints, slaughtered animals, disappeared children. I could attain such an exceptional height that someone on the ground might think me an eagle, but uncontrollable curiosity and a nascent taste for risk compelled another appearance.

Guards on duty either slept or occupied themselves in endless chatter. Such a waste of speech. Blessed with half their ability I would set myself right with everyone and protect the territory from every threat. Oh how I would help them if only they comprehended my speech. This elder Daniel to whom they defer, perhaps he might have some patience with me.

His house seemed identical to that of my birth. I slipped down the chimney. I climbed the steps in silence. I heard snoring, the loudest from a room with door ajar. I poked it open with the end of my snout. I feared my steady beating heart would wake them. Whatever life I had, better it end than not attempt this.

Daniel slept alone, still on his side of the small bed, preserving his late wife's impression in the mattress. Beside the bed a sheet had fallen. I cut two slits in it with a fingernail and let the rest fall over my body. Wings packed tight behind me, tail coiled best I could, all the words I wanted to say gathered in my lungs. I shut my mouth so not to lose my words and disturb the sleeper. I allowed the least bit of breath to escape through my teeth.

"Pssst," I said. "Pssst."

The sleeper stirred but did not wake.

I tried again, this time nudging the bed with my body. "Pssst."

"What? What?" said Daniel, his eyes opening. Confronted with a standing bedsheet, he seemed to think he was still asleep.

"Shhh," I said. "I come in peace."

"Are you not some dream?"

"Do not alert the others. Let them sleep and awake tomorrow safe."

"If I am asleep," Daniel said, "let this nightmare end."

"You understand me."

"Your voice is unlike any I've heard, though I have never heard a bedsheet speak. Perhaps my pillow would speak in tones more soothing than your disturbed rasps."

"It is a great joy."

"Tell me your name, oh most peculiar bedsheet."

"I am called 'The Beast,' a living dragon, the accursed devil of Leeds."

"No name at birth?"

"No more than screams."

"But why should I believe you are not one of my grandchildren having some fun? If you are the beast you claim to be, reveal yourself, and if you promise not to consume me, I promise not to alarm anyone."

"I am not a grandson, but a sort of nephew, though my father wasn't your brother."

"Before I grow impatient, pull the sheet from yourself."

"Reactions have not varied, I warn you."

"If you do not drop the sheet, your mother will punish you till the return of spring."

I spread my wings and the bedsheet rose and fell to the floor.

"I am scared beyond belief. Egads! Titan's descriptions inspired such a costume, surely. Now let me sleep."

"Sadly, it is I. Repentant sinner, damned, accursed, humbly asking forgiveness."

"For so horrid a beast you speak with earnestness and passion. But why trust you?"

"Grandfather?" a young voice said—a girl rubbed her eyes and stood in the doorway. "You talk in your sleep again."

I turned toward the voice to see a child no taller than the door handle, in night gown, hair tangled with sleep.

All the tension of this contact transformed when I saw her. I lost control of my voice. Endless beseechment sprang from my mouth in a screech. The girl was unhappy with the sight and the sound. Daniel then took up a sort of sphere he kept by his bedside and hurled it at me, striking the side of my snout. The girl stumbled toward the stairs, and I moved toward her. I was stunned by the sphere that hit me, that loosened a tooth. She might fall down the stairs, I thought, as I stumbled, my legs unsteady, unbalanced. I fell toward the girl, righted myself, crouched, wings spread in the narrow landing at the top of the stairs. I reached for the girl and attempted a soothing word but it came out wrong, all at once again, accompanied by spread wings and outstretched claws. The child flung herself down the stairs as Daniel stood and aimed another throw that ricocheted off my leathery wings. I dove for the girl, catching her before she hit her head on a step, but I caught her in my claws, never having touched a human, and the girl screamed, as much from fright as pain. Traces of blood appeared where I had touched her. At the top of the stairs Titan and Japhet and their wives emerged. Japhet aimed a musket but hesitated before firing for fear of hitting the girl, and in that second I escaped up the chimney.

Open air, an hour until morning, shots fired, a searing incision where wing meets back, I tumbled, more shots, torches, another ball in my body, in my meaty rump.

"Cease your fire, I come in peace, to help however I can," I tried but words came in a rush. My failure to express myself in human speech forced me to run at the nearest musket and cut its bearer's throat with a swipe. Another raised his weapon and I leapt into the air, landing on his head, which I removed like a cork from a bottle. I feared I would have to battle them all. Pain surged, as well as regret at escalating the carnage of my birth night. Eyes shining red, I heard a scream unlike any ever, and now another assailant ran at me, more shots, one hitting the man who had screamed. I ended his misery with a claw to the neck, and looking down I saw it was Titan.

Never a chance to undo this. Let them come. If one thinks he might kill me, let him be a hero.

Men charged and fired, hitting each other too often with unsteady shots. Those who made it close to me lost their lives.

Terrible-tasting men, I spat out their flesh. After a minute of battle, those who fancied themselves valorous discovered how much they valued their lives. They retreated to watch from the edges of the clearing.

And then Dade, with torch in one hand and book in the other, strode toward where I sighed, a breathless, bloodied monster.

Speaking to me and all those who might retell his words, Dade raised his voice: "O cursed and infernal beast, I brought you to life, I control thee. I am your lord and master, friend and devotee of all that is good. Thy murderous tendencies know no future in this country. Begone! Begone! Accursed beast! Satan's spawn if not Satan himself! Begone one hundred years, and only return helpless and humbled! Begone, one hundred years gone! Oh beast of Leeds, hear me and begone!"

I would grant all those living time to die in peace, my tale ascending into legend as I hid along the barrier islands, perfecting speech and taking time from trying to connect with men unready to confront my form.

I ran faster than any beast on earth, wings searing, unable to carry me into air.

"Begone, begone," said Dade, and I was gone.

Widow of the Island

F THROUGH POWERFUL SPYGLASSES those aboard tall-ships and ketches saw me off the coast of the long and narrow barrier island, they would attribute the sight to sea sickness, lens distortion, shimmering oases. One hundred fifty years to improve speech, heal heart and head, make peace if not with men then at least with myself. I flew and fished, made friends with a special gull. I dug a pit in the sand and covered it with a roof of driftwood protected with clamshells. There I practiced my speech, tried out the words I heard in my head, said each as often as I could to my fearless bewinged friend. I only say this gull was *special* because all others kept their distance. This one seemed fearless, perhaps because its brains were rattled from screwing its head to one side as though to better comprehend my speech. My happiest moments from that era were when the gull cackled, as though it sensed my language had improved, when my words rolled and crashed and withdrew into others, inspired by the sea. This gull offered more companionship than I deserved in exile. I needed time to strengthen my resolve to ensure that my eloquence one day calmed those as yet unborn. Five generations would advance humanity until all children were born with innate respect for beings like me, surely.

Each year I saw more traffic off the coast. Excursions along the long and narrow island revealed settlements of fishermen to the south who sometimes explored the north but never noticed my home. If I ever encountered a man and communicated with one, I doubt I would have been able to screech, for day after endless day repeated in silence until I saw a woman along the shore.

She wore a long white gown that trailed beyond her like receding surf. I dared not come out of hiding, believing that the pastor had truly banished me. *Begone, begone, a hundred years gone* reverberated daily, but had a hundred years passed? Trees had risen, only to fall during storms. Weather had cycled, but how many times? Had I tripled my sentence? Each morning this woman walked along the shore. As she neared, I disappeared, shy, guarding my solitude in my clamshell lair. I heard her song but when I peeked from my burrow I did not see the mouth from which her song emerged. A body occupied the long white gown, it seemed, a white hat with a healthy brim and bow, a white veil, too, but I could not see through it, the mesh making it seem empty. I detected bodily curvature, but through the veil I saw nothing, not a hint of chin or nose or cheeks or eyes. Still, her song kept me company. It was an easy song, without words, overheard from lips I could not see. I figured her face was as drawn and as narrow as the island itself, her cheeks the color of pale, smooth sand.

There was a primness as she walked, her dress indistinguishable from the foaming surf. The sun rose and cast above my head and then set beyond the bay and mainland a step south, rising lower, the weather colder, then warmer, and each day in the morning the woman passed and again in the evening she returned to wherever she had left, the same every day for several cycles of hot and cold. Other than the greenflies and the occasional gull, I counted her as a sort of friend.

I followed her from a distance one summer afternoon, compelled by an impulse to discover her home. Did she just walk all day, every day, the whole island, back and forth, resting at either end an hour before carrying on north or south again, singing that same melody? What an odd woman, I thought as I followed her, flying high above the shore so the train of her dress looked like the tail of a comet. I hadn't flown over the southern parts of the island in some time, but it did not surprise me to see many small homes there, each with its sandy yard. Off from the main square of the settlement on the island, I watched from above as the woman walked from the shore though a cleft in the dunes to a house almost reclaimed by sand.

I waited for the sun to drop over the horizon. At dusk I soared lower, seeing that the first level of the house had been covered in sand, its windows boarded other than a side door and another on a third-story balcony from which she emerged to hold a lit lantern, standing straight, not singing, facing the sea, hat always on.

Each night for years I followed the woman and each night she stood on the balcony holding a lantern, staring at the ocean. She stood there even in terrible storms, soaked, hat on head, veil over her face like a sturdy curtain.

I longed to contact her but could not. It would have been like disturbing the sun.

How many years passed I do not know, but whatever pressure within me that kept me so long on the island one day released. I flew over the mainland, exploring the endless pines, hovering over the cities of Philadelphia and New York, amazed at the density. Oh to settle atop a rooftop among those squat water towers, the open-air washing and soot. I walked the streets at night and did not stir a soul, no one even glanced my way. But I wanted an expanse of pines and sand, and before long, near my birthplace, I found myself attracted to an enormous construction, isolated from the world.

The house did not seem abandoned. One night outside it I found a rabbit chained to a pole, the words *For you* on a sign. The occupant of the house had chained a rabbit like a fisherman who pushed a raft out on a pond and dropped a baited hook into the water, hoping to catch a behemoth. I did not know what this fisherman intended to do when the line stretched ahead and pulled him under.

The man did not see me remove the first rabbit, I now know, though he discovered odd prints in the spot he had cleared of grass in the hope of finding such evidence.

The next night he stayed up, but snoozed at the critical time. Again he missed the rabbit's end.

The next night I swooped in, I gulped the rabbit down, licked my chops, and left.

He did not disbelieve his eyes. The next night, the same. Perhaps he thought I had lost my legendary aggressiveness. But if I attacked him, what better way to die?

I hovered out of sight behind the house. The sun slanted though western windows. Calm, quiet, a bowl of water at his desk. He removed his glasses, wet his handkerchief, and ran it across his eyes. He hesitated lighting lamps but did so to reread what he had written.

Clear and moonless, the sky absorbed the color of the surrounding pines. In those last moments before complete darkness, he visited his rabbit pen and picked out a sacrifice: the fluffiest charmer of a lop-eared Londoner. If presented at a county fair, it would win awards for girth and grace, its nose so twitchy even the callous would call it cute. I was glad he offered it tonight.

A rabbit's life is dedicated to the detection of threat. A quivering ball of tenderness, its mind is committed to its body's continuation, a minor, automatic part compared to what's devoted to fear. Long oval ears shoot fear through flesh the same for a snapped twig as the approach of owl or fox. Nose and whiskers, the nerve center of fear, register disturbances like a bat's radar. Great leaping abilities, of course, though the man had fattened his rabbits so those powerful legs couldn't lift their bodies far off the ground. With added girth, their threat-detection skills became more precise. His rabbits shivered on warm autumn days at the clamor of falling leaves. No chance of escape from omnipresent threats made these rabbits cute, cuddly balls of constant alarm.

Night fully arrived, the man sat in a simple wood chair on the porch, eyes moist, sucking back his breath, afraid of alarming me with too excited a huff. The specially chosen lop-eared Londoner was chained out front.

I crouched out of sight in a tree. A bat flitted and disappeared. No other monsters. So soft the night. He brought out a blanket, pulled it to his eyes. His back seemed sore and, from constant repositioning, it seemed his buttocks had gone numb, which was favorable, perhaps, because otherwise he might drift to sleep before I consumed the rabbit.

Blanket over nose, hat on head—its brim greasy from a decade of touches—slanted over his forehead, and through that slit between brim and blanket, clarified by glasses, he observed the animal as it registered an unusual disturbance. For hours, the pure-white, lop-eared Londoner had sat there, pink eyes open but otherwise calm. Now its ears rotated and rose as high as they went. The nose surpassed its usual curious state to something more like alarm. Some combination of sound and smell sent its legs a message to flee.

It tried to rise. It hopped, heavily, a baby step toward the man, away from the threat it perceived. Another burdened hop toward the porch. And another. Midway through the next the chain went taut. The rabbit sounded terminal alarm. Its tail turned toward the woods, and perhaps for a moment it felt safe. Or maybe the chain and collar and the inability of its body to fulfill natural instinct paralyzed it. The only place it could flee was to a space inside itself so close to sleep it resembled living death.

As the rabbit like a fishing bobber signaled something near, the old man removed blanket and hat. His brow was bald and spotted, a long gray collar of hair on his jacket's shoulders. He revealed himself so not to startle me when I appeared. Treat it as a man, he'd thought, and it will be a man. Treat it as an animal and it will attack as an animal.

He treated me like an animal by offering a live meal, but once I appeared he treated me like an esteemed visitor. I needed him, he knew, for he needed me. It was not the first time such creatures had found mutual comfort.

The rabbit did its best to disappear, escaping its fear like a child covering eyes with small soft palms. It came as close as it could to nonexistence, still as a stone. He heard the snapping of an enormous towel, a musty, whooshy flapping, and there I was. He later told me he'd thought at first I resembled a disfigured sprite, but once I opened my wings again I was gorgeous, an angel descended from family lore.

When young, he had heard of a beast in the pines banished more than a hundred years ago. He identified with the story of a son who had damaged his family and set off into the wild.

I watched him on the porch and sniffed at the rabbit. Ears up, hopping away but held back by a chain, it nearly hanged itself in mid-air.

"If you are the one who puts out these rabbits," I said, "I thank you."

I emitted these words without excessive rasp. He neither seemed fearful nor able to reply. I wondered whether my first words to a human since last I spoke to Daniel Leeds were understood.

"Thank you," I said. Again he seemed not to have heard.

He stood and stepped toward me on the porch.

"Do you understand?" I said.

"It's not a matter of understanding," he said. No more than five feet from me, he held his blanket like the cape of an amateur bullfighter. "If I throw this blanket over what I see, it will fall straight to the ground. It's a matter of belief."

"You understand me?"

"As any man," he said.

"My heart soars."

"My head spins."

I licked back excess saliva. "You raised these rabbits?"

"I hope they appease your hunger. My flesh, by the way, is old and bitter."

"Except at birth, I have never devoured someone unprovoked."

29

"I only hope you accept an offer of friendship. I am old and alone and familiar with your story, though I'm sure you have histories that escaped family lore."

"All I know is what I've overheard," I said.

"Then we have talk ahead that will interest you. But first, a feast."

He pointed at the lop-eared Londoner that seemed calmed by the conversation, not understanding a word.

"Will we share it?" I said.

"Save me a foot for good luck."

I tore the animal from its chain. I pulled a long, meatless legbone from my mouth and snapped it at the ankle.

"I'll set it out to dry and clean, thank you," he said. "Quite a sight. You devoured an animal in seconds that took much longer to fatten."

"Your time was worth it," I said, breathless and bloodied around the jowls.

He offered his blanket. I used it to wipe fur from my mouth. He then invited me inside for tea.

"I have never tried it."

"A relaxing stimulant."

A world was opening. I stepped uneasily inside the house.

The house in which I had been born could have fit in the main room here. Daniel Leeds's house could have fit in one of the unfurnished rooms I saw down the hall. Larner held a hand lantern. For now, all I saw in the windows were reflections of man and beast, each the same size in body, though my horns and wings made the man seem smaller. I did not know how my height rose and fell with each step. So much spring in these legs. My body around the middle was as full as Larner's, but his skin was wrinkled and soft. Cheeks as round as the lenses of his glasses, each circle of flesh drooped like some viscous substance that had settled over time.

His gait was slow and even and considered, as though his natural state were horizontal, not vertical. Hat now off, his forehead was slanted like a steep hill, lined with gullies, freckles, and spots.

I had only been indoors twice before. This time I would only attack if tricked to trust this man who then unleashed a trap.

He made his way to a desk toward the rear of the room. I raised myself off the ground, stretched out my neck, and lifted my snout to sniff potential lurkers: dust, mothballs, candle wax, mildew, cobwebs, lantern oil, the husks of rabbits I had devoured. Any saboteurs had disguised their scent against my most developed talent.

He lit a candelabrum. The room revealed portraits and landscapes, oils in heavy frames, old dusty books on shelves from ceiling to floor. I'd like to see him reach for one of those high volumes. I hadn't yet laughed in my life but I'd heard these pleasurable barks. Maybe it was something I needed to practice, just as it took so long to control my voice. Since stepping into this cavernous estate I felt something like mirth arise inside me, maybe related to having what might be a friend lighting a candelabrum and offering a seat.

"Sit?" I said. The chair seemed comfortable for a man with a traditional rump more than a ten-foot tail.

"Yes. Please do. Sit. Perch? Make yourself comfortable."

I approached the chair. I stood on its seat. I crouched, leaned back, wings folded, tail coiled. "I have never sat," I said.

"I'll teach you whatever you would like."

"Much to learn," I said.

"All these books are yours to study. In them, you will discover commonalities more than differences, especially in the epics and myths you seem to have stepped from as naturally as you entered my home. Does this interest you? Or have I overshot my hope? I did not expect for this night to begin as such. I expected it to end much earlier, and terribly."

"But you had no weapon?"

"Let me show you the letter I wrote before nightfall."

He held up a sheet and pointed to his signature.

"Our studies may as well commence with the letters of my name. It is Vance Larner, see it here. If I read this to you, you will know why I sat and waited for you, ready to be struck down, but hoping for a happier end."

He leaned on his desk, the pages close to the flames, nearly enough to set his writing alight. As he read, I emphasized his pauses with huffs and snorts.

"These may be the last words, an affirmation of years alone on this estate. My mind is as clear as ever—I am sure of this—free of missteps in the travel of thoughts. Yet what follows is an account of a beast believed in only by the young, the deluded, and the old seeking to scare the young. My visitor is the long-standing threat of these lands. I saw it alive last night. Tonight I will attempt to contact the beast. If it destroys me, it shall be months before a traveler finds my remains and this note. It is a peculiar endeavor to write of one's imminent manslaughter, but I am unafraid. If the beast I have seen is unreal, I am physically safe yet doomed to an uncertain mental future. If it is real and greets me with violence, such an end will prove my cogency. No one of sound mind would befriend this beast, of course. Anyone who valued life would barricade doors or escape in daylight and only return with armed witnesses. Instead, I will contact this being who I believe may be a relative. Such coordination of movement among its composite parts, wings and tail and snout, claws and hooves, an unfamiliar torso of short golden hair. So unlike any man, so unlike my father or mother, whose own father I believe was the son of the beast's father's first wife. My mother passed the story to me of a family descended into madness and neglect and lore after my great-grandmother fled the colonial Jersey coast. The thirteenth son of my great-grandmother's first husband's second wife, now known as the Leeds Devil, is not my blood relation, but the focus of enough shared history to make me think of beastly features in myself. I am man in form but in spaces concealed we are otherwise similar. Such exaggeration derives from gratuitous introspection. Whoever languishes in thoughtful reenactment of the past falls prey to cruel beasts. Memory is louder when alone. No roar shall match the one inside me untamed by healthful solitude. If tonight I meet my end, I am willing. And if an end does not come, if this remarkable beast and I protect one another from sorrow, tonight will redeem me. I am responsible for my actions, past and future. Now I only hope that the present hours pass so I may once more engage the world, even if it costs me my life."

I asked if he could prove the link between us.

"The last Genuine Leeds Almanack was never published for wide distribution," he said. "All copies are believed lost long ago. But this one remains, long declared a hoax in attempt to quiet an uprising of rumor. It mentions the disappearance of William Leeds, whose wife and two sons had left him, whereupon he engendered a dozen children with another woman before leaving his family shortly before the horrors they experienced. A look at the pages he published in early almanacs reveals an unhinged mind. But if one proceeds from an acceptance of the man's sanity, if read in terms of the initial stages of the struggle for independence, the words change shape. Courage and meaning emerge. I trust my great-grandfather was sane, for a thread of him runs through me. And I trust I too am sane. Your presence here confirms it."

I snorted. *Sanity based on my presence.* Was this what it felt like to laugh?

"Glad to be of service," I said.

Larner smiled. I felt a surging unknown when still. Soaring, yes, I knew that feeling. All I wanted now was to see this smile again.

But then the suns of his eyes seemed overcast. A depressive front steamed from his brow and descended across his vision.

"My god," Larner said. "If my wife and children could see me now. Years of hard work, steady earning, homelife disappointment, all led to this night."

Once upon a time, he said, he had been someone who had more than he needed, who could no longer endure the demands of Manhattan, including wife and children who rebelled at every turn and unnaturally aged him. His wife, their two sons and three daughters, and all their spouses and children—the immediate family was like some multi-headed dragon. *Disrespectful* was not the word for how they had treated him. *Disgraceful* was better. They expected luxury as one relies on the daily rising sun. If he had been more volatile and blasted them, or if he had been more a miser and withheld affection and praise, or positioned himself miles above them and condescended like a midsummer thunderstorm, it may have been different.

He had been soft, sensitive, silent, acquiescent, almost servile until he sent them up the coast one summer and left a note at home explaining where upon their return they would find sufficient funds for consecutive lifetimes of indulgence.

Money had been attracted to him as though by magnets, yet having been born into it, he never seemed to have a need for it. His persistent dream had been to free himself of omnipresent desire around him. Or at least attain the open stretches of time the last decade in the pines had provided. For a decade now, he raised livestock and made irregular excursions to Philadelphia for books and other essentials required to pass the days alone. A Swede had built the house with the hope of turning the region into a retreat for anyone with money attracted to the endless protection of millions of pines. But no one came other than a handful of friends who stayed for free during autumn masquerades.

Education would make me more of a man, Larner said, and I wanted that more than anything, not yet secure in my own odd skin. Cursed at birth et cetera. As I told Larner about the Pastor who had banished me, I watched as lore alighted as real life.

It was nearly dawn. We neither yawned nor lost our animation. Night grayed as the candles dropped. Day rose like crystalline water, enhanced by thick panes of glass imported from Sweden, a land Larner said was mostly ice.

"But why did you venture from the island?" said Larner.

Slowly releasing the rush of words that came to mind, I told him of my clamshell home and creeping development along the southern coast and bay. I mentioned the woman who walked along the beach every day and stood on the balcony holding an unlit lantern through storms.

"I wanted to talk to her but how?" I said. "She had no face, and yet she sang."

I listed my other companions over the years: wind, sand, salt, seaweed, sun, stars, surf, crabs, clams, gulls whose courage I rewarded with scraps of food. Storms, too, I described, great sets of waves, low tides, red seas. I released a century's worth of impressions of a world that had been my only companion. The mysterious woman who walked along the shore, singing, veiled, holding an unlit lantern, faceless, Larner recognized as the widow of a sailor whose ship had crashed along the island's northernmost rocks. The entry to the bay was treacherous, so now ships preferred the southern inlet, but it took many disasters before the lesson was learned. Lore had it that a widow walked the beach in search of her lost sailor.

"But why without face or head?" he said. "That's not part of the legend."

He said there was another legend about a pirate decapitated after helping Blackbeard bury treasure along the northern coast. But this woman was not a pirate. Why would she be headless? And why would she walk the beach forever? And how, without a head to hold a pair of eyes, would she manage to see her husband return from the waters? And if this sailor saw her, even if his skin were stripped by thousands of fish and his bones were encrusted with barnacles, how would he feel to emerge from icy ocean water after so many years to see this woman without a head waiting for him? Would he recognize her? Or, thanks to her fidelity, would he overlook the fact that she now had no head?

We slept most of the next day. Larner did, at least. I needed only an intermittent hour. Not so with an old man who spent the day snoring as I explored the house, the longest time ever spent inside. It seemed like a labyrinth of endless corridors in which space expanded and with it a sense of possibility. It was like living inside the royal oak I had spent so much time atop on Daniel Leeds's land, a long trunk with numerous branches, a place that seemed to have a life of its own—a mind, too, and not a cordial one.

I was sure the house had it in for me, manipulating me toward some unforeseen pitfall. This Larner lured monsters with delectable rabbits, seduced them with friendship and kind words as the monster, like all monsters, stepped from monsterhood toward, it hoped, a semblance of human decency. The host then let his prey wander his endless home and caught the gullible monster in a trap of disorientation.

Outside, whenever lost, I soared and established my position from above. I was not yet frantic enough to burst through a window, that is, if I could—the Swedish glass seemed so thick an attempt to break it might prove fatal, even for me. Through the walls Larner's faint ALLOOOs sounded like they originated inside me, achy vibrations in my bones, felt more than heard. If this was what it meant to be a man—to build such terribly branching hallways, to banish and curse, to seek and destroy, to differentiate like this—why learn their ways, study their language, emulate their behavior? Much better to spend time with the greenflies and gulls that worshipped me, the maggots in salt-wet driftwood, the gleaming curves of porpoises, the holy sight of a whale breaching the ocean surface, its spout and spray more serviceable and beneficent than that remarkably odd and varied species that referred to itself as *humanity*.

"ALLOOO!"

What if I panicked and punished Larner for failing to warn me of the house's complexities? How ridiculous to survive the night only to have his home incite, by architectural idiosyncrasy, his end? Larner had surely imagined a more strapping beast, with pectoral muscles like a pair of shields, a neck of ropey veins, vibrant brick-colored skin, more a traditional Satan than this ungainly miscellany trapped in its body like the most uncomfortable man.

"ALLLOOOOO!"

I moved in the direction of his voice but came no closer to it. At first I had sensed bemused appreciation for whatever drew me to this estate. Toward the center of the pines I should stay, venture deeper into it, and more thoroughly enclose myself from those unwilling to accept such an unfamiliar configuration of limbs and skin. A shriek formed within me. Lost in the contorted wings of the house, there was no escape. An hour ago it had seemed a sanctuary, not a living hell. My human heart (autopsy would reveal it) pumped desperation as it restrained a shockwave that would charge these corridors with terror. I sounded like a whipped dog. A scared dependent creature. And hearing it, registering it, an exhalation fogged the air in front of me as though my breath were smoke. A living dragon, they said. If only fire burst from my lungs . . .

Larner called ALLOOO. There I was, a child lost in some crowded marketplace as evening fell and the faces of vendors turned gruesome in the lantern light. I ran claws across my head as though shearing myself, wings back, tail coiled and tucked between heron-like legs.

"Allooo," quietly now, "allooooo," more like *shush shush* to ease discomfort. "Allloooo, all's well, all's well, I should have warned you from wandering this way. This must be more than you can handle so soon upon ending your exile."

How soft the voice, yet all was less than fine. I never expected to display such sensitivities to my new companion. Better to roar and keep him from stroking the stripe of fur across my forehead.

Impossible to trust someone who took me seriously, who offered sympathy as though he derived pleasure only from placation.

I attempted a short roar. But too accustomed to sighs, I chortled, as though I had mastered at last the art of laughter.

"We'll take a trip," he said, "We'll call on the veiled woman, bring her flowers, woo her perhaps, see if she can't teach us a thing or two."

I envisioned open travel on land with Larner, trees the only walls on either side of the road.

Late September light—sky and rivers letting out a last gasp—opened a door through which I imagined a more beautiful life. Larner's own father had not made it past his present age, he told me. His mother had gone a decade before that. Rarely did one reach winter, let alone the depths of autumn. Yet Larner claimed he already occupied the afterlife. I was evidence of his ascent.

II

I must have seemed like a walking armoire, wearing scarves, coats, a braided jacket across my shoulders, a hat cut open to accommodate my horns, old boots on my hooves, the soles removed, the uppermost leather tied to my legs with rope. I saw the world through peepholes in a simple mask. I wanted to raise my wings without dislodging the many satiny capes draped across my back. I was Larner's guard, dressed like an exploded wardrobe.

The mist brightened but did not burn off. Once we hit the road to Umbria to the southeast, it was a straight shot from there to the island. A web of sand trails crossed these parts. No maps tracked their layout other than in travelers' memories.

Not far from Umbria we met morning sorts, messengers and laborers and farmers. None seemed to notice us until a man stood in the road. He wore faded black clothes so tight they seemed fused to his skin. He had no meat on him, other than a ropey waggle neck. His arms seemed longer than average, the exposed wrists and forearms scabbed and bruised.

"Tax," the man said. "Tax to travel these roads."

"You cannot tax what you do not own."

"To keep you safe."

"From what?" Larner said.

"Pay now or regret."

Larner whispered to the wardrobe beside him: "What do you say?"

"Walk on," I said.

"What masked clothing seeks to pass?"

"It is my dear friend, Mr. Merriweather," said Larner. "Burned in a fire not long ago, he must wear fabric rubbed with soothing lard and herbs."

"Show the burn or both shall wear funeral shrouds."

The man revealed in each hand a small blade.

"Now, now," said Larner. "If Mr. Merriweather reveals himself, you will cause no trouble?"

"We must be sure he's no escaped prisoner or kidnapped kid."

"Mr. Merriweather, it is your choice," Larner said. "Shall we sport him a trifle or show him what had once been your hand?"

This man who demanded taxes reminded me of Dade, though worse off. The eyes were sunken and his exposed scalp was reptilian, the flesh like sunbaked earth. He seemed in misery. Yet he was accepted as human, no matter how he maintained his humanity.

I could overcome our obstacle with a swipe. We could be on our way. But it's better to become human via humane treatment of humans. Even such a questionable one.

I worked a claw out from a sleeve of the braided coat.

"Does this please you?" Larner said.

My fingers were long and overknuckled. At each end were conical nails, sharp and thick, more like horns than fingertips. I clicked their ends together.

The man leaned in to inspect my hand. I aimed a finger at his nose.

"I trust you'll let us pass," said Larner. "Quite a misfortune for Mr. Merriweather here, but as you can see, misfortune is often accompanied by unforeseen benefits, such as protection from bandits on the path to Umbria."

The man stashed his blades in his belt, behind his back. "Fires turn hands to that?"

I snapped my hornfingers and pointed the longest now at the man's heart. "We owe you no answers," Larner said. "Let us pass."

"Or pay with your life." I let some rasp enter my voice. I regretted the threat, but I enjoyed the pulse of anger, the risen strip of skin along the uppermost part of my spine.

"Anyone asks, tell 'em you okay by Branley. Way is paid. Your way is paid."

"Thank you, kind sir," said Larner.

I returned my hand beneath its garments and growled to speed the man along.

Larner stopped me and whispered: "He may slip around an unknown path and gather a posse to meet us in Umbria. We must move now in secret."

I unfurled my wings and the garments fell to the ground.

"Lie upon the sturdiest cape," I said.

I took up its corners and tied them together so he lay bundled in a makeshift sack. I wrapped my tail several times around the knot and secured it in my claws, and then I spread my wings.

In the distance, pines gave way to beach and water. In the other direction was the tower of Larner's home, the path we'd been walking, perhaps even the man we encountered, scampering to Umbria. "Mr. Merriweather" could drop Larner far below to the underbrush, but he trusted me. He could have ordered me to dispatch the thief. A sickly meal. Those purple wrists. An intruder upon the race of man, more so than someone with horns, wings, and scaly skin.

My wings open and strong, flapping a few times and then soaring as we descended, our path through the air rising, rising, and falling though clouds. Wet with mist, we saw silent breakers on the coast, boats in the bay, a tall cargo ship perhaps conveying the widow's century-old husband lost at sea.

Larner, if he fell through the fabric of the cape, his bones would snap, never to appear in the stories of grandsons, the heirloom legends. His own mother had brought such life to the stories. When she told of the nor'easter the night the thirteenth son of Mowas Leeds was born, young Larner smelled the rain that lashed his cheeks and saw lines of liquidy steel travel parallel to the ground. When she said the words *lightning flashed*, he covered his ears ahead of the thunder. He closed his eyes from fear when she told of the beast feasting on its mother, the midwives, and the children before shooting up the chimney and into the rain, washed clean of gore.

Larner now peeked over the edge of a cape, as though in the basket of a one-man airship, and heard the surf as I brought him down gently on a dune.

The cape sprawled open and Larner rolled onto sand and grasses. We made it in a fraction of the time it would have taken in wagon and ferry. And we made it apparently undetected. No armada waited off shore, cannonballs pounding the dunes, skiffs filled with men intent on capturing and displaying me for profit.

Tumultuous surf pulled back from flattened land, leaving a glassy stretch that lightened until salt-spray and foam slid shoreward again before it pulled back again, tumbling shells and driftwood toward the horizon.

"Have you flown me to the moon?" said Larner. He had never visited the ocean here, needing no rest from his island in that ocean of pine.

Sand moved more than one thought. With no one to dig out the excess, the hole where I had stayed was almost filled. The clamshell roof had fallen. Not much of a sanctuary.

Larner studied me now in the open light of day. I could tell he thought I seemed weathered. The flesh of my face was covered in fine short hair beneath which it seemed scaly, neither mammal nor reptile. My wings were smooth, pale, nearly transparent flesh.

We stood there in silence as he looked at my spread wings.

"Have you always been this way, Mr. Merriweather?"

"This name brings me joy, but is it my first or last name?"

"We could say the first is *Merry* and the last is *Weather*?"

We started along the shore toward the widow's house. Larner walked easily while I stood straight, my senses, like those of the rabbits I had devoured, set to detect the least threat.

"You trusted I would not drop you," I said.

"I worried more that the capes had been weakened by moths or wear unknown."

"Ended by a moth, your whole long life. It is terrible, yet I find it amusing," I said.

"A marvel how you mirror my speech. Part ram, horse, kangaroo, pterodactyl, and apparently part parrot too," he laughed. "In your mouth, protected by such teeth, no doubt one may find a chameleon in place of a tongue."

We walked to the south. Some boats on the horizon were too far off to discern us.

"Much more to go?" Larner said.

"Shall we fly?"

The sun overhead was a pale orange disc, the clouds more like smoke than anything innocent, gray celestial vapors beyond which it was surely blue, and beyond that all was more difficult to understand than my existence on this beach.

We walked along the flat sheen between shore break and beach until I started toward the house. It was half-consumed by sand, or protected by it like bulwarks against storm seas.

"From that balcony there she waits each night with a lantern," I said.

"How come no brave soul interprets the light as an alarm, the woman signaling for help as her house sinks into the sand?"

"It is possible she does not exist."

"Do you believe that?" Larner said.

"We will see if we enter the house."

"You are brave now."

"Your company makes me so," I said.

We walked to what we assumed was a second-story window— no telling how many stories lay beneath the sand. It could have been a tall tower once, only its uppermost reaches now exposed. It must have been glorious.

The windows were shuttered but unlatched. We stepped into the shadows. The floorboards had warped. It smelled musty, briny, like dried seaweed, in places sulfurous. Undulating yellow bands seemed to hang in the air.

"I detect an underlying scent of seagull corpse," said Larner.

"No one is home," I said, "but her presence settles on my skin like dense fog."

"No man senses such things. Consider yourself lucky."

"Or cursed."

Upstairs, there was a large open room, empty of everything other than doors that opened on a view of the sea. I cracked one and then the other. Sea air rushed in and Larner's fear decreased.

"It feels like being on a ship run aground," he said. "It will sink beneath the surface thanks to our weight."

"Just an abandoned house on the coast," I said.

"Maybe the sailor returned and they left for a distant shore?"

"Every night she returned and stood on this balcony, even through the worst storms. If I had imagined her, she must still reside in my mind. If I see her and you do not we will discover her origin."

"A scientific experiment that only requires a night awaiting the supernatural," said Larner.

Afternoon sun revealed blue sky. Far over the ocean, tremendous clouds stirred white capes and surf. From the balcony, we watched the shore to the north, waiting for the breakers to assume the shape of a gown. The sun moved behind the house—we would not see it set from where we were. Throughout the afternoon, like a gunship on the horizon, a steel-gray storm—in places black— signaled distress. We did not mention these dark formations or interpret the lightning. We were too far away to hear thunder. We enjoyed its entertainment, thankful it had missed us by miles. The house would have withstood such a storm, protected by the dunes that devoured it. Protected, threatened. It was almost night.

"She should come soon," I said.

"I hope she brings a sandwich or some salted fish."

"Can you make it?"

"I can subsist on this." Larner's hands cupped either side of a generous midsection. "And you?"

"That last rabbit should suffice."

"We failed to remember flowers, chocolates, trinkets to win her affection."

"I have nothing to offer except my curiosity," I said. "And maybe she once somehow heard me imitate her."

I listened for her song but only heard the primitive rhythm of my heart.

And then I crouched, wings back, head lowered, tail coiled. Larner crouched, too, peering over the shaky banister.

"Quiet now," I whispered.

" 'Tis her?"

"Shh. Hear now?"

"Nothing."

"Listen."

Larner tilted his head toward what he hoped might be a melody. "Nothing," he said.

"The side entrance."

Larner covered his mouth with his hand. He seemed aware that he was crouched on the balcony of a sinking shore house, accompanied by a speaking beast descended from family lore, awaiting the arrival of a headless widow whose song he could not hear thanks to insufficient human senses but that seemed to pervade the air and vibrate my bones. The porch doors were still open. Inside, the house was darker than the moonless night. But then the darkness brightened.

I nudged Larner to the northern corner where we waited. I opened my wings and overwhelmed the salt air with the scent of my leathery flesh.

III

A white walking gown raising a lantern lit with aromatic oil: it was difficult to tell if she saw us. Larner heard her song now, faint as it was, muffled by the tulle of her dress. Her presence was ghostly, the gown occupied by an apparently gorgeous form, the veil as empty as ever supported by an unseen shape. We stood against the banister, like ants in amber. She held the lantern and did not waver. Entranced, unable to break the spell, we waited for one another to take action. But her unmoving silence sent thoughts reeling. Possessed by her ritual, drawing her lost love from the surf, so completely did she inhabit the past she did not notice that visitors had appeared in the present. I understood her longing. We both searched for a man: she for her husband and me for the one I would have been had I not transformed at birth.

Larner was a detection device who alerted me to the presence of the unusual. "This sight makes you seem common," he whispered.

I controlled the rush of breath that might have poured from me unrestrained. "I will take that as a compliment."

"Not only headless," Larner said, "but handless. The lantern emerges from her sleeves."

"Animated only by sorrow and desire."

"Perhaps one of your impressive fingers might poke her?"

"Why should *I* poke her?" I said.

"You are my protector, are you not?"

"It's just a dress," I said.

"Then poke."

I pulled a weathered post from under the railing and pressed its end toward where a thigh might be. The board dented the dress without resistance.

Larner nodded. I stepped ahead. There was no end to the board's entry.

"More dress than damsel," he said.

I scraped the board along the balcony's floor, scooted it under the dress, and then lifted.

"Raise it higher," he said.

I raised the dress. The lantern did not waver.

"Now remove the lantern from her grasp," Larner said.

I gave Larner a look of disappointment.

"You take the lantern," I said. "At the least movement I will hurl her into the sea."

A rounded handle emerged from the glass bell of the lantern before it disappeared into the dress's sleeve. Larner ran his hand along the handle's edge, held it tight, and yanked, perhaps too hard, expecting resistance. It gave like the gray head of a dandelion.

Larner put down the lamp as the dress's arm slowly dropped.

"Now what?" he said.

"All these years as she glided along the water I felt we shared a search for innocence lost, she in her dress, pure and serene, me in these wings and weird heron legs, awkward and cursed. I expected to meet her tonight."

"Then it follows," Larner said, "that the dress is an outer wear of innocence. Beneath it, your wings and scales can be comfortable and unseen."

"Are you saying I wear a dress that walks by itself?"

"Is it not possible that you—my dear Mr. Merriweather—are the sailor she seeks?"

I never once thought her lost sailor was someone like me.

"You say you seek innocence," Larner said. "Here is a garment worn by the pure."

"But I am not a woman."

"I ask you, Mr. Merriweather, do you take this gown to be your wife?"

"Oh really now," I said.

"Until death parts you. And if you cannot die, well, until the dress becomes a yellowed shred of fabric. For now, raise her over your head. The train shall hide your tail as the veil obscures your face."

His back to the sea, lightning far off, Larner lifted the lantern high and directed me to stand to the right of the dress.

"My dear Mr. Merriweather, do you, a man of remarkable appearance and extraordinary history, cursed by the community while still inside your mother, cursed at birth by your own mother, cursed by nature to transform and commit acts of unspeakable instinct, do you, Mr. Merriweather, my only remaining friend on earth—if this darkened beach is not some sliver of the afterlife artfully imitating seashore—do you take this bodiless embodiment of innocence that traveled the beach and stood on this balcony for a century, not in search of some lost sailor per legend, but to lure you as a bird's plumage attracts its mate? This gown wears its innocence upon its sleeves and will take not your hand in its hand—it being

49

a dress without hands and you being a beast with intimidating horns for fingers—instead it offers its every inch as cover for your current form, what you deem a misfortunate compendium—*do you, Mr. Merriweather,* take as your lawfully wedded wife—as lawfully as my pronouncement and this lantern allow, with the surf and night sky behind me on one side and the country stretching ahead on the other as witnesses—will you pull this dress over your head and let courage animate the dress the same as the spirit that presented it to us this evening? *Do you, Mr. Merriweather,* accept this dress and agree to consider your innocence thereafter restored?"

IV

My new wife concealed me, horns to tail. Wearing her, I searched the dunes for crab apples I enjoyed late in the season. A sleep-deprived Larner ate on the balcony. He shielded his eyes as gentle breakers turned a greenish gold.

"The dress is lighter than those capes at least."

"So our travel will be easy."

"It is a solid walk to the ferry."

"How does it feel, your first day of innocence regained?"

Trailing breezes from the storm kept us cool as we walked the shore. Only a few shacks toward the dunes. Most lived bayside.

Larner mentioned all the aisles he had walked with his daughters, unions overseen by family and friends. Each now seemed replaced with the joy of the beast beside him. The innocence of it made his spirit as light as the mist that rose from the shore break.

The dress was a second skin, loose and silky other than the starchy veils through which I could see well enough. Larner poked fun at my century alone with gulls and greenflies and what I had once thought a woman who sang to me as she walked the beach. A melody of longing, and still I heard it unplayed within me. It propelled me step for step with Larner. How animated he had been as wonder possessed him, the depressive front across his eyes burned off by spectacle.

As we walked along the water, Larner said he must give me a sort of wedding gift, a list of the thirteen essential virtues delineated by Benjamin Franklin in his autobiography. Referring to them as a recipe for moral perfection, Larner relayed them from memory, and asked me to repeat them until we both were sure they were lodged forever within me:

"The first is *temperance*: eat not to dullness, drink not to elevation. The second is *silence*: speak not but what may benefit others or yourself and avoid trifling conversation. The third is *order*: let all your things have their places, let each part of your business have its time. The fourth is *resolution*: resolve to perform what you ought, perform without fail what you resolve. The fifth is *frugality*: make no expense but to do good to others or yourself, waste nothing. The sixth is *industry*: lose no time, be always employed in something useful, cut off all unnecessary actions. The seventh is *sincerity*: use no hurtful deceit, think innocently and justly, and, if you speak, speak accordingly. The eighth is *justice*: wrong none by doing injuries or omitting the benefits that are your duty. The ninth is *moderation*: avoid extremes, forbear resenting injuries so much as you think they deserve. The tenth is *cleanliness*: tolerate no uncleanliness in body, clothes, or habitation. The eleventh is *tranquility*: be not disturbed at trifles or at accidents common or unavoidable. The twelfth is *chastity*: rarely use venery but for health or offspring, never to dullness, weakness, or the injury of your own or another's peace or reputation. And, finally, the thirteenth is *humility*: imitate Christ and Socrates."

Step for step, we walked as though hand in hand, as a rare southward breeze directed us toward a village of fisherman and those who needed an island to increase their sense of worth. Ahead, we saw the central steeple, wide-porched mansions removed from the shore and bay equally at the island's midpoint, protected on either side by shacks. I had only perceived life here when concealed by a loose netting of clouds. Now we crossed dunes on planks that gave way to streets half-buried in sand.

If anyone bothered us, Larner said, we would not linger: we're rushing to get this bride to her wedding ceremony, need to arrive in a hour, just outside Umbria, must hasten to the ferry or forever blame whoever delays us.

"And remember," he added, "if we are threatened, a simple growl should suffice."

"A growl from such a gown should unsettle anyone."

Larner stepped more quickly toward the bay.

We passed an open area with a central gazebo around which men and women attended to midday duties.

"It is just beyond—the dock—ahead," I said.

Larner laughed. "To hear that voice through those thick veils," he said, "it brings me joy." This happy spirit possessing Larner seemed more conspicuous to the island community than the anonymous bride, for it truly seemed he was a happy father taking his daughter to the mainland on her greatest day. It may have seemed stranger to some that the gown was so luxurious and the clothes worn by her escort surely cost more than most on the island earned in a year. Yet we traveled not on horseback or carriage, nor had we secured a private vessel across the bay, but instead opted to take the sloop each passenger helped row across the water.

On the sloop, a man possessed by rum and more than sufficient commitment to the democratic spirit suggested that the bride must also row, citing a rule that applied to all except the pregnant and the sick. Since her gown was so exceedingly white she might prove her innocence by taking an oar.

"It is her wedding day," said Larner, "and besides she is exceedingly frail and tired from our journey down the shore from the northern settlement."

"It washed away years ago."

"A shack, where we prepared her betterment."

The man cited a grandmother, age eighty, who once had rowed. He was quickly shouted down. He was drunk and all else seemed sober, dissatisfied with a confrontational stain upon the perfect weather.

Larner approached the captain at the stern. He whispered about how his daughter was terribly scarred, unable to show her face, hence the veils, and yet it was his wish for his daughter to have this special day, her one blessed moment on this earth, for the man she would marry was blind and cruel, life ahead would be ceaseless sorrow, and so would the captain accept a small note to ensure that his daughter enjoyed a day of rest and pleasure before a lifetime of service on the mainland.

The captain pocketed the note Larner slipped to him. A hand on the cutlass at his hip, he told the drunkard to shut it or be thrown into the bay.

The drunk muttered doubts. He asked to see her skin. It was common at the time for the shore and wild pinelands of the eastern coast to shelter fugitives. There they were obscured from all those lacking knowledge of the sand trails.

"Show us your pretty hand," said the drunk.

Larner touched the bride's shoulder to quiet a rumble he anticipated and feared. "She cannot be seen," he said, "not an inch of her flesh today."

"And why's that?" said another man nearby.

How terrible if they clamored for me to reveal my skin, a general rebellion on the boat, led by a drunk. Larner had remained silent alone for years, but last night's ceremony had opened a long-closed door in him.

"Friends," Larner said. He looked at the captain expecting paid support. "We have no time to suffer a lengthy speech that might win your favor. So, simply, row on and forget the presence of my humble daughter, no more important in the grand scheme of your day than a common moth. Give her no thought. Let us proceed."

"Such protest surely obscures a strange truth," muttered another passenger. He wore no hat and shielded his eyes from the glare.

"My daughter's dress glows in today's sun, brighter than a beacon guiding endangered ships. Heed her brilliance, respect this special day, and leave us in peace."

The captain approached the wedding dress and said, "If we are to believe your words let us hear one from her. Or will we not be able to hear her voice through such thick veils?"

"A word and you'll leave us in peace?" Larner said. "Not the most pleasant melody emerges from her crippled mouth, I warn you."

"Crippled?"

"Aye, a fire. Long ago. I wished not to reveal this, but it is the reason she covers herself thus and marries a blind man. Please pity my poor daughter, whose voice has been affected by inhalation of smoke, though her ears remain as sensitive as her heart."

"So we know she is not a fugitive, let her speak."

"Speak then, my dear. Tell them of our haste."

From beneath the series of thick veils, I said, "We are in a great hurry on this my special day"—thinking: this is no better than attempting passage with wings exposed. I tried to make my voice sound feminine, but it came out odd, of course.

"A woman, you say!" said the drunkard. "Please. Unmask him! Not a woman, and most likely no free man, either."

"Acrid plumes damaged her voice."

The captain turned to Larner. "Let us see her hand before we travel on in peace."

"So disfigured it is you will forever regret the request."

"Show it," the hatless man said, and the others grunted agreement.

"Show it," said Larner to me. "Let their curiosity be sated. Serve their selfishness."

I inched a hand out of the sleeve. At first sign of aggressive reaction I would tear off the gown, grab Larner, and fly us over the sea, safe from this world of so-called men.

I held out my hand. It was delicate enough to pass perhaps for a woman's.

JRZDVLZ

I am the Leeds Devil

LATER LEARNED that Branley Jukes—thief, mental defective, father of three—met us on the road to Umbria, doubled back along a footpath, entered a tavern called the Bucket of Blood, and relayed the encounter's innocent beginning and nearly tragic end: "Sinfulness such a creature harbors, without doubt, whose existence foretells horror to come." It was not the first time Jukes had ranted about a talking chicken or a stranger more cow than man. The tavern crowd did not trust him any farther than they could stumble at the end of the night.

The Jukes family had long worn the crown of fools. But no one found these jesters humorous. Above-average height, below-average weight, they walked with a jerking motion inherited Jukes to Jukes. They kept their mouths shut as though ashamed of their teeth, but their eyes they opened wide, staring into a distance where their gaze melded the branches of a dead elm with distant laundry on a line, combining these until they swore they witnessed something remarkable, if not a devil than a spirit no more damned than its beholder. That generations of these odious idiots survived was an unfortunate miracle, most thought. Many hoped that each successive Jukes would be the last. But when confronted with a potential mate, instead of uttering incomprehensible, delusional rants, they somehow managed to woo.

Each generation of Jukes deposed itself well before old age. That he talked of horned fingers and a satanic growl seemed proof that the current Jukes would soon proceed down the path of his forebears. Many wished he'd get on with it. Three days straight he talked. And then news arrived of a couple on the ferry, an old man and a woman in a white wedding dress. The old man claimed she'd been burned and deformed, but when she revealed a hand, it was clear of scars and delicately boned yet nevertheless masculine.

This story substantiated, in Branley's mind, the claim that some mysterious creature was about, one that perhaps was two separate forms, an old man and something so hideous it must be concealed from sight or else cause an uproar.

Jukes now maneuvered all conversation to the presence of this monstrous pair. They were responsible for the death of Farmer Chandler's cattle last month, he said, as well as every accident and negative variation in life. Leaves dried and fell and the light weakened and rain came colder and breath could be seen from one's mouth—their presence brought these changes, so claimed Jukes.

Once this mysterious pair no longer existed, he said, we would live in paradise—everyone accommodated. Jukes then displayed an unexpected investigative diligence. He analyzed every cloven footprint, sniffed at every turn for monster and old man, scrutinized elderly couples to see if one were not disguised, even nosed around wedding receptions to ensure excessive veils did not obscure a beast in place of a bride.

Nathaniel Leeds oversaw the press at the Umbria newspaper and distanced himself from the spoken-word world of the tavern. Illiterate Jukes had forever passed Leeds as though he were words on a page. But now the former approached the latter after thirty years of no more than a nod.

"Mister Leeds. Honorable Leeds," said Jukes. "Please confirm your relation to the Leeds Devil."

Nathaniel Leeds laughed. "No one has ever mentioned the similarity in surname other than my father, who said it related to a legend based on an old almanac we possess. My father asserted it was composed for monetary purposes, but he also said the Genuine Leeds American Almanack could be as valuable as I wanted it to be. I value its connection to predecessors. Impossibilities in the text— the monster that slaughters its family—I have always understood as sensationalist hoax."

Nathaniel Leeds had also always understood Jukes as crazed. Jukes' father had been unpredictable: at times noble; at times volatile; at times he'd help anyone who needed it; at times he was reckless, dangerous, liable to beat with fists those he had helped. Now, this current Jukes—younger than Leeds by half—haunted the tavern and sand trails, and preyed on travelers through the pines like some utterly unremarkable beast himself.

"Mr. Jukes," Nathaniel said, his voice searching for tones suitable for confession more than lecture, "as I have aged, I have taken more interest in descriptions of William Leeds, in fact, than the so-called Leeds Devil. There is a fantastic call for information about him in the form of an annotated man, as well as excerpts of William Leeds's apocalyptic writing from previous issues. These may fire your imagination as they have mine. The family history my father handed down—I am more stable than my distant relative, of course, but the era is easier now. I believe the obvious fantasy of the beast was conceived to regain readers lost to the work of Poor Richard Saunders. Confronted with such competition, their compendium

59

of predictions, prophecies, and sundry usefulness they transformed into a purveyor of simple hoax. It was original and ambitious, and charged with such violence, it would have restored their almanac's reputation had it been widely distributed, so entertaining, if not necessarily functional, were the drawings and prose."

Leeds's words fed those blue-white, all-too-open eyes, and once Jukes thanked him excessively for the information, oh how Leeds regretted it. The tavern soon burned with so much talk about the Leeds Devil that it seemed Nathaniel might soon find himself at the center of renewed interest in the hunting of witches.

Jukes ran with the news. He knew no division between history and fiction. "It's true, true, all true," he said. It became a chant, an incantation. Those in the tavern retold his stories to charge otherwise dull evenings with the imminence of slaughter. Peace and quiet were like a layer of ice—these tales pressed down until a boot cracked through. A week after his first visit to Leeds, Umbria seemed to shimmer. Any minute, Leeds's skin might turn scalier than old man's sclerosis. Was it not possible that beneath hat and coat were horns and tail?

Leeds meanwhile proceeded as though he'd never said a word to Jukes. He did not act—had never acted—like a beast. He had always been reticent and hard-working, preferring *The Crier* to a society of open words. But ever since his children had left and his wife had died, some said he had not been the same and perhaps this heralded a shift of shape. Something was not right with him, anyone could tell, and yet he withheld that peculiarity, gracefully, stoically, very much unlike Branley Jukes.

Jukes wore his sleeves long. He liked to tie a noose around his wrists and hang from the rafters. It pleased him to see the faces of his children when they found him. He savored the sight. When Branley was six, his own father properly hanged himself. Hanging from the wrists gave a sense of what the noose had done to his father's neck. His children untied him. Blood-black bruises wound around his wrists like the handcuffs of an obscure sentinel.

He had not hung himself by the wrists for weeks before he met us on the path to Umbria. But now he believed we were the ones who needed to hang from rafters until the evil in us dripped out and returned to its source in the sand.

He had not hung himself since his focus turned to rooting me out, capturing me, killing me, and bringing about eternal paradise—the end of disease, misery, shame, poverty, death. But now Jukes tossed the rope over the strongest beam. He fished wrists through the loop and pulled it tight with his teeth. He stepped from the chair. Sinews stressed. Cruel thoughts magnified complaints beyond anything sane. All frustrations took the form of that threatening growler. Pain in his wrists scorched territories within him and a corresponding X marked the beast's location in Umbria. Discovered hanging and helped down, Branley soothed his wrists in cloth soaked in fat and hurried to that spot. He peered through the window of a home to see Nathaniel Leeds leaning into a book, inhaling its essence.

"The book," he said, "if I get it I will get the beast, if not, no eternal paradise, no ever will we never die."

Pine needles carpeted the woods a soft orange. Anyone could creep around and not be heard, even a tavern-born troglodyte like Merkins, a former teacher who wore a beard that reached his cavernous navel. He did not value his remaining days too highly, but he did look forward to many more drinks before he reached the afterworld, and so he consented to Jukes' demand for company. They waited until night. The trees revealed black limbs. Leeds's house was isolated from others, and so they did not fear being seen. They stood at the window.

They saw Leeds remove the Genuine Leeds Almanack from a glass case and a wrapping of silk. By candlelight, he read closely, attentively, hunched over, and then he leaned back. Eyes closed, he held his breath and exhaled before he returned to the pages.

"Might he ever tire of it?" Jukes said.

"Must be a splendorous work," slurred Merkins.

"The book of the beast," said Jukes.

"A righteous man would savor another book, would he not?"

"Accursed histories. The way he sighs he sees his future there," said Jukes. "Leeds the same as the old man I saw, shifts shapes, costumed now as a man."

"We should neither break into his home nor assert ungranted authority," said Merkins.

"We act in best interests and rightful causes," said Jukes.

"Only Sheriff Hopkins has that power."

Only Jukes had seen that claw, only he had heard Leeds's story, only he had made connections, only he had brought the beast to life, only he would track it down. He would not submit to an authority other than his own awful obsession—fantasy would not

bow to official realities—the law worked for pay instead of the fulfillment of undeniable instinct.

Jukes knocked on the front door. Leeds opened it as though
wary it might fall from lack of use. He let them in. A two-room
cottage in which one old man had made himself comfortable
through many winters. He had lined the windowsills with evergreen boughs and lit oil lanterns so the room glowed. A cone of
cinnamon smoked on a silver tray.

"Mr. Jukes," Leeds said, "a pleasure to host you."

"The book," he said. "We come for you to read it."

"The almanac?"

"Merkins comes with me, do not worry, a respectable man,
most respectable."

"An honor, sir," said Merkins. "Most agreeable home you have."

"Why tonight, of all nights?"

"Brisk and blustery, perfect for deviltries."

"Not so devilish," said Leeds. "I read from it nightly and never
tire."

I watched through the window as Leeds read Japhet's account
of my birth. He read like a performer. So familiar with its rhythm
and texture, his visitors for a time seemed enchanted. Midway
through the reading, however, Jukes and Merkins shared a look.

"The game's the fresh meat, isn't that right?" said Jukes.

"I don't understand," said Leeds.

"The game's the fresh meat, do you believe it?"

"I understand your words but not their intent," said Leeds.

"He doesn't understand," Jukes said to Merkins. "A mark."

"Of what?" said Leeds.

"You know nothing of fresh meat?"

"Is this some riddle?"

"The game's the fresh meat, I say."

Leeds pronounced the opaque phrase, rounding out the words instead of slurring them, saying each slowly and clearly as though proper enunciation might break the code.

"The game *is* the fresh meat!" shouted Jukes.

"I neither understand this phrase nor why I let this madman into my home."

"Can you imagine me a madman, Merkins, when Leeds's so mad he's no inkling of what it means when we say fresh meat's the game. Do you see him with such a bitty bearded face, cruel fingers, horns hidden, saying *I'm* lunaticked ... when I *acknowledge* the game is fresh meat, and yet he denies it. Do you think if my fathers or his father or someone even farther down the line of fathers left a record to say why it was they did what they did, do you think I might invite someone to my home to hear me read from it? The game, you see, *is* the fresh meat."

Branley shot his sleeves so they fell about the elbows. Leeds saw the bruises on his guest's wrists. He seemed almost to understand this talk of fresh meat.

"First," said Leeds, "I did not invite you to listen to my relatives' story. Second, I knew your father. He was not an unkind man, though few understood him, for, like you, he was not easy to understand. He was a man whose sensitivities, whose tenderness, gave way to regular violence. I did not know you discovered his—"

"You tormented him so he roped the roof, you churned the oceans that took my grandfathers, made my mother run into wildfire, my grandmother swallow mercury, it was you, the beast, the fresh meat, the game. It was you, the quarry, the hunted, the target. Let's sees your horned hands. The beast himself here, those horned fingers, let's hear again that growl."

"I have told you a number of times that the beast, if it exists, is not my relative by blood. This is a simple almanac, something I read to fill my time. You cannot hold it, but Mr. Merkins can look on these pages and see that what I say appears here in print."

Merkins sat with excellent posture, but leaned alternately to the left and right, like a bearded metronome about to nap.

Jukes slapped Merkins' shoulder. "Confirm what he reads."

Leeds politely held the back of his hand to mouth and nose. Merkins must have smelled of stale brandy, whiskey, mead: sweet scents cutting through others more sour.

"Merkins?" said Jukes.

The words swam one into the next: if reading the Constitution, he would not have recognized *We the People*. Merkins raised a cracked red hand over an eye.

"It says here," he said, "it says ..."

"Yes, yes, what's it?" Jukes leaned forward, suspicions confirmed.

"It says the beast is this man here. It says the beast is a dangerous bird."

"*A dangerous bird?*" Leeds mocked, incredulous. "It says nothing of the sort."

"No, no, right here, right here." Merkins pointed to an arbitrary line.

"*Sinister.* Yes. That word appears. *Wings* are mentioned. Yes. But—"

"You want me to believe you when mine good friend Merkins here, a schoolteacher, once the finest, confirms you untrustable."

"I see the words clear as the flame of that candle and your friend covers an eye to read yet might as well have both eyes shut."

"Oh here we go, here we go, Merkins, now this old man forces us out of his house, and how will he force us out with no strength in his arms at all? How might he manage, you think?"

Now covering the other eye, squinting, Merkins said, "Well, it does say here he's the beast. It says a man like him will haunt the land forever and not until he is deposed will we know paradise."

Merkins was not drunk enough to forget that Jukes carried knives—he'd often seen Jukes sharpening them—and he knew Jukes liked to throw them. They were not something Merkins wanted to enter his heart. And so he chose to let Jukes hear what he had wanted to hear. Yet if Jukes attacked this poor old man, Merkins believed he would protect him best he could.

"Take your finger from the book," Leeds said. "It's filthy, and the book is delicate."

"Merkins, he values books more than his lives."

"I value my peace and sanity," Leeds said, "and you are upsetting both."

"Transform then, beast, to protect yourself."

"If I could I would to run you out."

"He threatens us, Merkins! He threatens us with transformation and death."

"I have coins and modest jewels from my late wife. They are yours if you leave."

"Hear that, Merkins. Show us shiny things, all smiles and peace. So easy he thinks it is. Gives us the book and we spare you."

Leeds held the book as though some force within it protected from intruders. Perhaps Jukes was right about its abilities. An impossible beast might burst from the pages and protect those who loved it. If only the drawing of William Leeds emerged to annihilate these intruders.

The book was not much taller than the fists that gripped its sides. Leeds closed his eyes, pulled the book to his chest, and threw his arms toward the men again. He shoved the cover at his guests and unleashed a breath he'd been holding since he read to the men, before they had arrived, before any of it—a breath he had begun holding before his wife died, before his children were born, before he himself was born—a breath he'd started holding when the creators of the almanac encountered competition from Benjamin Franklin, when they concocted fictions to secure advantages for their practical compendium, when William Leeds walked into the wilderness away from wife and a dozen children, when they came to this country, when dissatisfaction spurred them to cross an ocean to this unproven place.

Leeds released his breath in a shockwave shout. So uncommon in his silent home, it seemed the windows would shatter once ears stopped ringing with the violence that had come from him, propelled by blood more than voice, from veins more than throat.

"Feisty, isn't he?" Jukes said and stood. He reached for the blades strapped to the small of his back.

"Leave him in peace," Merkins said. "He's no harm. Let him rest. Look at him."

All Leeds had to defend himself was this demonstration of his lack of defenses. The book he held in front of him like it could ward off evil. He stood frozen as though the men would leave if he tightly closed his eyes.

"You think I can throw a blade through the pages all the way to his skin?"

Jukes held a knife out so the handle pointed at Leeds, who saw no evil, heard no evil, as though his shout had devastated his senses.

"Flick wrist, pierce book and heart, nights end, summers stay forever. A blade that changes night to day, famine to feast."

"Let's make it back to the Bucket for a glass," said Merkins. "It's a book—no more, no less—and it's a man, no better or worse than any other."

"You read from it, you read from it, and you said it's the beast, you read from it and said the beast's in it. Look at him and tell me he's not the beast, skins thickening, hardening, scaling into rightful self. I see the beast in this statue of a man. I throw this blade at the book without wasting more words."

Merkins moved in front of Leeds. "I could not see the words well enough and only said what I said to appease you," he said.

"Move away now so I can do what needs to be done." Jukes flipped the blade he held in the air and caught it by the handle and with his other hand removed another knife and held both blades out.

Leeds's eyes were shut so well he probably hardly heard what Merkins had said. If Leeds's eyes were open he would have seen a swift movement in front of Merkins who stumbled toward Jukes and collapsed. Jukes flipped his blade again and pointed the handle at the book and threw it, one eye squinted for accuracy. If his eyes were open, Leeds would have seen the blade tumble toward him and enter the Genuine Leeds Almanack, dead in its center, and not continue through to skin.

He held the book so tightly it did not tear or fall. If Leeds's eyes were open he would have seen Jukes pull the blade from Merkins's throat and wipe the blood on his gasping friend's leg. And then Leeds would have seen Jukes step ahead and flip the same blade that had downed Leeds's defender and he would see the blade tumble through air again to enter his chest. His grip on the Genuine

Leeds Almanack loosened, the book dropped, he lived for another moment on the fumes of what had been his life, legs liquefied, and there on the floor Leeds would have died if he had not released his grip on life the moment he had thrust the book at Jukes and exhaled that shout, hoping a fiction might emerge from the pages and protect him.

II

Jukes lifted the impaled book like it was unrelated to the man at his feet. He extinguished the candles, stepped around Merkins and Leeds, and then slipped into the night.

He headed toward town as though conveyed by the path at his feet. At the door of the Bucket he hesitated, impaled almanac in hand. An ordinary man may have taken this time to escape before the bodies were found and the hunt was on. But Branley Jukes was extraordinary.

He pushed open the door. Safe place, he thought, no one looks for me here, invisible like old smoke, no one knows where I went, what I did. Look at them alive in paradise, no one knows it's the end of sorrows, our only trouble an overabundance of ease. No one knows they've entered a new realm now, summer heat will rise with the sun and never leave again, the beast slain by a most valiant Umbrian knight. Once they discover the beast they'll rename the town for generations accused who sacrificed themselves so I could save everyone.

All he wanted was to relive that moment with blades out, oh such confidence and control, lives at the mercy of a flick of the wrist. He must have realized a blade was still lodged in Leeds's chest.

"Let it stay," he said, "so they know who slayed the dragon." He said this loud enough for it to be heard.

The bartender seemed like years of ales and porters and sausages, as well as the small, repetitive movements of service, had stuffed a much larger man inside a smaller one's skin. He watched Branley fiddle with the handle of a blade impaling an old book. Branley often seemed agitated and his knives often held everything from partridges to snakes to cobs of corn. That he now had a book seemed like progress.

"What'd you spear there? Something dangerous?"

"Better to see yourselves tomorrow."

"Tomorrow then," the bartender said.

Jukes muttered something so animalistic the barkeeper thought it best to turn his back and polish glasses. Branley muttered more. The exact stream of vehemence, the specific words, did not matter. They were less words than sounds that represented his thoughts more closely than he ever could communicate. His usual slurred speech was a concession to society. His true speech slithered, hissed, a sinuous, twining, toxic cord that forced him to hold his mouth tight.

The smoke in the Bucket never cleared. Whites of eyes reddened so the average unsquinting patron seemed to weep. A startling sight if one were to push open the heavy door and see the pink flesh, like the exposed upper gums of a demented smile, around Branley's eyes. The sockets of his skull made him seem more skeletal than ever. His cheeks were sunken and ashen and rough with stubble, unshaven since he began his hunt. His mouth was twisted in unintelligible, nearly inaudible speech.

That suspicious pair of travelers on the way to Umbria. If he'd ended their lives, everyone would be in paradise now. Drink did not still the memory of what he'd done. He decided against another and left without goodbyes.

His home was less a cottage than a shack, the roof high and arched, like some underskilled carpenter's attempt at a turret. Hunters found it, peeked inside thinking it abandoned, and ran when they encountered Jukes' wife and three children wearing squirrel, raccoon, and rabbit pelts caked with mud. A dirt floor was covered in fresh pine needles, straw, leaves. A refuge from Umbria, from what's civilized. They did not starve or overly want, protected by innocence.

He could make it back with eyes closed. No trouble under a full moon. The shadows of the trees were no more demonic than how he moved among them.

Home sweet home, he found his family asleep on beds of straw, covered by sheets that looked like shredded flags.

He sat on the ground with his back to a wall as his family slept. He lit the nub of a candle and saw the rafters from which his father had hanged himself, the rafters from which he had hung himself by his wrists. He felt the bruises. Now that the beast was slaughtered he would trim the discolored skin. He removed the blade from the almanac. This book in which everything he needed to know might be learned. He stopped on the picture of William Leeds. The bearded head emerged from the starburst crater the knife had made in the pages. The drawing was faded, pale, almost disappeared with time. What good was this punctured book if the spirit of the beast were not sucked back through this hole, ending its hold over the region so pines untwisted and stood tall and trunks thickened and limbs elongated, fanning wide, bursting to shade the area until sand became soil and everyone lived off mushrooms and moss and mammalian delicacies protected from winged predators?

He woke before his children, before his wife, this woman he had made suffer for years. She could have found some troll beneath a bridge, an ogre who had stowed away on a plagued vessel, and done better. Without her, he would not have made it too far past seventeen, when overrunning energy had endangered him. She had stilled him, harnessed him, optimistic, a woman he never would have been able to secure if he hadn't set himself across her spirit, like algae on a summer pond, until she became uninhabitable.

Georgia slept next to three children in a corner. Two boys in their early teens and a younger girl. Branley had been the only son of his family, his sisters taken once they reached fourteen, available to anyone who needed a wife. Only Branley was left to see, at age six, his father hang from the rafters. Branley's two sons seemed as though whatever genealogical affliction inside them was dormant, or at most building pressure, preparing to erupt with the end of adolescence.

He looked at them as they slept, straw in tangled hair, and he had hope. A sense that they might not die before he did, at the minimum, and more so that once he stepped outside that morning the world would be renewed. Eternal paradise. Their father crowned King of Umbria, a country onto itself, and from that morning on the Jukes would be first in a long line of royals, immune to the surge of hereditary insult.

He stepped outside. The sun was not all the way up. He could see his breath. He held his fists tucked in the sleeves of his tight black jacket. One ear he raised toward town. He had eradicated the region of the beast and brought about eternal paradise.

The breath that emerged from his mouth was not what he expected to see. As he wandered from his home and into the woods a hundred yards off, the morning was cool and easy thanks to mist, the woods patterned in traditional autumn hues, branches not any more monstrous than the limbs of trees at dawn.

From where he stood, his house looked like an outhouse. If paradise did not fall from the sky or emerge from the earth, he would soon be wanted for murder. It might be better to run.

He wandered from the house and then returned. The underbrush was covered in foliage, the earth insulating itself for a long cold winter he would not see. He entered the house. Where he had slept on the floor he saw almanac and knife. Only one blade. It was like he'd lost a limb.

"You're back," Georgia said.

"Tell them I'm off for Manhattan Island. Tell them I left three days ago."

"Tell who?" said Jermaine. His boys and daughter sat around a cauldron Georgia had heated for a breakfast of reheated tea.

"Who comes looking, tell them I'm gone three days."

"And when will you return?" said Georgia. She was dressed in rough wool rags that had never been any color other than gray. Her hair was streaked around her temples as though pressure there had aged her most.

"If summer comes and never leaves you'll see me again."

Georgia shifted a log beneath the cauldron. Her own family hadn't slept on straw mattresses or survived on sick chicken eggs and the milk of a recalcitrant goat. Her family had died around the time she met Branley, and soon after she replaced mother and father and sister with children of her own. She had thought herself chosen to save this man. But it had long been clear that whatever force existed within him was far too strong.

"Good then, good," she said.

"Good," her eldest son echoed.

"Good," the younger son said, echoing his brother.

Their sister kept quiet. Her ten years had been darkest night. Her brothers looked to her, expecting her to speak, to side with them, to join the revolt. More than her brothers, she had inherited her father's open eyes and mouth shut tight. Her straight black hair was roughly cut at the shoulders, and her skin seemed as though she rubbed her cheeks each morning with dust that made light eyes stand out all the more. She turned them on her father. In them he saw that no matter what happened that day or the next or in the coming years, whatever it was that lived within him would find expression in this girl.

Such departures call for speeches. One started to rise in Branley, words by which his children would remember him—his epitaph, if the image he cut were a gravestone. He looked at these people taking their last look at him and remembered his last look at his father's feet not three strides from where he now stood. Just standing there he burned himself into their memories. In that way he inched the Jukes line a step ahead, sparing them a memory like what he had seen and ceaselessly saw of his father hanging from the rafters. They had only seen him hang from his wrists, an exercise in sorrow. He wanted to rid the world of sorrow as it was caused by the beast who had a hand in his father's death, his grandfather's death, everyone's death, Jukes or not.

Nothing was what his father had left the world with, and Branley Jukes would leave the area surrounding Umbria with not much more: the impaled account of the origin of all its evil his only possession other than the knife that had pierced it.

It came from his bones, his blood, somewhere that rarely spoke: "I am the Leeds Devil," he said.

His children heard him as they stared at the fire. In those flames they saw something more steady and peaceful and altogether fatherly than the form that said these words that made little sense. Before they could break their focus on the fire and pull a log from beneath the cauldron and smack their father across the jaw with its molten end, he slipped into a morning that was bright-shining and warm, if not eternal paradise.

A Vortex of Pandemonium

HE JUKES stuffed what they had into sacks and followed Sheriff Hopkins and his men to Umbria, surrounded like prisoners, like they were the ones who had murdered. Once in town, they were deloused, separated, and distributed among families optimistic about raising the children and restoring Georgia's respectability. Children expressed good and evil if they encountered either principle in excess. Umbria would err therefore on the side of benevolence. Charitable dominion would amount to justice. Socializing the Jukes out of existence would avenge Nathaniel Leeds—even Merkins. It was a matter of security: something had to be done before the children became like their father. Trouble need not be inevitable, argued the Altruists, although they worried that the widely considered satanic father may soon return to claim his wards in person or spirit. Each adoptive family ignored at first concerns about the lineage but the threat of transformation opened fissures over time. They might not become volatile, depraved, wicked adults, forever in pursuit of illusory monsters, but they would experience some ever-extended childhood in which they failed to take responsibility for themselves and others. All was done to make the Jukes feel welcomed and cherished and capable of evolving from their near-feral state. But there was a condescension to this. It became something of a competition to see which family best polished the raw material they had found in the woods.

The Greers, the family that hosted Georgia Jukes, led the others. She had been raised unlike her children and this socializing experiment offered another life. Accustomed to so much daily labor, she worked on the house's upkeep and her studies as she learned to play a musical instrument that spun a telescope-like construction of thirty-seven tuned bowls on a spindle powered by a foot pedal. Moistened fingers pressed to the spinning bowls enabled the player to sustain melodies and harmonies, an advancement on the art of those who made music on the rims of wine glasses. The armonica had once been popular, played by Marie Antoinette and Mesmer and its inventor, Benjamin Franklin, among thousands of others. Georgia took to this pastime, hypnotizing herself with rolling glass bowls and the tones a light touch of her fingers produced. It was extraordinary how a savage beast could soothe itself playing this instrument. She rendered simple melodies popular at the time, slowing them so each note hung in the air as long as possible. Since each bowl was coded with a stripe according to the spectrum along the rainbow, she seemed to see tones suffusing the space above her with color as she played. She blended them and maneuvered them and interjected a white-striped bowl so the sound shifted toward dissonance. She lingered on these white bowls and saw round sounds in the air dent and collapse. Her time with Branley had seemed like one long white-striped dissonance that turned her into mud he molded into something she never imagined she would be. He had changed her and she had allowed herself to be changed.

It was a remarkable form of therapy, one the family who housed her had not anticipated. She sat for hours at the armonica and played in a way that seemed therapeutic for the inhabitants of the house, as well. In its most popular era, the instrument had gained a reputation for casting listeners into obscure states from which they never emerged. Glass bowls on a spindle held a strange power. Many heard something so haunting and gorgeous and eerie and pleasurable it was believed that in certain hands this instrument might cause turmoil, even madness. After disappearing into such open tones, what would one rather do than return to that realm of pure spirit? It was no secret that players and listeners alike often suffered depressive states. They had listened too long to the celestial spheres. Sensual messages reached them and romanced them with the suggestion that perfection were achievable in life as in sound. That life was far from harmonious intensified the temptation to return to an enchanted state. It soon became evident that aversion to dissonance can be a kind of madness.

Three years of regular exposure to benevolence had passed since their father disappeared. The boys were sixteen and seventeen, the girl almost thirteen. Although divided among separate families, the Altruists allowed the Jukes children to maintain close enough contact. Once every couple weeks they reconvened to walk the sand trails their father had haunted as they indirectly considered his demise and their uncertain and by all accounts inevitably tragic future. They often explored near the coast, attracted to the ruins of a doomed village. Unchecked vegetation overwhelmed abandoned iron works and random houses charred by wildfire. What once had been Leeds Points now offered endless adventure. The Jukes kids found shards of pottery and tarnished plates among the ruins. Last time there they even discovered a locket in the shape of a coffin.

The Umbrian Altruists were excellent educators who'd installed fanciful language as the boys' favorite recreation. December tried to pierce the sails of their wind-blown phrases, but speculation about the tiny silver coffin sent armadas of talk into battle.

"The tomb of the king of a race of diminutive natives!"

"Opening it curses the discoverers with certain misery!"

"The pines swarm with minuscule combatants fiercer than tigers!"

"Everywhere we *don't* look, there they are!"

"They possessed our father, slipped into his bloodstream!"

"Only our mother's tears kept us from this peculiar infection!"

"Now so long without her, opening the coffin will release the curse!"

"Let it loose," said December, "if it shuts your mouths."

"She said let it loose, Brother," the older Jermaine said to Gus. Already taller than their father, a recent spurt had made the elder's spine, neck, and limbs seem overgrown. There was something lupine about his movements as a result, emergent jerkiness inherited Jukes to Jukes, and adolescent volcanism still marked his face. "But do you have the courage to open the tomb of the tiny king?"

"Those already cursed are impervious. Ancient curses benefit our sort."

"Two negatives multiplied make a positive," said Jermaine.

"Let us be released from the curse our family has suffered forever," said Gus, so much squatter than his brother he often doubted they shared a sire. An omni-allergic child whose swollen freckled cheeks concealed ever-replenished deposits of snot, he had been half-blind until fitted with glasses yet still seemed wary of an unclear world.

"Give it to me." December snatched the little coffin from Gus's hands and snapped its little latch open and held it so they could see what's inside. Thanks to life with the Altruists her face had brightened, her cheeks no longer in need of an insistent scrub. Her straight black hair, no longer cut at the shoulders by her mother with a dull handsaw, was long enough now to frame the object of their curiosity.

December opened her light eyes wider as the boys shaded theirs.

"Look closely for hidden treasure," Jermaine said.

"A sufficient quantity," she said, "perhaps could buy our freedom."

"No treasures shall we discover greater than the precious metals of the mind and heart afforded to us by our new families," said Gus, sniffling all the while.

Now on this warm November day, they proceeded northwest from Umbria instead of toward the ruins near Leeds Point and, beyond that, marshlands and the bay. The empty coffin hung on a cord around Jermaine's neck. He hoped it contained ballast to steady every memory of his father. How his grandfather had died, his great-grandfather too, what his own father had done, he hoped this coffin hauled in their stories and revised them until they all ended happily ever after. They passed their old home, visible now that the trees were nearly bare. They did not speak of it, as though to see which of them had been most successfully civilized, a state that required no memory of living like hairless cubs, surviving on tea and cranberries and small game and fish from the Mullica. They maintained a good pace, lithe bodies empty of the sorrow and static that accompanied nature's descent into winter, into areas they could not recall.

They came to the Mullica. A ferryman on the other shore offered to row them across. They walked north along the bank instead. After a mile the river narrowed and there was a bridge and a path leading to a house larger than all those in Umbria combined, a sprawling construction of wings interconnected by windowed corridors.

Seeing this uncommon cathedral, it seemed they'd discovered their future resting place, or so Jermaine thought but did not say, afraid such statements might be understood as unstable. It was the type of utterance they had been counseled to avoid. Indulgence too often in first thoughts became habitual weakness, especially for children of a man who'd streamed words from his mind, unfiltered by tact. Put thought before speech, the children were taught, like horse and carriage. Mouths were gates restraining wild animals: release of one eased the release of others until the world reverted to savagery.

"It can't be a single place," said Jermaine, "more like a string of palaces."

"Who could live there?" said Gus.

December shrank as she looked at the tower of Larner's estate. Apple trees grew in rows, none too tall, as though less than a decade ago the area had been leveled. The air smelled of fermenting fruit, not yet in the thick of the orchard. Time enough there and they would stumble into the river, drunk on fumes.

Jermaine loped toward the house, a lone soldier invading an army, as his siblings held their ground. December crouched as though to hide behind her knees. Gus crossed his arms low across his belly, protecting upset guts the best he could.

"A house like any other," said Gus, "no need to worry."

"What's that?" December whispered and pointed toward the entrance.

"What do you see?" said Gus.

"Through the trees, along the ground," she said.

Jermaine returned to their side. "Let's wait," he said.

"For what?" said December.

Coming toward them, a white apparition in the orchard. December started across the bridge. Her brothers looked at what walked toward them as their sister's legs propelled her down a footpath along the other side of the river. Her brothers ran, too, more not to lose her than to flee the orchard, or so they later claimed.

December had no trouble distancing herself from that bridge. She saw her brothers running, if not screaming as she'd be if she were closer to whatever she'd seen. Her first thought when she saw the wedding dress: her father's story was true.

Jermaine and Gus caught her, nearly to the ferry.

"Does it follow?" she said. "Did you see it? Do you know what it was?"

"I saw a wedding dress," said Jermaine, "but that cannot be."

"If father saw what we saw and—" said December.

"We chased after you," said Jermaine.

The ferryman was so settled in middle age his skin resembled chalky stone. Like his father and grandfather, he floated everyone across the river unwilling to swim. One could wade with careful paces along the coppery silt when it was slow and shallow. But who would do so as the ferryman watched? Now the river was swifter, colder, wider. Bridges had been built nearby but few walked to them when they could punt across here. The ferryman had a dinghy for larger groups, but mainly served solitary travelers.

"Seen a ghost?" he said to December.

She had expected something reassuring. "An apparition in white," she said.

"And these, your brothers, they also saw it?"

"We all did—yes," she said.

"I have seen a much more terrifying sight." The ferryman paused, unwilling to continue until they pressed him. But his three visitors stood as though a thin film now existed between them and him.

"Have you seen this dress," December said, "like the one that consumed our father?"

"Your father?"

"Branley Jukes, who—"

"You are his children?"

"Did you know our father?" said December.

"I knew to warn travelers of his presence. He did more damage to my business than the worst winters, but now I see he stole so his young ones might survive and become children as healthy as these three." The ferryman seemed caught in a spell. "Excuse me. Yes. Terrible what happened to him."

"What was that?" said Jermaine, on guard, taller than the ferryman by a head.

"You must know better than I do."

"Do you know what became of him?" said Jermaine.

"Some believe he took the form of the beast he talked about and—"

"What is the house there?" said Jermaine.

"Only every few years do I see its owner. Rumor is he's not alone, but, as I mentioned, that orchard harbors something far more chilling than a dress."

The children stood as he communicated as though with someone well beyond an arm's length. "I have always been here," he said, "my father had always been here before me, and those who have passed through have always told us what they have seen and heard. Forever we've invoked legend when we fail to explain peculiar circumstances. We throw baffled hands in the air and assign misfortune to a mysterious force. We blame the Leeds Devil. Recently the beast has been seen, there have been sightings, many, many, but people keep largely quiet, not wishing to remind anyone of your father, whose madness assumed the form of taking arms against it, whereas everyone else who's seen it, myself included, hesitates to mention it to those who might question our faculties."

"What have you seen," asked Gus, "and where?"

"I have seen it soaring overhead and stop to quench its thirst with river water. It has even approached me, cautiously, not at all ferociously. The feeling from it, my single lingering impression, was of fear—that *it* was afraid of me. Even if it's harmless as a water bug, it is too terrifying to treat as anything other than a threat."

"So what about the dress?" said Jermaine. "Should we tell the people of Umbria? Alert them?"

"I would not recommend it."

The ferryman took them across and did not ask for coins. Their father's absence had paid their passage several times over, he claimed. More so, in case one fine morning they transformed into accursed monsters like their father, perhaps they would remember his generosity and haunt another road.

II

The Trachtens, the Worthens, the Dorwoods, and the Greers, the four main Altruist families, met once a season to discuss how to raise the area to a more respectable level, fulfill their moral obligation to perform acts of goodwill, and advance already honorable reputations. It could have been worse. The families had enough sway that if they decided to move twenty miles south, the rest of the community would follow or otherwise suffer.

Jermaine's adopted siblings wheezed, snored, gasped, and choked, all three Trachten children in the same large bed with him, cuddled together for warmth as he lay on its edge. Not quite asleep he imagined his brother in a similar situation, not quite awake either, aware of another groaning house not quite his home. The Worthens always seemed distracted, their heads turned when addressing Gus as though to flaunt remarkable profiles, the nose, chin, jaw, lips united in service of some royal ideal. He sensed December's sleeplessness at the Dorwoods' home, where she lived with two girls her age who, in the presence of their parents, showed December how to handle cutlery, for example, but treated her like a fork with twisted tines when alone.

The Trachten kids slept enveloped in nothing close to silence as Jermaine slipped from bed already dressed and made his way out of the house to the woods without anyone wondering where he went so early. The arms they had stored were hidden among sticks and enough moss to protect from rain but still showing in case they had trouble finding the spot. Once Jermaine found them, excavated them, and dusted them off, he squatted, surrounded by the misshapen shadows of the pine trees. The soil was cold and moist and, minute by minute, he watched it in a hypnotic state as it steamed into light fog. He remembered how he had once been indivisible from the woods, calm and wild. Every effort now was made so he moved and spoke in ways the pines never knew or seemed able to support, its soil too porous to tolerate such uprightness. If he disappeared into the woods, his brother and sister would wander to that spot and stand over him. He'd overhear them say he was too willing to lose himself in acceptable behavior—and he thought the same about them. They needed a day of disorder.

Gus found his brother against the trunk of a rare deciduous tree, collapsed into himself more than crouched. The ferryman had said he had seen a beast, something in the air, a monster, and they would end that rumor by proving it true. His night was troubled because this day might disrupt what had been established these past three years. The Worthens had taught him a way of life along a path he had always hoped to live, if only he had known such procession were feasible. Strength, humility, generosity, intelligence, upright-ness, he could chant a list of virtues, words that entranced like a long-unknown spirit realm that had always existed in some figura-tive next room. The world as it appeared consisted of undiscovered empires if one knew to call *an oak* representative of endurance and strength and nobility, *a stream* representative of all that was delicate yet on the move, and when he considered the world within him, he understood it as endangered. How he smiled in mirrors at the Worthen's house. Reflections he had never seen in the woods except in puddles. His smile he now knew related to the word *ashamed*, a bashful smirk, even when sincere and happy, as though something in the musculature of the face, the round and impure cheeks, the uneven measure of his thin dry lips, the moist and heavy eyes, sus-pected the release of control that allowed an expression altogether fragile that came from something even more fragile within only suggested by a mirror. Gus therefore perfected a reflection of what he saw in the Worthens, what he would like them to see when they looked at him. An expression of happiness agreed with the unasked question: do you wish to continue in this world? And the world now began with the Worthen's home and the Umbria area and his small spot in both.

He had shaken his head in all directions, before his father had left, instinctive rejection of the wilderness he had known. Civility he built brick by brick, raising a wall to protect where he was from where he had been. His older brother collapsed against a trunk in the woods, nearly a head taller than him now, so much longer in the limbs, looked unlike a brother at all. Guarding muskets disguised overnight as sticks reminded Gus of their previous life in the woods. If he were armed at that moment, to rescue Jermaine from the miseries of their former life, he would have taken ten paces ahead, aimed, and fired.

Ten paces ahead, his brother's head turned and nodded. Gus expected his brother to stand and shake hands as civility required but Jermaine sat and told his brother to wait for their sister.

Gus hovered over his brother like he might kick his knee and make him stand as was proper, but instead he collapsed in uncaring leaves and together waited for December. After a time, they heard innocent whistling in the woods, a child hunting pheasant feathers.

December, her hair restrained in two long tight braids for the occasion, was too aware she was alone, she was rarely alone, and so she accompanied herself with sound to ease her dread. It was like she walked to her own funeral, her energy seeping with each step into the woods.

Her brothers leaned against a tree. She saw them and her whistle became a light-hearted greeting, her solitude replaced by these two with whom she'd always felt as though she were alone, so familiar they were she might have continued along by herself.

"Come sit," said Jermaine.

"Why?"

"Sit with us."

"But why?"

"December. *Sit.*"

She screwed her face but pressed herself into the space between them.

"Now what?" she said.

"Be silent."

"Why?"

"December."

They sat in silence until they passed into a state of innocence, before they had been brought to Umbria proper, before they had seen their father hanging by the wrists, before they had known they were human: a space where they existed but did not know it. Only for a second did they sense this before a leg moved or a branch snapped or leaf fell or they heard wood chopped in the distance or imagined me, in all my hideous fragmented glory, wheeling over the outgrown apple trees surrounding the estate.

"Shall we, darlings," said Jermaine.

They had lost all their blood while leaning against the tree. They had disappeared a moment, and now with each step they returned to life. The sky had whitened and they squinted. A leafless glare seeped into them, weakened them. They passed where they had lived and the separation between now and then widened and clarified.

They hiked toward the orchard before they reached the river. Cutting northwest, they avoided the ferryman. They felt like the only moving part in this wilderness, aware of the inevitable appearance of another moving part. The ground sloped toward the rear of the house, which sprawled away from them, the orchard on its other side.

"If we entered the house and—" said Jermaine.

"What if an army occupies it," said Gus. "Or if we force open a window and—"

"We'll circle the building and wait for whatever awaits us," said the elder.

The house was a pulsating leviathan in the woods. It seemed set to imitate a landslide and crush them like some vast and malevolent worm. They hesitated toward the river. The air became colder. They thought my dress had assumed the contours of the sky.

I intended to welcome them. I had spent time in the orchard and around the river, staying as far as I could from Larner, who let me live in peace. Now that I regularly assumed the shape of a man, the question was what would I do. In conventional shape, altogether wingless, I couldn't soar over the woods, surprise a deer and feast on it, let alone smell or hear so well. All I could do was walk through the orchard on long flat feet, speak to myself, sit by the river, admire the whorls in soft fingertips, and gaze into my reflection.

I had seen them come and run off. Had they seen through the dress and my disguise of skin? Was I still only something to run from? After seeing them flee, I stored the dress in a cave not far off and spent days perched atop the house's tower, from where I could see to all horizons.

I admit that I often tried to avoid Larner, my first and only friend, my crucial tutor, who had developed an obsessive interest in Benjamin Franklin. He attributed all inventions to him whether they pertained to Franklin or not. He suggested that William

Leeds had journeyed to Philadelphia to confront Franklin after insults related to Titan Leeds appeared in Poor Richard's Almanack. The famously libidinous Franklin must have become curious about my mother Mowas when he heard William mention her, and so Larner concluded that the seductive British solider who sired me was Franklin in disguise. Larner now only saw the world in terms of the thirteen commandments determined by Franklin and described in his autobiography that one must follow to attain moral perfection. He pronounced associations among Franklin's thirteen commandments and the thirteen original colonies and what he deemed the thirteen signs of the zodiac, having invented a thirteenth constellation that assumed the form of the thirteenth child of Mowas Leeds and reigned over a mystical thirteenth month, also originally invented by Franklin.

In short, my only friend had ceased to exist long before his death.

Lacy white sky let through enough blue to strain my eyes. What I understood as my most human part saw three humans come, and so I leaped from the tower, an extraordinary jump, and as I began to fall toward the ground I opened my wings and soared as high as I could to where the air thinned. Larner may no longer be in possession of the majority of his cognitive marbles but he was right: I was an improved human variant, a beneficial and superior virus, that everyone should contract so they too could one day rush through the atmosphere like this. The world fell away and could be seen for what it was, so peaceful and empty of all those who sullied it with acceptable human forms and virtue. I hovered at the highest possible point, letting my wings fill with the world below, and then I dove like a spear thrown at the earth's core.

My belly skimmed along the river and I dragged my tail to create a wake. Three children walked the banks of the river heading toward the bridge. I passed at maximum velocity and then shot up and circled back to the bridge where I landed to wait. The children threw themselves into the muddy banks. On the bridge, I held my wings as wide as I could and released a sound I hadn't let myself make in years, a sound I had learned to control so it would be intelligible in common words. It was time for these children to hear it for what it was and maybe learn to make a similar extraordinary sound themselves.

I stood on the bridge, spread wings, and howled. The children kneeled. They seemed to experience something that surpassed fear, that almost resembled peace. It felt so good, I could howl like this forever.

The children shaded eyes as though the sound were responsible for the glare. Once I stopped, in quick hushed speech, they said I seemed smaller than they'd imagined. They'd pictured something so large it could not fit in the house. The ferryman had described more of a dragon than this beast no larger than a man once the wings were closed.

"Shall I shoot?" said Gus.

"We must get closer or wait until it makes another pass."

Jermaine loaded his musket and crouched as though hunting an animal that didn't know he was there. He crept with weapon held out like a blindman's cane.

Gus started after his brother and tried to load his weapon as he hurried.

December lay against the muddy riverbank. Her braids had come undone and she seemed on the way back to a half-feral state. She looked at her brothers hunting something that could not exist. "Wait. What if—"

Wings down, I seemed to them no more than a kangaroo-shaped heron with the horns of a ram, vaguely snorting from my canine snout.

"Almost there," said Jermaine. I could not be anything other than the beast his father had once met. Those long pointed fingers. Their father had not been insane—meeting me had set him off.

Protected by muskets, they had courage. They did not run.

The girl said, "Our father!"

Jermaine fired as December pushed him in the back. The shot met river water. Gus, primed, held off as his sister threw herself at him.

"Father said *I am the Leeds Devil*," she said. "What if that's why his father hanged himself and his grandfather walked into the ocean, to stop transforming into this beast?"

The same girl who had run from a white dress moving through the trees, now confronted with my howl and an even more impossible sight, stopped them from finishing their father's work and restoring the family name.

"You endanger us all," said Jermaine, who packed another round into the snout of his rifle.

"He doesn't attack," said December, "because we are his children."

"Shall I restrain her," Gus said. She flailed her elbows and he stepped away as though she herself were fearsome.

"Hold your fire until it flies toward us," she said.

"Better to react than force unfortunate action," Jermaine said.

The next shot they heard made them fall to the mud and slip in it and curse. Like a surprised pigeon I leapt into air.

"My god—" December pointed toward what hovered above them, wings open as though the sound of their commotion kept me airborne. They hushed and I fell on them, my body warm and meaty and soft, wings enveloping them.

"Stay here, stay here," I said, as though they had a choice. Another shot was fired and I heard it ricochet off a rock and snap a branch of a tree along the river.

A musket was fired into the flesh that protected them. I swarmed into the air and for a second gave a look of violence to the smaller boy who held the smoking rifle.

Another shot came from the direction of the house as Gus reloaded his musket and December screamed at all and no one. Larner came through the woods between the house and the river. He was unkempt, unshaven, altogether gray, bedraggled, armed. He yelled something the Jukes could not hear. I flew at Larner. Jermaine fired but I was out of range. The old man fired again. Jermaine fell into the river. Eyes wide, mouth shut as though holding her breath underwater, hair wild, December pulled him toward the banks as Gus ran at the old man. I airlifted Larner to the house as Gus pursued. December stood over her eldest brother. She held her hands to his chest where the ball had entered. Her brother might have been looking at eternity. He tried to say farewell to his sister but all that emerged was hemorrhaged air. She pulled her brother from the river another foot. Her father had led them into an ambush.

Gus crashed ahead toward Larner's door. He threw his shoulder into it, possessed. He ran into the house screaming as though if he demanded it with sufficient emphasis Larner would offer his throat and a sharp blade to ease the extraction of revenge. He ran through rooms, overturning chairs and knocking over vases and bowls, a whirlwind loose in the house. He ran down a corridor, turning sharp corners down one corridor after another. He opened doors on empty rooms and furnished bedrooms covered in dust.

The water seemed a translucent sort of brown, reflecting the white sky. She seemed to sense nothing more than Gus screaming in the distance. I reappeared beside her and did not do anything but look at the long-limbed boy in the muddy banks, the life already left him. To keep his body dry, I picked him up and carried him through the air to the bridge where I stood over Jermaine's body and spread my wings and howled again, softer, a different lament this time. How would she relate the news that Jermaine had been killed, Gus had chased the killer, and the beast her father had hunted now tended to her brother's corpse?

"If it laments," she said to no one, "how is he not our father?"

III

They may have found her sooner if the wind had blown toward Umbria. The ferryman may have discovered her kneeling beside her brother as a tower of smoke emerged from Larner's estate, a twisting monument atop an era of my life. The sight meant more to the girl than it did to me. I wanted to comfort her as she scanned the trees. This was her birth into worst possible times. But no one who sees me ever seems relieved. I am never welcomed, not even when needed.

I could have shepherded her from above, a protector out of sight, ready to swoop. Meals I could have provided, raw or charred.

I could have followed her so she sensed my presence and thought herself under my wing. Or I could have overcome my fear of fears of me and openly escorted her.

Right when I resolved to fly her to the outskirts of Umbria, she started home, entranced, as though her eyes no longer adjusted to darkness. A wolf stalked her. She would have attracted the attention of innumerable predators had I not emitted frequencies only they could sense. It would take the night to return. I could carry her though air without disturbing her if she stopped to sleep. Her eyes were open as she walked, yet it was clear she only saw the moment she became finally and totally alone.

Rain fell as I hovered above her, wings spread, doing what I could to keep her dry. Riverbank mud sucked down her shoes. She didn't even notice, not walking fast enough to feel much pain. She thought I was her father, a man who had said he was me. I would do what I could to protect, if not *parent*, her. The word was a riddle thanks to what I had done to my own mother and the uncertain identity of my sire.

Larner, in his lattermost years, had developed a theory about my father. It was conjecture I argued against by lifting a finger and poking his belly with a horny nail. *Crackpot* described the theory in general but it proceeded along these lines: I did not exist as anything more than legend. My father was neither William Leeds nor a seductive Briton soldier but a man of lasting importance who initiated a hoax to discredit the name of his chief competitor. Like the almanac and the colonies now known as the United States of America, I was a composite of disparate parts. I was known as the *Leeds* Devil because Poor Richard, another figment of this great man's imagination, had wished to slight the popularity of the *Leeds* American Almanack. Franklin had concocted his attendance at a witch trial in Mount Holly around the time of my birth. Some say the famous key–kite–lightning experiment was also a hoax. Larner attributed my existence to Franklin, the genius around whom all revolved, from whom all emerged, a black hole that devoured credit for all human progress and emitted such a bright and lasting light, my humanity only a mercurial, competitive glimmer in the eye of a founding American father.

But what were the chances that none of this was happening? Was I the one now with post-traumatic stress syndrome, as they'd eventually call it? Hovering above the girl, I was no more than a poor beast, worrying all the time about my so-called humanity when I should have been concerned that I didn't exist, that none of this was real.

The scent of smoke traveled on the wind, but neither the wind nor the smoke existed? Heavy mist sogged the hair of the child I protected, but neither rain nor child existed? The town of Umbria existed and did not exist? Yet every day our eyes opened on a world that never questioned its existence.

If Franklin were my father, if I were only a legend he had sired, if my existence had derived from his wish to smear his competition by associating it with a ridiculous bestial composite, my origins could have been worse. My father could have been the thief who begot this child now drawn home through the night, her trouble just begun.

What a state the girl was in, and yet she made it to the outskirts, the first shack farthest from the church, the homes of those most removed from the town's center, the roads unformed and pocked with manure and great stinking fissures and gaps. She continued to the center, slower now, automatic. I rose out of sight to see all below: an imperfect grid along the Mullica, civilization only a feat of pruning, optimistic woodwork, shale roofing against the suffocating forces of endlessly surrounding wilderness. To the east, the ocean mocked them all. If only they could see such a sight, how would they behave, how would they transform, how renounce unrealistic expectations of perfection?

The next stage in the girl's life would require supreme patience. How would she withstand questions and accusations, criticisms and conclusions regarding her character, all mixed with self-congratulation among those who had doubted the Altruists' instinct to reform the Jukes?

At first she'd had fresh skin, sparkling eyes, a smile that calmed stirred emotions or gained someone's favor who may have intimidated her. The unmistakable rightness of her youth, open, curious, unfiltered, in part made the Altruists help the Jukes after their father's disappearance. Elders remembered Branley's youth before harsh weather eroded him inside and out.

Everything charred, razed, cleansed in a way. The house had been about to crumble well before Larner had lost his capacities. And from those ashes rose in Umbria a force directed against the innocent arrogance, they believed, of the Altruists. Their moral obligation to serve created a superior air, their imitation of Christ a sinful pretension. They solely wished to reinforce their standing with transparently manipulative outpourings of charity. The dynamics of their do-gooding were altogether loathsome, their opponents contended. There was no such thing as generosity. All giving was tainted by expectation of equivalent return. In that respect, the Altruists, it was argued, were as impure as any degenerate they sought to reform.

As though an aftershock of the rift between Confederacy and Union, the town split at first on what to do with the girl. Arguments, editorials in the *Crier*, raised voices at the Bucket, sermons, hushed conversations by candlelight, all were shot through with concerns for the girl. There were infinite complexities to their lives in terms of health and sustenance and any number of the consequences of the minor cruelties of life, but instead they focused on December Jukes.

One side suggested she be sacrificed how her father had sacrificed Nathaniel Leeds. Be done with her and the Jukes lineage forever. The other side insisted that her treatment would filter through all aspects of their existence, through large and small decisions thereafter, to how they spent their days. The girl's shadow in the town darkened as her existence attracted suspicions of supernatural powers she would use for good or evil per what what those who invoked her name believed. And they all invoked her name.

December was not accused of anything, although many blamed her for numerous maladies. Ignoring shouted objection from her Altruist family, she was held, not in prison with thieves and drunks, but in a single windowless shack with a rolled dirt floor. They kept her there as though caged. The Dorwoods seemed relieved that she hadn't been killed outright.

Whenever released for exercise or to bathe, crowds jeered her, and others rose against her detractors, the town so unsettled by her presence that many among the Altruists began to think they should send her to Baltimore, Philadelphia, New York, or Boston, somewhere she could be anonymous, where the history of her family would not follow. It was in everyone's interests, most agreed, for December Jukes to leave Umbria. The town may otherwise erupt.

Never had a child taken such a hold. Some sensed they were infected by her, the girl caused sorrow, enflamed passions, the empty look in her eyes reflected the gazes of those who reveled in worst thoughts and feelings. With this virus in the air, more became infected or fought the infection. Arguments emerged in favor of the girl's innocence, the need to keep her in town and rehabilitate her to teach everyone a lesson. With consistent and thorough application of our best instinct, we could change the world. To such peaceful, positive arguments, the Anti-Altruists countered with vehemence, with such hatred toward the girl, that they seemed maddened with whatever condition they'd developed since December returned from that doomed trip up the river she'd taken with her brothers.

The Altruists in turn became possessed with their opposing force, animated by their enemy's furor. Those aligned against the Altruists, anticipating imminent aggression they perceived, dragged December's mother through the streets, displayed her as a monster infected by copulation with Jukes, the devil himself, father of the spawn that led to the death of good old Larner, someone they now championed as representative philanthropist and dearly departed righteous entity all should emulate. They knocked December's mother in the street, pelted her with refuse, the first real move toward open violence the town had ever taken. It was clear that something had happened to the mother's nervous system. She now only played the armonica as though through those sounds she accessed paradise—and otherwise she seemed in an accelerated state of decay. The mother's corruption was obvious by the way she no longer recognized her own daughter, the girl in effect orphaned, the essence of her mother's brain a sort of charmed mush.

Such hostile parading of the Jukes mother led many to believe the only way to restore order was to put the girl, and thereby the entire town, out of their collective misery.

It was one young life, they argued, damned to a future of criminality and outright insanity. It would be charitable to drown her in the Mullica.

The idea spread. The call for it sobered passions. It was a sort of capital punishment levied against the girl, her father, the untold history of horrors perpetrated through time by their progenitors. By staunching something in this girl, her brothers both dead, her father presumably dead, her mother of no blood relation to the Jukes, a victim more than anything, they would cleanse humanity of an impure link. It was all for the best: the girl would be released from her trauma, the town's conflict would end, and the Jukes' mad spark would be snuffed. If the Altruists were genuinely interested in bringing about the best possible world they would support the plan.

The Altruists argued however that putting December Jukes to death, to even consider it with any seriousness, was the first step into an abyss from which Umbria would never emerge. The Worthen father gave a speech and was pelted with mud and rotten vegetables, ridiculed so obscenely that he moved his family to a saner settlement to the north. Worthen had been an initial proponent of redemption for the Jukes, but once he crumbled, the other Altruists fell silent one after the other as the rest of Umbria articulated a rationale for the elimination of a thirteen-year-old girl.

December seemed almost feral, lost in chaotic thoughts, removed from pleasant encounter with anyone. I kept an eye on her when I could, overhearing everything, the town failing to consider the possibility that their rationalizations for murdering a child were no match for justice levied against them by the so-called Leeds Devil.

The Umbrians were in no hurry to do away with her. Holding the girl as a centerpiece for their hatred brought them together. She was an unlikely unifying force, a figure around which to rally. Once she was gone they would only achieve a similar state if they found someone or something else to oppose as one. For now, the plan was to walk her to the Mullica after dressing her in a white gown and transform her murder into ritual sacrifice. They would pave her way with cherry blossoms and rose petals and release white doves as her feet touched water. They would wed her to the river, return her to the water, and by doing so, restore their community to its former state. Sacrifice of a young girl was a beautiful idea, most thought. The town joined together like a happy family detailing every last element. It would be unforgettable, beneficial to all. For an air of seasonal rebirth, they chose the first of May, when days lengthen and the green of the world embodies tenderness itself.

Until then, they treated her as a rising queen. Attendants brushed her hair and oiled her limbs. December became a daily remainder that all have only so long to live. No more than thirteen years old and yet the day of her death is determined.

As her treatment improved throughout the winter, December emerged from her trance. It would have been best to hibernate within herself until water filled her lungs, but now she understood and replied to speech. She would not say what she had seen, but she responded to her attendants, who were not much older than December, rewarded for good behavior with positions as handmaidens of the doomed girl. By proximity to her, it was thought they might comprehend life's fragility.

As December regained her faculties, her privileged attendants began to covet what they could never secure. They too wanted to succumb to the coppery waters of the Mullica and thereby benefit everyone. Each was willing to martyr herself if promised elaborate, maudlin, festive ceremonies, especially if it assured a season of peace in Umbria.

The attendants decided that for each to attain and surpass December's stature, they needed to cause a disturbance for which each would be put to death before December's proposed marriage to the Mullica. No one expected these girls would aspire to exceed December's reputation. The attendants were the sort who had forced December to dig a burrow of secret tunnels inside herself, like a mole. Yet now these girls seemed charmed, even worshipful. They treated December like a hidden gem, the search for which they devoted their short lives.

"December," they said—in their mouths her name was an aphrodisiac—"What can we do for you? How can we please you?"

They outdid one other with garlands of compliment. These girls, their scents, the absolute bouquet of them, was cruel reward. The sight of her father hanging by his wrists. Her own wrists circled in bright rings the girls made of strands of dyed hemp. Her return from mist and creek mud. That mansion in black inferno. Its dark roar.

IV

I could have reduced her cell to splinters or removed the roof and snatched her out, but then I would have needed to fly throughout the country, an omniscient, bestial crime-fighter who righted all wrongs. Who has ever come to free me, to save me, to release me from history? Why have I been damned to access the thoughts and feelings of all those with whom I have an affinity? A gift and a curse, extrasensory and inhuman, akin to flight and never seeming to die. That everyone I'd known had aged and died supported theories of my non-existence. It is a particular sadness of the immortal to outlive everyone. Consider the weariness of Poseidon surveying the ever-changing coastline, nostalgic for the shape of Pangaea, the ecstatic appearance of islands upon their fiery steaming birth above water. If I were a sort of god, I could influence December's situation without detection. Have paparazzi ever captured Poseidon surveying the Atlantic coast? I'm more of a beast of a man, alas, possibly immortal and definitively aware of the fragility of those unlike me.

Sheriff Hopkins was found in bed, hands flat against his chest, middle fingers meeting at their tips, his black mustache a covenant with death across his grimace. It was unexpected, considering his age and health. Nothing was out of order in the room but this was no natural death. A delicate cut ran across the stomach. A fine knife or needle had left a tattoo of dried blood. The mark looked like the head of a ram, its curling horns bracketed by wings like mine. Some called it the mark of the beast.

They wouldn't openly slaughter. Their actions required artfulness. If they had hacked the sheriff in the street, they would have been overtaken and destroyed, stamped out by the men they wished one day would sacrifice them. To supplant the sacrificial virgin they needed to make her forgettable. Branley Jukes had murdered two men—they would exceed that number until everyone feared for their lives.

After Hopkins' murder, the beast was seen again. Some claimed it was Branley Jukes in natural form, stalking his daughter's capturers. Regardless, something far too large for flight had descended into the branches of an oak that under its weight thrashed as though in a windstorm. A man and not a man.

That was the extent of news I detected thanks to civic scurrying and commotion. As far as I knew, the only ones with anything to fear were rabbits, doves, quail (particularly), a fawn at most when gluttonous. I tried to limit myself to corn and other vegetables, but we all succumb to instinct now and then. If one of her attendants wished to slit December's throat, what could I do? But if I had a chance to intervene I would.

To say Hopkins had represented order to the town was an understatement. His words had come in intelligible, predictable succession. His smile was even and slow, consistent in its ability to calm, and he'd seemed strong and compassionate. He was the sort who took a knee as though to pray or examine the dirt when collecting himself, trying to enter as deeply as possible into the complexities of a situation, opening himself to concealed shreds he would miss if unable to occupy the moment. His removal from the town had put them all on edge. No one protected them now.

Some said they deserved it for agreeing to put the girl to death. Others said it was the girl herself who had done it, or at least she could be blamed. An airing of concerns stirred their confusion and fear. Voices relaying hysterical exaggeration and nonsensical psychosis united to improvise dissonant hymnals to Umbria's state. Some said the Jukes had always been sensitive to instabilities in the land and atmosphere. Something about the terrain of this spot with three thousand miles of water and three thousand miles of land on either side, existence here experienced unexpected shifts as water and earth pushed and pulled one way and another. The death of Nathaniel Leeds was the first shot and now they were at war with some evil among them. The only way to appease it, obviously, was to sacrifice the Jukes girl. And those who protested that this plan was the truest demonstration of evil were howled down to such a degree they feared for their lives. She had to pay as soon as possible, they said, and so December's attendants accelerated their operations.

Armonica at rest beside her, Georgia Jukes was discovered in bed like Hopkins, another ram head and wings carved by a light hand into her stomach. If she had gone first, it's possible that Hopkins would have discovered that December's attendants had done it. But his successors were more or less inept. No apparent struggle. Skin that had stretched when pregnant with December was now tattooed with a pagan visage. News of her mother's death seemed to come from another life. Her mother was already far too gone, so perhaps it was better, although she thought of little more now than spending an hour, let alone the rest of her life, outside again. Not long ago she had leaned on the trunk of a tree with her brothers. Not long ago she had slept in a shack in the woods with her family.

The way Hopkins's successor, a comparative halfwit named Sampson Torp, told December about her mother, it was as though he thought she already knew. The newly appointed Torp examined her face for an intimation of guilt, a sense she'd made her trackless way to her mother's bed where she ended her mother's life, motivated by the fact that her mother had failed to recognize the death of her sons and capture of her daughter.

Something in Georgia Jukes had opened once they'd removed her from the woods. The specter of her husband had held her together, but once he was gone, beyond the rounded tones of her armonica, she had lost all shape. No one could say whether the instrument attracted the mad or whether it accessed something mad inside them the music externalized. Some believed her music had invited the devil to her room. It could not be a coincidence that they had also discovered an armonica in Hopkins' sleeping chamber. He was not known to play it. Some believed the true culprit was, in fact, the instrument invented by Benjamin Franklin.

Every armonica was smashed in the central square, the shards carried to the Mullica. For some, if no such instruments existed in Umbria, security would be secured.

December's attendants thought punishment should have reached them by now. Someone other than the incompetent Sheriff Torp should have discovered a footprint, a fingerprint, or through careful investigation deduced how Hopkins and Georgia Jukes had lost their lives. The town had gone so mad they blamed a musical instrument.

On the morning of their sacrifice, as they envisioned it, the water slides by like coppery oil, its red enhanced by new green boughs and flowers of every color, some as tall as saplings, and once at water's edge the girls see everyone transform into half-flower human-sized daffodils, irises with crocus children accompanied by yellow-rose servants, followed by marigolds, the air suffused with pollen dust and a steady hum, an open vowel, nothing more. The girls wave goodbye to family and friends and kiss all goodbye as tears meet the warm and flowing water. On each forehead they feel the touch of Umbria's attention, anointed, celebrated, everyone so thankful, wishing them well in the afterworld, everyone in bloom with a paradise to come. As the girls step into the water and submerge, their ceremonial veils spread as they float and rotate down-stream like imitation water lilies.

Such a peaceful, joyous, celebratory, perfectly clear May morning no longer seemed possible. After the smashing of the armonicas it seemed that, unless the town calmed, its citizens would unleash their fear in another violent event. The girls now envisioned their inevitable end: cooked on a spit and consumed by all.

Each day proceeded as though torn apart by their guilt and their ceremonial dream, and yet each day they visited December who, unlike everyone else, reflected no change. She rarely smiled, her body thin and tender and tensed, expecting a flurry of punches or even a knife in the neck, as though she could sense that the girls' attention was now an act.

The bartender of the Bucket of Blood lay dead in his bed. On his bloated hairless stomach they found a ram head and wings. The pagan image leaned to the left this time, rushed, dug deeper into the flesh, a sketch more than a diabolical mark executed to perfection. Nevertheless, this matter was not widely broadcast as the Bucket was shuttered and searched and they held everyone who had ever entered for questions.

Among themselves, the attendants insisted not to have done it. Each swore it hadn't occurred to her to repeat their atrocity alone. None could imagine how she might seduce him, coax the poison into his mouth, and drag him to his final resting spot without at least three others or the help of a man.

But what about you and your older brother?

He'd never conspire with me. He'd throttle me, simple moralist, you know that.

But your uncle knows no morality, drinking partner of that murdered Merkins, maybe he avenged the pints the bartender had failed to stand him?

If we didn't do this then who did?

A devil?

There is no devil. We are the devil. We did it.

The devil is our dream, our desire.

The devil is December Jukes, full stop. We blame this on her.

But she's done nothing.

She's done all.

Since her return it has been mayhem. And we have behaved as though possessed.

We are not to blame for any of this. We have done nothing.

We know we've done terrible, twice.

For all we know we did what happened last night, too.

But we didn't.

Who can say what happened?

One thing we can say is December is to blame.

No one else is suspected of extraordinary powers.

But what now is our desire, our dream?

V

Umbria whirled in ragged circles around her unmoving center. All now transformed into something less than human. To see behavior devolve complicated my urge, my need, my hope. The more I watched these people, the more I thought that not even the highest power might comprehend their actions. All sense of order and justice and good seemed upended by fear. They planned to marry the girl to the Mullica, but the longer she lived, the more the town did itself in.

Another three bodies were discovered, no marks on their stomachs, no hidden armonicas, not the holders of titles of particular importance. They were anonymous members of the community, seemingly chosen at random, or chosen per dissimilarities, and these three sent the town into open madness.

No one thereafter would let themselves be alone. The weather had warmed and it was wet, the center of town a mud pit that might soon see Umbria's extinction. All spent their days in plain sight, a joyless celebration intended to advance one's innocence and achieve protection of the masses. Viruses spread among them, excremental maladies, hacking coughs, unending phlegm spat at the earth. Pregnant mothers held their stomachs and tried to evade pervasive terror. Men on knees clucked along with rags on their heads, hoping to discover a cure for visibility. Some rode piggyback to become superhuman, trying to glimpse a far-off moment of peace. Into trees others climbed and from there were safe but exposed to the sight of civil disorder. Beatings, lashings, flailing of self and other. Hands together, some beseeched heaven for a remedy, only to receive a secular knee to the nuts. Slop was spilled and filth strewn as though one must keep all trash airborne. Bandaged skulls, bloody limbs, the new leaves a testament to the season's cruelty, hair pulled out in clumps, a wooden leg used to ram the door of a dwelling, no one trying to bring peace. Confusion became so severe on the ground it seemed the sky had opened and from it poured armies of rebellious angels, overgrown mosquitoes, sexually suggestive manta rays imitating harmless orchids, beams of light solidified into glowing silver trumpets, enormous worms, gargantuan crab shells, an egg twice the size of December from which perhaps a sense of order might soon hatch.

I watched human citizens transform more or less into beasts, the evil always concealed in the land now out in the open. In comparison, I was a tender flower, forever repenting as they churned to prove their innocence. And then out of the unhinged and improvised ceremony of sinfulness, a cry emerged for the sacrifice of the town's most precious and innocent: the attendants surrounding the damned.

They took refuge with December as madness raged. They wanted to run outside and stop it, and yet all along I reveled in it. Every fallen moment of humanity made my state seem more common. Few devoured their family, yes, but look at Umbria: did it matter if the ravaging came at first breath or when everyone was fully developed? What was the benefit of advancing age if all purported good would be tossed into a swirling cesspool of worst urges? I revealed myself then, flying above, through them, among them, but either they were blinded by madness or now I fit right in.

It was Umbria's last gasp, this proclamation to round up the children who attended December. The chaotic sprawl funneled toward the humble holding shack. The attendant's parents, most of them, assented, convinced that sacrifice was for the greater good. One mother objected, but they dragged her into the woods.

That no one spotted me, that I didn't distract from the fury, suggested how far Umbria had fallen. Yet all I did was fly among them, another element of nightmare, hovering above as the door to December's shack was torn from its frame to better accommodate the men who pulled out their quarry. December, too, they extracted into daylight but let her stand and watch what they did with the girls who pleaded their case through cries and kicking at first, and then once their innocence was presented as the reason for their sacrifice, they screamed their guilt for the first two murders, statements laughed away as the stuff of panicked minds offering whatever preposterous claims might set them down.

Each child was strapped to a beam of oak and held aloft, muttering confessions, calling themselves killers. The town entire trundled en masse, hooting, roaring, like a bloated sidewinder snake, as it made its impassioned way to the river, the color of which now seemed stained by bloodlust more than cedar bark.

I watched December watch them as they went to the river. She followed, no longer the devil's spawn, now a bystander to sprawling ill will, a madness in comparison to which her father's seemed manageable, preferable to a civilization's collapse.

Speakers at the river competed for the common ear, each intoning bombastic judgment upon the girls, sentences the river would execute: In the name of the Lord and the common good, so our safety and commonality might not be slighted, we relegate our purest urchins to propagate their innocence throughout the area so it might return to a state of grace. These children are our saviors and today shall forever be celebrated and their sacrifice be honored as the most recent holy covenant of heaven and earth, and as we cleanse our illness in these waters we shall listen for their final words expressing accomplishment of their duty. The Lord too suffered forsaken, and these children, the lambs of our flock, have struggled, their innocence stirred by aghast countenance and preposterous confessions of crimes they never could have committed. Now as we release them into paradise, we expect to emerge into a state of grace surpassing any achieved since these colonies transformed into country.

I would not intercede. It wasn't worth the bloodshed, the hysteria. Better to pass into legend and limit myself to a witness role. And so the girls were introduced to their groom—the extra-animated Mullica River—warmed perhaps by their struggling bodies. How quickly the girls' desires had shifted. The ends were the same (sacrificed), but the means lacked the posturing, the planning, the graceful determination, and of course the respect accorded to those ascending to the pantheon of holy martyrs. It seemed everyone wanted to kill off their most promising aspects, their hope. Like some eugenics program in reverse, they exterminated their privileged and most promising so the rest might rise in emulation of those removed.

The Mullica accepted anything offered it. The girls were no exception. The succession of wavelets on its surface broke open and shifted toward spitting whitewater, like woodchips airborne after the fall of an ax, and then it settled and returned as though nothing had happened. These masses along the banks of the Mullica did not witness everything become orderly as their unrestrained actions gave way to patience and respect and reasonable plans. Voices fell after salutes and hallelujahs, and in that silence they sensed that before paradise were achieved they would need to finish the work they had started. To restore their former state, they first needed to reunite December with her attendants.

She had almost blended into the crowd. She had watched as the girls tied to weighted oak were introduced into the river, dragged across its soft, inky, withdrawing flesh. Her father had said he was the Leeds Devil, but the Leeds Devil in human form was a disappearing act, something almost like death, out of sight, with no hope for return. Yet if she looked up she may have seen a shadow move across the uppermost branches of the trees, a presence if not quite her protector.

December would not struggle or run but give herself up as though happy to relinquish doubts of the last hundred days in favor of the certainty of no future, or at best transform beneath the river into tadpole, algae, water spider across the surface consumed soon enough by trout or crane. She preferred this fate to a future around those she'd orbited but could never live among without violent impact. She was a comet. Beneath the Mullica she would be celestial.

I restrained an urge to give into basest desire and punish humanity. Everything I learned of them convinced me of my rightful inclusion.

It was then, as speeches soared and weights were attached to a beam of oak that would transport December into the Mullica, they saw him. The sight must have rivaled the natives' first glimpse of conquistadors on the backs of stallions, for if anyone had ever appeared from some distant land, inherently superior with a powerful obsidian horse beneath him, if anyone could sit as upright and as natural as though the beast were an extension of his body, it was this man. He was accompanied by two others, fat and thin, the voices of contrary advice and attitude most likely on which the great visitor depended, both atop gray fillies that seemed more like ponies next to the central man's steed. Behind them, teens followed on knock-kneed quarter horses, though the effect was of an undefeatable army. The crowd parted to where December lay on the bank of the river, bound, silent, ready for sacrifice.

The crowd gave way without struggle thanks to the extreme vitality of the arrival's steed. Proud across the chest and neck and hindquarters, it was the apotheosis of horse, so much so it edged into other orders of animal: lion, panther, god. The animal seemed to absorb all possible goodness into its hide and project it outward. That a man rode this horse was remarkable. The sight mesmerized them in their weakened state, like news from the world indicating how far Umbria had fallen. December's salvation was more dramatic than escape into skies. The man on the horse seemed drawn to the scene like a conquistador to some lost city of gold. He offered to buy everyone's land. All accepted, wide open now to the prospect of change. And so the paradise they sought was attained, in a way, and Umbria's ruins surrendered to the woods and fire and time.

The Dream of Pure Water

TEXTILE MILLS, iron works, paperies, tanneries, hundreds of thousands of citizens spewed filth into rivers. All tributaries became open sewers, all water impure, all life endangered. Pestilence and stench mixed with the rattle of plodding mortuary wagons through brick and cobbled streets. In elegiac gridlock, funeral processions en route to burial grounds stalled at intersections. The port received cargo from the tropics conveying mosquitoes, insignificant as eyelashes, thirsty for human blood, carrying yellow fever. Those in the know covered their mouths. Those with sense left the city, draining a population weakened by death and disease. Immigrants filled occupancies and contributed to urban atherosclerosis as unregulated industrial waste mucked the rivers. The city had risen like a wart, a lump, a tumor. No Mid-Atlantic winter of sleet would ever heal it. Outbreaks of typhoid and cholera challenged mortality records set by yellow fever. No mosquitoes this time, just mess, and those responsible for public good were leaders of private industry who entered the city from pastoral retreats, repeating the word *purity*. Fresh or filtered, pure water must be served, somehow, before the streets of this long-thriving site turned viscous with waste.

Purity, the word itself, when Wharton said it he saw a pane of glass and tasted cold brilliance through the translucent spike of an icicle, a representative apparition, a model of civilization. But he wasn't prone to abstraction. His mind revolved around enterprise, speculation, investment, private energies unleashed to spur public good. Quaker roots, ascetic tastes, spiritual parents, but unlike to the north, no Puritan ethic dissuaded entrepreneurs from applying energies to large-scale industry. First bricks, then zinc, then nickel, then iron, Wharton advanced fortunes his parents' families had won in shipping, and his nickel was used to make the country's coins—all very good, except for the stench, pestilence, and contaminated streams that jarred his sense of order.

Filth-teeming veins. Unregulated chaos. Only private hands, Wharton believed, could mold public lands. His plan for renewal was simple: invest in cranberries.

East of Philadelphia some dozens of miles, between the Delaware River and Atlantic Ocean, most of the land was covered in pines, a region aptly named the Pine Barrens. It was hardly deserted or stripped of resources but instead offered sanctuary from sullying forces that came from the encroachment of people and their work. Iron works there failed as industry moved to richer sources to the west, and the trees were used for charcoal and cedar and wreaths and cones and holly come Christmas. Over time, bogs and marshes and otherwise dry terrain proved suitable for cranberries. Acres of pine were cleared and the sand sculpted into furrowed rows for the primary agricultural product of the state's southern counties. Wharton had a hand in it, too, of course, having sold his interest in sugar beet farms to purchase as much of the so-called Pine Barrens as he could. Something about the stark territory between western river and eastern ocean attracted him—quick access to the shore and travel by sea to New York or Baltimore and beyond—but mainly it was those waxy red jewels, and soon after he discovered a far more valuable resource.

It is unfathomable, he wrote, that such land can draw one to it with something as innocent as these berries and soon after reveal the savior of one's home city's ills. Purity is there, unadulterated innocence in the waters, all concealed by spiky landscape common men might deem a waste, not understanding potential so often beneath unpleasant surfaces.

Wharton purchased an estate ruined by fire. The land had once been used for a pulp mill after a failed attempt at a bog-iron works, later it was transformed into a resort that had also failed before an eccentric lawyer spent the last years of his life on it accompanied, it was said, by someone in a white wedding dress who curious observers had seen on the grounds. The house was consumed by wildfire that regularly wasted the pines, the body of the old eccentric was found in the ashes, but no trace of the woman or her dress. Rumor became legend and merged with tales of the Leeds Devil who conveyed escaped slaves by cover of night, carrying them in its claws or entwined in its long tail, flying at great speed a hundred miles north, an underground railroad high above and out of sight. Yet no rumors circulated among the freed of a beast offering extraordinary air travel.

On Wharton's land near the Mullica River, these stories seemed like innocent entertainment. At best, the legends might scare all those interested in taking advantage of resources that existed not as obscure speculation but as *fact* beneath the pineland's surface. Those legends weren't as troubling, in any case, as what he had encountered when he first arrived in Umbria. And he couldn't see how legends affected the capability of a freshwater aquifer to relieve the stench and fever, the sickness and sorrow, and the general misery of an uncertain future for Philadelphia.

Wharton conceived the idea when a local told him that if one ran a pole ten feet into the sand it spurted coppery water altogether pure. The sand of the terrain filtered rainwater and stored it protected in underground lakes unfathomably endless, renewed with every rainfall. Topographical surveys documented it. This water would save the city better than any attempt to filter its polluted rivers and streams. From beneath his lands he would import innocence, purity, renewal. He would convey it by pipe and aqueduct and store it in reservoirs outside Camden and then deliver it to faucets via tunnels running beneath the rancid Delaware. It could be done, it would employ thousands, and it would save the city.

Pure water was needed, and just to the east it was endless.

Wharton would oversee the project from a moderate dwelling rising from the pines. In a clearing to the west were reconstructions of the original iron works there, excavated like the ruins of some great society instead of an early venture in American industry.

His interests in this property and project, his advisors said, came at the expense of lucrative exploits elsewhere, but Wharton felt best here. He and his family took long autumn vacations. He envisioned the lake beneath the land that surfaced as bogs and ponds and rivers, coppery and pure. He sensed the inevitability of success, as he had since he first proposed the use of his nickel in the country's coins.

Any idiot could rate gold and gems but to value worthless ores, to turn these into common currency by application of imagination and will, to recognize the savior of a city in copper-colored water, that was what men like Wharton were good for, and for every man like him a dozen others united in opposition. Hundreds with more practical ambitions, without that transformative spark in the eye—well-meaning councilmen lined up against Wharton like those who had persecuted Christ. *That story*, of all stories, he valued. It supported obstinate avowal of his most persistent interests. Minor figures have always ganged together to peck at those like Christ and Wharton, who did not waver.

His only failure had been in bricks. All of the city was brick. Houses, streets, sidewalks. He had been too young and there had been too much competition. A fire took out two city blocks and Wharton rebuilt it with bricks. Bricks from London, waterproof bricks, bricks that expanded with heat and adjusted. But bricks led to zinc, white zinc, zinc oxide—the leading industry in Bethlehem—and a wife, Anna, and children, and then nickel. Zinc and nickel and bricks. From rocks in the earth he made a fortune.

Wharton looked to the ground for solutions, and now he looked underground to save the city. Quantities of water beneath the pines, endless millions of gallons: *gazillions* they said. The council proposed to channel filthy water through sand and charcoal and boil it and treat it before sending it back to people. Their technique was so elaborate and unproven, failures were inevitable. The most elegant correction was wholesale conveyance of endless quantities of pure water. All it required: thousands of shovels and a single genius engineer to access it, harbor it, maintain its purity, and transport it by canal to reservoirs where the water, like fresh blood, would be infused into a city dying and dry. Instead of celebrating Wharton's option, instead of recognizing its obvious good news, his competitors united against him.

Wharton purchased land adjoining acres he already owned. He advanced the initial stage of his strategy securing rights to as many acres as possible before they were wasted on the cultivation of cranberries or corn or cedar.

Zinc and nickel had made him a leader of industry on par with Carnegie, but essential regions of his ambition remained untapped. "Do, do, do" he had ended letters to Anna when courting, instructing her how to live an honest life. But what good was private fulfillment if it did not include public good? In every hand in America, in Germany too, his nickel was in the coins. Now he wanted his water to animate bodies, purify them, something so good it inspired good in them.

The council voted for filtration beds by a single vote in favor, swaying the majority. Thousands dying of typhoid, and after long hesitation, they deemed other interests more pressing. They should be served warrants, the do-nothing slags, forgetting the people they swore on the Bible to serve, as though that book were filled with fictions and swearing upon it was only a formality required to enter privileged society. In the name of helping threatened citizens, influential lawyers and businessmen sat on the council to protect their interests, each a dragon on its horde.

Wharton never would serve on such a council. He was too busy to endure idleness like that. A sort of living hell, he thought. Doomed to listen to duplicitous, flattering, curlicued inconsequence. All sounded good and, on the surface, advanced a semblance of intelligent, well-meaning society, but it was all only idle talk and elaborate hand gestures intended to display fingerfuls of rings. How many years would it take to advance their scheme, perfect the mechanization, put it to use, repair malfunction? As they aired tentative plans to filter the water, Wharton purchased tens of thousands more tracts adjoining others he owned, assembling an empire, convincing owners of nearby land to sell their shares in the name of public good.

By the turn of the century the uninterrupted possession of one-hundred thousand acres was complete. His land ran with bogs, rivers, marshes, swamps—pure water to serve Philadelphia and Camden six times over a day. So much water, the city could become an American Atlantis. Or better yet: the New World's Venice. Gondolas on Market Street. Fins more common than shoes. If it's pure water they wanted, Wharton had more than enough. Brackish streams and typhoid-breeding tributaries could be cleaned, sure, yes. In the meantime, the city needed a flood.

"Oh if I were younger and not so steady how I would endear their faces to my fists," Wharton said upon his return from Philadelphia where he'd learned the result of the vote. "How I would beat them from shores and docks into the polluted waters. Make them fill their bodies until bloated. Waterlogged swine. If I were younger and not overburdened by menhaden fisheries, iron works to the north, the far-flung operations of my empire, if I could focus all remaining energies on the restoration of the original city, not some agrarian ideal before the rise of industry but more toward what it could have been: a functional, living place that distant cities might not scorn—birthplace of liberty, the stars and stripes, the Constitution, all the inventions of Benjamin Franklin—they scorn it when there should be hushed respect. I should mention my city with pride, sullied by unregulated indulgence, public good never on the minds of private coffers, never on the mind more than the accrual of monies needed to maintain escapes from the city, a place they demean with words and actions, thereby increasing the value of sylvan holdings with every detrimental passing of urban day into night. The swine ought to slather in their own muck. Contract typhoid like street urchins. Die. That would help them recognize the help I offer, the help I may never be allowed to provide.

"Boies Penrose had listened and seemed in support of my proposal, but I could have told the senator anything as long as I suggested I might support his candidacy. Stand beside me. I'll stand beside you. I'll donate to your campaign if you support my plan to ease travel to London by constructing a seabridge or tunnel. Sure, sure, he'd have said. Charmer, flatterer, willowy cavity filled with popular whim. If such men populated the country a century and some ago, how would we have fared against the British? Never would have dared revolt. Why did they even bother? All in vain. How these councilmen associate themselves with the founding fathers. Invoke revolutionary spirits. Replace overthrown royalty with empty pronouncements.

"Braddock and Vermeule and I, we could turn the city into an amphibious paradise. Or at least a place where citizens enjoy a functional, livable life, free of disease, so commoners perhaps have the health and energy to revolt. Now, how can they petition positive gain when even my last attempt to speak was met with yawns and exits so swift that before my brief speech was complete I was interrupted because quorum was no longer met. Perhaps I should not have prefaced my talk with commentary related to their idleness and accreted failures? Perhaps I should not have held them accountable for the toll on life and livelihood? Perhaps if I had flattered they would have heard me out. Or maybe coming from an elder respected worldwide, their pride was too great to withstand injurious words, to endure statements perhaps somewhat misconsidered, I now freely admit, related to their similarity to swine per the Book of Matthew? Perhaps such allusions had no role at this meeting? Perhaps they had heard how when sharing a platform with Theodore Roosevelt complaining of trusts and collusion I whispered loud enough for all to hear that greater men had been impeached for less seditious comment? Knowing this and other instances from a life of public appearance and private discussion misrepresented as rumor, perhaps the councilmen considered my reputation more than my proposal and the state of the city? Swine.

"Braddock and Vermeule and I, if a dozen years younger, thirty years younger, still in our firebrand prime, oh how we would have debated and demeaned them, let our arguments loose, amassed supporters, our enthusiasm for restoring the city's original state so infectious we'd restore the place by running through the street, a golden burst of example by which all would right our shared problems one by one.

"But now we are old, I am old, tired, without the energy or capabilities to commit to pure water. We must attend to other industries, profitable ones, or else sink in the current depression of economy, city, and soul, never to emerge. This venture in the pines, my great folly.

"Franklin stood before the British as a diplomat, greatly ridiculed. He stored that poison in his heart, engaged Britain's natural enemy in France, and took his revenge. Perhaps I will have the same fate, though by the time I avenge myself upon them we will all be gone.

"Does it matter if we players are no longer on stage? What matters is the stage is filthy, its conflicts unresolved, its state desperate, its solution unknown. I will include in my will language relating to desires for my lands to serve Philadelphia, enable its citizens to live no different from elected nobleman, those swine who rut and snort in troughs of luxury.

"Unornamented elegance in the pines, my retreat almost Spartan, reliant on woodwork, skilled labor, attentive carpentry, broad porches facing southwest, a widow's walk overlooking the pines all around, ocean mists on clear days. But this house, other than chandeliers and silver and china bowls, needs nothing that might remove my family from the wilderness we cherish, the freshest air, a wholesome ambit from which man is not meant to live too far. When I speak of luxury I speak of avarice more than wealth. Ostentatious displays intended to reinforce in their owner a sense of pride in the accrual of items valuable to few. A man wallowing in filth and excrement, dying of thirst, if offered an amulet, what good is it? Every time he would choose water over extravagance.

"We sleep to the sound of the Mullica running through the mill, a quick fall where dammed waters reflect trees and skies, so spirit-restoring it must be shared with everyone, one day, and the waters beneath these lands must be shared now. My legacy, a lifetime of industry, a rejection of idleness—when I rest in the pines I refresh my energy for battle to come—a legacy I wish passed down after my death, which must come soon. These lands I want to serve the people who need them, either as water provider or sanctuary. How these lands have refreshed me time and again, and how I imagine they might support others the same. What I fear is misuse, development without responsibility by swine possessed of avarice instead of responsibility and foresight and universal burden to uphold best interests without sacrificing them in the name of profit. These lands should pass into the possession of those deserving, those who might drive out the swine who sully the city with snorts of self-concern. And if I do not die, I stake my immortality on restoration of the city's original state. Let us hope I do not die until I see these resources unleashed, or that those who follow choose wisely, which I might add is an easy decision to discern: just ascertain the beliefs of those in power and take the opposite tack, for it is always right."

II

That commitment to industry and abhorrence of idleness might make him wealthy, he had never doubted. Outlay of energy returned as profit or else he deemed it wasted. That such expenditure might sustain his presence on earth beyond his death, he had never hoped, and yet as death approached, the woods would remain in his name. The pines, despite towns wiped by fire, preserved legend better than cities where history was forgotten as lives dispersed across a continuous present. On the porch of the mansion among ancient trees and the Mullica River, the landscape appeared to him as it had to the first Europeans who had traveled there, the natives who had fished and tracked game, the more recent history of the acres themselves, the resort that failed to attract European aristocracy, offering no real luxury or impressive vistas to which idle souls could travel, summits paralleling their success, and from the widow's walk all that could be seen for miles was wilderness interspersed with swamps and marshes and, in the distance, the sea, the sky. No place for aspirational aristocrats.

But Wharton had no need for an impressive landscape to encourage generous self-impression. He needed immersion in this land mistakenly called *barren*, undervalued by those unable to appreciate contorted pines and vines, scrub oaks, ink-black bogs clustered with lily pads, extra-green in contrast to sediment-rich waters elsewhere copper along the banks of turning streams, winding and twisting in a way no rational hand would ever plan.

Imagine the councilmen claiming authority over the pinelands and razing the forest, bricking it, rerouting Philadelphia's rivers so they flowed to some newfangled treatment plant. Wharton had never doubted that slavery was existentially unfortunate, that the owners themselves had wished to end it, but also he had believed that all had been caught in their ways. Migration to the north of freed slaves he thought would be a boon if the cities were ready, not already overwhelmed by European rabble. Those formerly enslaved migrated north to work machines instead of fields, removed from African jungle to Southern plantations to Northern streets, with nowhere for their waste to run but into the drinking water. How long would it be until he fielded a proposal to route their sludge to the pines? How far off could it be? How long until some swine remembered Wharton's insults and voted to pipe excrement to those scrappy lands to the east? How would he rebel against such a proposal, and if passed, how war against it?

Braddock and Vermeule, now almost elderly as well, might just sigh and let the world pass from achievable paradise to realm of living shit. Not too far off, Wharton thought, but how would these old men fight off a plan to pollute pristine lands if rational pathways were reversed, with purity flowing not to the pollution but pollution to the purity? And yet how could even one of the most successful industrialists of his age protect against swine possessed by avarice, self-interest, ignorance, evil? Was it possible to leave the dream of pure water behind? Is it possible to make them see just by closing his eyes?

He envisioned his head as the pinelands entire, the ponds his eyes, and he closed those eyes and gases burst from the waters and floated to the city and suffocated them all, or at least infected those in power with concern for the city's current and future state.

Overhearing talk on the porch with Braddock and Vermeule, these three old men so concerned with pure water seemed unlike others I had met. Larner had been more bedraggled than these men

128

who sat on the porch looking west as though ready for some entertainment, a parade of quail, anything more than the words I heard while hidden by nearby shrubs. The three of them on the porch in their fine clothes, expressions wizened, eternally unimpressed, resigned yet ever-ambitious, optimistic veterans who respected themselves, their histories of accomplishment, and what remained of their outsized will.

Braddock and Vermeule on either side of Wharton were like stump and vine. Braddock overflowed his seat. He seemed to rumble even when still, finely aware of the imminent threat of a broken chair, the possibility of embarrassment all too present thanks to experience. He tensed his thighs as though channeling weight through legs rather than down through rump. He squatted more so, resting as lightly as possible. Vermeule, with long legs one around the other, seemed lighter than his chair, nimble, as though his entire body might elevate if he raised an eyebrow. Ethereal, half gone, he seemed further along the process of unbecoming, almost angelic, and his voice when he spoke was soft and smooth. Between the two, Wharton was a landlubbering admiral whose presence commanded by virtue of issuing orders for decades, staring down questions and responding with indubitable authority. He wore a beard shaven only beneath the ears so his chin seemed twice as wide as the lipless gash of a mouth hidden by whiskers.

Braddock and Vermeule glanced at one another and toward Wharton as he spoke, but Wharton settled deeper into his reclining chair, squared shoulders, and eyed his land. He seemed like some savant whose words were spoken long ago by the land and filtered through every impression of a lifetime, and then he smiled at a thought, an assertion, and seemed again as present in mind as he was in body.

Their stature and speech were removed from the land more than any I had ever seen, as though stewardship required separation, their dress and gestures too precise, their language honed, whereas the rest of humanity I had encountered—even Dade, the old pastor who cursed my mother—had seemed more like shadows than these broad-based surveyors of the world. I stood on the widow's walk, perched there some mornings before dawn. There I saw the ocean, the lightening sky, and it seemed that these men enjoyed such sights at all times—sitting on the porch they saw to all horizons—and maybe it was this all-seeing sense that interested me. Unlike Larner with a blanket pulled above his nose when we first met, or Titan and Japhet shrieking in their printing shed, these three might brush me away with the back of their hands.

Ever since my chance to save December Jukes, I had not helped anyone. I once tended to a baby bird fallen from a nest, helped a lost dog find its way home instead of devouring it, but after years with Larner before he lost his faculties completely and came to such an unfortunate end, I spent time alone doing very little, the dress hidden as I explored the territory. New leaves filled out and dried up, year after year, yet nothing like that ever happened to my horns or wings or teeth. I didn't seem to age in any way, as though I did not exist. But it was during this time that dispersal of my legend truly began.

I flew to the cave and slipped into the dress. It was like showering after months of trekking through mud. It took some time to settle into the flesh, the feet, the hornless head.

The men were still there by the time I approached. Wharton's eyes were closed. He seemed asleep. Vermeule took more interest in his fingernails than Braddock's speech, which stopped when he saw me cross the bridge over a dam in the Mullica.

Braddock nudged Wharton. Vermeule untwined his legs.

"Do you see it?" said Braddock.

"I confirm a man in a dress—nothing else," said Vermeule.

"I see nothing," said Wharton, "except a sight I've never seen."

I walked toward the men, without timidity, proud of every step. I stood in front of them, just off the low porch.

"May I join you?" I said.

"These are private lands," said Wharton, "and this is a private conversation."

"I have lived here for years and would like to help however I can."

"We have a maid and a manservant. But thank you for your interest."

"I only appear like this so not to startle you."

"How less startling might one appear?" said Vermeule.

"Obviously disturbed," whispered Braddock, "and perhaps in need of a meal."

"I'm not hungry, thank you."

"Then why should we not drive you away?" said Wharton.

"Because I was born here more than a century and a half ago, because I lived here with the man who lived here before you restored this estate, because I overheard you talk about delivering pure water to the city, and because I think I can help."

"Just what we need to overcome the councilmen," said Braddock, settling into his seat. "A young man in a wedding dress."

Wharton at that moment may have remembered his speech before the councilmen, the difficulties sustaining their interest after insulting them, and now this young man stood before him. They had sat for hours, making no progress, circling the same notions, the same complaints. Perhaps this appearance was fortuitous.

"I am prepared at least to listen," said Wharton.

"Do you intend to protect these lands?" I said.

"We intend to save a city with what runs unseen beneath these lands, leaving them undisturbed except in areas where we channel the waters."

"And so then if you are not enemies I can perhaps influence those who challenge you, for I have uncommon powers when not in this dress."

"Not of sound mind," said Braddock.

"I can show you what I mean."

"If you must," said Wharton. "We are all eyes."

I lifted the dress over my head. They stood in protest as though the elasticity of youth were momentarily restored, but I soothed them, saying, "Sit, sit. Let us talk of those who oppose you."

"Deception of an extraordinary order," said Wharton.

"Quite an impossible sight," said Vermeule.

Wharton had heard of course that his land was haunted by the region's odd spirit, compacted into strange form as though the sky pressed harder and created extra pressure that twisted the trees and expelled this wonder from pockets of hell beneath the pines. The water was one thing, pure, perfect, but then this beast trying to soothe them with civility, despite appearances, was something else altogether.

The skin of the legs intrigued Wharton the most. It seemed covered in crustaceans, stiff and brittle, less bone than iron, like mechanical poles. I figured he looked at my legs to avoid the rest, my neck like a wildcat's leading into a horse's head, with collie snout and long teeth, completed by the thick curling horns of a ram.

"No sight can compare to this," he said, "yet if you focus on its eyes and close off your vision to just its voice, this beast, though inconceivably composed of various animals, seems human in essential areas, the mind and most likely the heart."

"A most impressive proposal," said Vermeule, "one to which I respond with astonishment, so intimidating a sight when it opens its wings."

"How I would have impressed my ideas upon the councilmen had I similar capabilities," said Wharton. "No sooner had I begun my speech then I stood before them in all my glorious purity until something like this beast spread its wings in City Hall. I would soar to the ceiling of that domed chamber, shadow all light, the way the bright sun of my plans was blocked by the cold and lifeless moon of their interests. I should have transformed into something like this beast, snatching with extraordinary jaws those who walked out, men I would not hire to oversee a scoop of mud in a mason jar, men who now control the city's future, how I would have dispatched them from their plight. Instead I reddened with displeasure as quorum was lost. Terrible, terrible."

Wharton collapsed in his chair. All those years of industry had whittled his constitution. All his systems were overcome by the sight of a polite beast that watched as Braddock and Vermeule attended to Wharton and called for help.

I sprang into the air and soared out of sight.

III

Summer gave way to mulled scents and eerie light. Battalions of clouds heralded winter. Men raised voices and invoked the presence of a spirit more than a man. Through heavy mist, they emitted calls as though to attract an exotic bird. No rainbow lorikeet or resplendent quetzal, I crossed the river, low, like an ordinary crane, and then shot high and circled like a vulture, surveying the area for snipers, not trusting these men (stump or wisp). Coast seeming clear, I descended like a sleeper awakening from a dream of flight.

Braddock and Vermeule had not seen me cut across the water or soar above them. Only when I landed in front of them did they realize their calls had succeeded.

"Oh my," said Vermeule.

"Lordie," said Braddock.

"Greetings," I said.

The men seemed unable to remember why they'd called in the first place. I waited, trying to appear deferential, hoping not to cause any more damage than I already had.

Vermeule seemed dazed, but Braddock, born in Manhattan, had spent most of his life among intimidating sights and never bowed. Advanced now in career and age, what did he have to lose, other than his life? He stepped toward me and spoke:

"We seek the help you offered. We believe you may be of service."

Vermeule now emerged from whatever enchanted state the sight of me had caused. He added: "Yes, yes, of service, we believe you may help us achieve Wharton's dream before he passes. Our plan is no more than a notion but perhaps you can advance it?"

Connection to their friend was stronger than fear for their lives. They believed in Wharton's dream, shared it, and as they spoke their eyes brightened, their skin tightened, propelled by a noble cause. They were motivated by more than profit: successful execution of this project, they thought, might best secure a spot in heaven.

Wharton died in the second week of January 1909. Among many accomplishments, his obituary mentioned failed attempts at resolving Philadelphia's typhoid epidemic with pure water imported from New Jersey, a proposal dispersed in his lifetime only in the form of pamphlets. Front-page announcement of such a plan, longstanding and unfulfilled, incited a minor fury. A plan had always been in place, conceived and advanced by Wharton himself, yet rejected by councilmen who favored costly, malfunction-prone, mechanized endeavors. The obituary also mentioned Wharton's land and the sanctuary there and his initial wishes to will it all to Philadelphia, a desire ultimately curbed, not trusting the city to use it well.

Braddock, Vermeule, and I met late one night, days after Wharton's death. The councilmen intended to devalue and then seize the pinelands. A land grab, Wharton's forces called it. Around a candle, they related what they knew.

"You are part of their plans. A smear campaign," said Braddock. Dark hollows beneath his eyes seemed affixed to his face, the uppermost part of a mask of exhaustion. The rest of him was as overpresent in the world as ever. "They'll terrorize the people into distrust of these lands and force their sale by Wharton's heirs."

"How can I—"

Vermeule interrupted, a stride ahead: "It was always about philanthropy, profit, increased production, improved health, better workers, and so forth, a flood of goodness for all beginning with the water beneath his lands. He discovered these lands, in a sense. The councilmen never considered their proximity and potential to serve their city. They considered the city something to manipulate to serve their interests. Pure water for the scuttling masses is not part of their portfolio of interests. Typhoid and cholera are consequences of urban life. If immigrants drawn to the outer circles of hell have a problem with the threat of illness, the councilmen believe they can return to where living is easier, or they can work harder, save more, muster resources to improve their state. Thirst for rising from poverty is a prerequisite for those who wish not to contract waterborne illness. Other arguments we discount and should not even pronounce, such as these impoverished citizens are damned, cholera and typhoid and dysentery and all other maladies are God's gift to the righteous, as if the Lord were doing what He can, what He must do, to eliminate wretched infiltration. As clearly as you hear my voice, I have heard councilmen opine that the Lord is in fact an *exterminator*. The poor of the city are pests, requiring elimination, and ..."

Braddock intervened: "My friend elevates his umber with such descriptions. He doesn't have the highest regard for the poor, nor do I, but we believe their state is mutable and that we can do what we can, as executors of Wharton's final wishes, keepers of his dream, to deliver pure water, as Wharton liked to say, the essential lubricant of commerce and industry, the most valuable natural resource, without which we all, rich and poor and everyone in-between, are merely bones in bags of skin."

"But my use?" I said.

"To stop the councilmen's land grab ..." began Vermeule.

"First, we must define it," said Braddock, taking over. "In their eyes, Wharton was more than a powerful industrialist. He was akin to Columbus, in that he alighted on a new world. Not just the water beneath it but its surface, all the crops, development potential, rail stations, timber, sites for prisons and military bases, and, perhaps most importantly in some minds, a potential permanent home for the poverty-stricken residents of the city, not to mention a final resting spot for its refuse."

I considered the flickering emanations I could see around us by candlelight. I imagined the surrounding darkness produced by mountains of oily, odiferous, obscene trash, blotting out all light and life with it.

Vermeule noted my fugue and snapped his fingers above the candle. I refocused and the candle seemed to brighten.

"Wharton still has loyalists. Many owe him everything, many have their ears open, many relay information of potential interest to us."

"What C.C. means to say is Wharton's grease has turned many wheels."

"And yet wrenches are now in the gears. More than that: they seek to wipe his legacy into the grave with his body. We now must stop it or at least complicate it."

I did not quote Larner's words that I was just a twinkle in the eye of a founding father, a mercurial hoax, a ridiculous composite lampooning various elements of almanacs and colonies, a frolicsome phantasmagoria intended to haunt the space between competing publications. I didn't want to call into question their conspiratorial tones, the assuredness of their actions.

Braddock continued: "Stearns and Daley, they're total swine, as Wharton liked to say. No others would seek an offensive now. Stearns particularly knows neither graciousness nor tact. Some longstanding insult must linger, some blow to his psyche, eternal hurt that can only be avenged upon the land Wharton once possessed. What matters: the dream of pure water is now reduced to an endangered drip."

Per Braddock and Vermeule, this Stearns contradicted every commandment Franklin issued as he strove for moral perfection. Instead of imitating Christ and Socrates, Stearns emulated some undead Teutonic villain, an aristocrat of arrogance, lord of extreme self-interest. Yet it's unfair to present him entirely as a devil thanks to obvious elegance and charm. That some seemed like citizens of another world, held to other rules, complicated hope I had for assuming an advanced state of humanity. Men like Stearns and Daley were the exception, not a model for me or anyone else. They twisted reality on its side, turning all heads until they were the only one upright. To protect the pines and achieve Wharton's reasonable dream, I agreed to set Stearns straight.

Phenomenal Week

FLYING THROUGH SNOW at night, each fugitive streak evokes an image, events recalled in associative order, fragments of speech, insubstantial meteors in a rush across the void. The flight to Stearns's estate was ecstatic passage back to the world of men. Snow seemed to fall harder, come faster. I folded my wings. Gravity shot me toward my target like a sentient missile. Unfortunate encounters loomed, the fear of them at least, or if not fear then shaky expectation, the sense that only in flight could I achieve a stable foothold.

Fight terror with terror. No matter how odious Stearns might be I must restrain myself. No need to eliminate anyone. Keep in mind the inevitable necessity of redemption. Do not believe the plans of Braddock, Vermeule, and Wharton are indubitable. Stearns may be the one who envisions a better world and makes it happen.

I descended toward geometric hedge work unlike anything seen in nature. The house itself was not immodest. Covered in snow, light from within it emitted warmth, hospitality, a memory of cups of chocolate Larner had made on winter evenings.

Behind the house on a patio covered in snow someone bundled against the cold. Like my beloved wedding dress once did, she held a small lantern. The snow had tapered to an icy dust. Each bit sparkled as it neared her light.

I took a position behind a sculpture of a rearing horse and its youthful rider aiming a sword at the heavens. The woman with the lantern was not singing, but there was a melody to her voice, a lightness and rhythm like the snowfall. She stood before a sculpture of snow nearly as tall as she was. It must have taken a day's work, an obsessive creation. I held my breath to better hear what she said. Her speech was an unintelligible sing-song muttering, not intended for anyone's ears. Snatches of phrases seemed like a story more than audible rumination.

Fire, brothers, beast, river.

Perhaps it was the ice on my wings and in the crevices of my hooves, but, although seeing her warmed me, I froze to the spot, unable to conceive a harmless introduction. If I approached from behind ... From in front or the side ... if I said her name, kept wings down, and instructed her as softly as possible not to fear ... if I hovered above the ground just beyond the sculpture, wings spread—the most dramatic choice, the one most likely to alarm her.

As I hesitated, she ended whatever nocturnal confession she enjoyed with the snow sculpture and joined the light from her lantern with that of others inside.

I emerged from my spot behind the statue and stood where she had stood, my hooves on the matted areas her feet had made moments ago. Snow had softened the sculpture's details. The wings were swept across its back, tense and ready and strong, the horns full and spiraling and intact, the noble horse's head and smiling canine face, the tail coiled behind legs rising from a block of well-packed snow. Oh to have such a stable base. But alas, for all its artfulness, this representation would only rise into the air once it evaporated.

Had she made it? Or someone hired by Stearns? Such representations were part of their plan. Or so I'd been told. A proliferation of likenesses. She had treated it with respect, almost reverence. That little nod before she went inside could have been a bow.

Through broad windows I saw an enormous fireplace without much fire in it. Portraits of Stearns on horseback and generic pastoral scenes in gaudy frames. She looked unlike what I thought she might become. Her hair was long and full and lightened. Her neck was wrapped in silk the color of coral that made her eyes seem like elaborately grained ovals of glass. The expression around her mouth seemed ambiguous, present and vacant at once, perhaps the fault of the painter or maybe it recognized a tendency in her to slide into the past. Every aspect of the house seemed intended to fulfill the expectations of visitors. The distance in December's eyes suggested her love for Stearns. The viewer was meant to marvel at Stearns for having such a wife and knowing such a talented painter, a currency among a limited set of citizens, as the rest drank putrid water.

A form appeared, a man's back. Stearns was so close. Did he see me? He turned and ran a hand through dark and gleaming hair. He smiled and hitched his chin toward a shoulder and said something I could not discern from his lips. He could not see me, or else he thought I was another replica, an enormous marionette he could manipulate without bothering with strings. Perhaps he had said "excellent" or "perfect" before extinguishing lanterns. A squat hurrying servant followed and left the room thereafter in darkness.

Unless the doors were left unlocked there was only one way in. The fire was now warm ash. They had screened off the chimney against rodents and birds, but without much effort I pried away the grating and entered what seemed like a primitive oven. I stirred a cloud of ash.

Saturday morning would not be far off, a few hours left for a nightmare to stalk this dream house. The moon now found spaces between clouds and, reflected off the snow, it lightened the room.

I sensed the presence of sleeping bodies. But I did not expect that some of these would be children. The scent was unmistakable. A quiet cry grew until someone shuffled from an adjoining room. Children have a sixth sense for the likes of me. Hearing and taste and sense of touch combine into a radar that, like with Larner's helpless rabbits, is ever-ready to sound the alarm. Detection of nightmarish intruders is intuitive for them, and yet, thankfully, they cannot articulate what triggers the response. An uneasy dream causes them to call for comfort, but rarely are dreams troubled by the actual presence of a beast.

My snow-wet hooves trailed ash as I explored. They would think the cloven footprints a prank, one among many that weekend, hoaxes of all sorts, as a brigade of craftsmen unleashed their work into spaces in the region's psyches reserved for fear of the unknown, the impossible, the supernatural forces that some might argue were inseparable from the imagination's creation of gods. Belief in powers beyond our perception makes one human.

If nothing else, I supplied a demand for monsters. Without monsters, what would unite many in fear and few in courage to show these beasts they deserved no place among men? Trouble started when one of us slipped from the imagination and interacted, or trailed hoofprints of ash down the hallway en route to a bedroom.

The monster's fear in these situations is rarely discussed. The beast stalking the sleeping residents of a house is not without anxiety. Pulse quickened, thoughts sped, and there was also a sense that I was being drawn through space against my will, that I was not in full control, that my actions were directed more by innate behavioral wiring than what I had wanted to do. Of course I worried that this might go badly. Indiscriminate savagery. Carnage. Bodies strewn everywhere.

Should Stearns aggress at most I would maim him, make him whimper and repent and promise to change until he pleaded and sobbed.

In my mind, I turned Stearns's agreeable and handsome face into something more befitting a rat, mixed with something more like Dade's expression of fractured stone, stained by uprushes of bad blood and worse thought, always trying to sway, to probe, to ascertain weakness and manipulate it for his own reward, his breath run through with alcohol, his form from the neck down a flame that gave neither light nor heat, that only sought to reduce everything to ash from which he would rise like the legendary Phoenix (no relation or acquaintance of mine).

For now, I wanted the sun to rise and for Stearns to see me not as artifice but as force of nature against him, the real thing among multiplicitous imitations, the original Devil of Leeds Point.

My legs were the kicker, these lanky stalks best suited for a prim water bird weighing no more than half my wings.

The saddest thing would be hope for romance. I was not deluded. I had seen my reflection in mirrors, panes of glass, the water of clear ponds, and the horrified faces of those who saw me. Whoever invented me—Benjamin Franklin, biological chance, or some prankster god—had paid scant attention to the parts of me, at least in my devilish form, required to engage in satisfactory acts of carnality. The horns of a ram, wings of a bat, tail of a rat, but not the endowment of a horse. Temporary pleasures and immersions in another I have seen occur among animals and men, a sight that hypnotized as though the gyrations, the alteration of tender, forceful, passionate embraces, the apparent suffering of it, seemed unlike something I would enjoy, largely because I could not imagine someone deriving pleasure from proximity to my form, wrapping legs around the spot where my tail emerged or grasping my horns to better balance atop me.

To think too much of such interests strikes me not as a unique human characteristic but something shared by all species, ant to virus. The whole world was about to unleash an inexorable spate of copulation, cruel breeding, green shoots bursting from life drained of color. Imagine that happening to one's own arms or the tip of the fingers, an outburst of flora, the birth of hundreds of stems giving way to leaves and further growth around one's trunk. It's almost painful, the repeated process, I suppose. The cycles of lust, or for some the constant presence of it. But with December, it's different. It comes from a desire to assist another, to release oneself from the world in favor of another. The sensation was similar to flight, an airborne-ness that came from projecting thoughts and feelings toward another and wishing the best.

December, now, was asleep, either beside Stearns or elsewhere. Stearns was surely a human being, same as I was, same as everyone. Maybe another facet of humanity was a inclination to say that any attempt to recognize natural complexity was misguided, things were simpler than they appeared, and enemies were better off with their humanity replaced by abstractions like the serpentine flame I imagined Stearns to be. He was a fire-bearing snake, a true devil, whereas I was a man in the shape of a collage of a dozen animals.

Either my eyes had adjusted and now what I saw of the night seemed more gray than black or the sun was nearing the horizon. The snowfall had resumed, maybe enough to cover my tracks, though of course not to hide the ash prints down the hall. The servant would soon rise. And so, with the urgency of a common vampire (also no acquaintance or relation) I explored the house for a hiding spot.

II

The home seemed larger once inside it. Hallways and doors and staircases, all unfamiliar, each a different fate. Most rooms were empty, as though waiting for a purpose. All seemed too spare except for a library of sorts, with more books than I would have expected, if nothing like Larner's stacks. Globes, maps, mostly local, but also framed depictions of the continents so old the boundaries seemed estimated, cloud-shaped, labeled with the names of countries now conquered or gone.

Hours passed as the Stearns family rose with the reappearing sky, the snow still falling, the sky gray, not quite awake, not as animated as their now-moving bodies, the world still a dream. If I stood still enough when discovered, someone half-asleep might consider me a statue. The first thought would not be that I was alive. Even if I moved, the viewer would question if she were awake or mad. No one came into the study. Instead, they ate. Conversation was quiet, muffled, functional. Their mornings were a ritual of ordered movement, unlike December's upbringing and Umbria's chaotic decline.

Her voice could have been anyone's, more British and slower than the flat, quick tones of the former colonies. Unseen in the next room, I imagined her grown, her features matured, her face drawn but in good health, something almost severe in her cheekbones, her eyes creating the impression that she hovered. There was something avian about her, restrained in Stearns's transparent cage.

All conversation targeted the children, two boys, named for December's brothers. I would spare them the sight of me, if possible, and not reveal myself as they finished their porridge and eggs. From the study window I could see the snow sculpture, its details covered in the morning's accumulation. The trees hung with it. A birch stooped to the ground like a loaded catapult.

Finally, the children were allowed outside, young boys, five or six years old, just the age to admire me and know I'm not an enemy, our difference not a liability.

Stearns and December moved elsewhere. I lost track of their movements. I stood along the wall farthest from the windows, trying to camouflage myself against the bookcases, transform my skin to the earthy hue of leather-bound volumes. The maid entered and took something from a table near the entrance to the room and then left.

My tail coiled and flexed and snapped like an angry cat's. I opened my wings and almost yelled something confrontational, set again to engage brave men. Maybe that would be the way to release December from restrictions that fell on her since that day at the river.

"Stearns!" I shouted. "I am here."

Something else that makes us human: our ability to restrain our compulsions, to staunch our urges. And another: cognitive somersaulting as a consequence of slip-ups, complete presence in the moment when body and mind pursue a single goal.

Had he heard me? Had I even yelled it?

I peeked outside the door, the larger room with paintings of December and the pastoral scene and a young Stearns outside on a magnificent horse, maybe the same one Wharton had mounted, a beast that had made me reconsider my uniqueness and strength. The statue of horse and rider outside must depict young Stearns astride his first love. I had not seen the likeness in the half-light last night.

The house seemed abandoned. I heard footsteps and then a door opened and slammed. I hurried toward the sound—no one jumped from the second level to spear me. I opened the front door.

White light flooded the foyer. Snow fell over tracks of hasty retreat. December and Stearns ran from the house to a barn, stumbling all the way. December turned toward the possessed house. Stearns kept on a few strides but then stopped.

I must have been a sight in front of the house: wings spread, snout open, laughing and snorting, reveling in their retreat across the snow as December stood unwanting or unable to move.

Stearns disappeared into the servant's quarters slightly uphill, perhaps expecting December would follow or maybe he had no concern for her. He only seemed to think about distance, putting more of it between himself and his house.

I was not a hoax. I could not be simulated by craftsmen.

December held her ground and looked at me with the conviction of last night's confessional, bowed as though the image weighed on her. I felt released from the night, the darkness of the house, the restrained time in the study. All that now seemed expelled into January sunrise across this pasture, the sun a pale disc cutting through clouds to create an eerie rainbow of snow.

Far to the side of the house I heard the children playing, accompanied by the maid, not knowing that their parents had fled out the front door. If I were a base and singly motivated monster, those young ones would serve as appetizers before an adult-sized meal. Life would have been so much easier if it had been simplified as such for me, every day my ghastly desires fulfilled. There would be no questions, no caverns of the mind to crawl from. So much easier to gorge on flesh and then sleep the sleep of the over-sated.

Now what should I do? A beast damned to indecision. Surely I was invented by Franklin, his humor showing through, my wings and teeth and general external beastliness juxtaposed with criss-crossing undulations of internal rumination.

Something must have stopped her as she ran. She turned to see that it had all been real. I had appeared to her at the river and protected her once. My presence now proved she had not been mad. She had seen me again, unlike her father. Not seeing me twice perhaps caused her father's descent, or so she may have thought. Imagining the beliefs of others differentiated humans from ram, bat, kangaroo, or crane.

I took to the air and descended to the rut through the snow Stearns and December had made as they ran from me. December's expression became all rounded eyes and open mouth. I slipped but regained my balance to greet her with a polite hello.

"I don't know what to say," she said.

"*Welcome* is always a good start," I said, with a deep bow, flourishing a wing like a cape.

I had looked forward to this encounter for as long as she had. She weighed her response as though she'd spoken to me many times when alone but now was surprised to have no control over what I said.

"Welcome then, Sir. It has been quite some time since last we met."

"Your circumstances have changed for the better I presume?"

"Blessed yet not without trials."

"I hope I didn't cause too much trouble this morning."

"Your arrival was unexpected."

"I apologize for the intrusion. I rarely call on dignitaries such as your husband."

"What brings you here? I ask but am aware of the likelihood of your answer."

I began to explain that it was more than just the hoax, more even than the possession of my territory and Wharton's dream of pure water, when Stearns emerged from whatever structure he had entered. He now made his way toward us, aglow with the sort of bravery that had damned men like him throughout time. He leapt across tracks in the snow he had made in retreat, following his steps toward the mother of his children. Stearns yelled something as he approached and, with a long pistol drawn, indicated that December should move away from me. He slipped and fell to his knees, keeping the pistol in the air. As he rose, with his spare hand he took a mouthful of fresh snow as though it might energize him through this confrontation with what? What could he imagine I was? As he rumbled through the snow, I saw that he had a small scythe at his side, prepared for intimate battle if the pistol did not end me.

We watched him approach.

"I won't let him hurt you," she said.

"I'm not concerned."

"He will not stop until you are flayed."

"I had heard he was diplomatic," I said.

"I doubt he considers these circumstances negotiable."

She raised her arms and shouted for him to stop, but he did not stop until he was ten paces from us. December stood in front of me as though willing to sacrifice herself.

"He is no trouble," she said.

"His presence is trouble enough," Stearns said.

Closer now, I recognized the man in the flesh from descriptions I had heard when in the pines and the portraits. No longer rendered in oil on canvas, he was older and more unkempt, clearly not in possession of his famous composure.

"I am here to dissuade you more than ensure your demise," I said.

His reaction to my speech was expected. It wasn't the first time such articulation impressed an assailant. But he shook it off and recommitted to whatever survival instinct now held him.

"December, step aside," he said. "Step aside so I can dispatch this devil, display its form, prove legend true, and end this era of terror."

"I have hardly terrorized anyone other than your family, and for this—"

"Step aside," he shouted. His voice forced its way across the space between us.

"You mustn't," she said, "it will do no good."

"Step aside," I whispered. "Let him do his worst."

She ceded the spot between us.

It was now a sort of duel. Stearns took aim to end me. I spread my legs and threw out my chest, opened my wings, and raised my snout at a proud angle, maximizing his target. The sting of the pistol's ball would be nothing compared to the sorrow he wished to inflict on so many innocents.

Something about my posture—wings open and held behind me as though in mid-soar, yellow pelt over the muscular lobes of my chest, the thick trunk of my neck and sinews of my throat—required my life to end in service of something beyond itself. It was a moment of martyrdom. My chest offered to the enemy, I sacrificed myself for the dream of pure water. A blast and rise of smoke and before it cleared I would be splayed in the snow, no longer an earthly form, my spirit dispersed into its essential shape: legend proved true.

I raised my eyes to the snowfall and then closed them in anticipation of the shot. But he would not shoot, so I coaxed him: "Let's get this over with."

I said this, knowing there was no way he could make an actual martyr out of me and parade my corpse through the streets, considered a dragon slayer.

He inhaled and released a stream of exhaust. I knew that at the end of that exhalation when the air inside him merged with the unreal morning atmosphere he would fire. There was a violent explosion of thicker smoke, and either the cold of morning and the excitement of the day combined into an efficacious anesthesia or Stearns had missed. He stared at the pistol, disgusted.

"If you are thinking about trying again," I said, "I doubt even a blast between my eyes would end me."

He reloaded, too aggravated to hear my words as December lifted herself from the snow, having flung herself for cover. She blew on her hands, more a spectator to this duel than anyone's second.

"Give it up," she urged. "He means no harm."

"The ultimate quarry. I dare not miss."

"I fear he will kill himself for you," she said, "so considerate he has been in response to your aggression."

Stearns seemed lost in the logistics of preparing another attempt to dispatch me into legend.

I retracted my wings to express impatience with his execution. "I am humoring you," I said. "If you'd like to transfer this dispute to a realm better suited to your diplomatic skills, it would be a pleasure. Otherwise, you are outmatched with pistol and scythe or even an army at your service. In an instant I can elevate out of sight or if so moved, although contrary to my preference, I could, in less time than it would take for you to plead mercy or say a final word to your wife, provide you with a unique look at your heart as it beats for the last time in my fist before I devour it and you expire."

The pistol was loaded but he lowered it. Sense entered his panicked skull. Reckless courage gave way to sanity now that I displayed the same fingers of horn that December had surely told him had haunted her father.

"So what is your preference?" he said.

"Waste that round and we will discuss what I have in mind."

He blasted a divot in the snow. I anticipated a deployment of words meant to sway and manipulate, and, as Braddock and Vermeule had said, twist reality until only Stearns seemed upright.

"To the barn," said December. "Let's spare the children, considering your effect on my father, on me, and on my husband most likely for years to come."

"Assuming there are years to come," said Stearns. It was clear his smile had eased his ascent. Intelligent, confident, off-kilter, it helped me understand how December had accepted him.

The barn sat at the top of an easy rise. It could have hidden a brigade set to fling sturdy nets atop me before removing limbs from torso and tail from core.

"I promise not to halt your forward flow through years as long as you promise not to make sudden hostile moves or launch traps," I said.

December seemed to have reverted to the girl I had met by the river. That look of wonder. For some, my hideous form seemed a feat of nature.

The barn sheltered hay and manure, appetizing swallows, and huffing horses, the personal transportation of the era. I pictured Stearns on that black rearing horse rendered in painting and sculpture. He had lived with images of himself atop a fierce and superior animal. It must have affected his psyche, no matter how wrong so many had thought him.

I asked what became of that horse.

"Olympus lives on in generations he sired. He had been a brother to me, but my father lost him in some negotiation that required he be delivered to Wharton's stables."

"I imagine it discolored your appreciation of Mr. Wharton?"

"I pledged to take from Wharton as much as I could by manipulating all available levers. When Wharton first discovered December long ago, he rode him, and when we met, December remembered the magnificent horse. That connection made it clear we should be together, both exposed so young to mighty Olympus."

"It seems outlandish," December said, "but it is true."

"Olympus," I said.

"Wharton treated the horse with the respect of someone with the means to do so, of course, but he did not realize the consequences of wrenching such an animal from a boy my age. He cleaved my spirit from my soul, amputated the best part of my life, and only years later did he sell us a yearling from which most steeds on this estate have sprung. I felt robbed and reduced, and I blamed Wharton for possessing that unique natural resource. His skill was to determine the value of something before others began to see it. Ore, the pinelands aquifer, Olympus. This horse, anyone might appreciate, but Wharton realized how its owner and master would be associated with the animal's extraordinary attributes. For me, I loved that horse, believed it an essential part of me, and because of that love and the loss of it to Wharton, years later here you are, ready to discuss, I presume, my plans for Wharton's lands."

"It is a moving story," I said, "but why avenge someone now deceased?"

"Because the insult motivates me, and motivation, whether noble or wrathful, leads to unexpected places. I thrive on that anger, and perhaps even Wharton himself would want me to use it if it helped me secure the future for December and our children."

"But you only think of yourself and the insult but not anyone you will harm. You think of your own children but not those you seek to displace."

"Untrue!" Stearns elevated his voice. He seemed cheerful, not combative. "I want to ensure that no young ones harbor such ill feelings. It is for their health and well-being we propose to claim possession of Wharton's lands so they better serve those in need. Wharton's plan to move the water to the city cannot be critiqued on a philanthropic level, but it would have cost too much and taken too long to perfect. I heard him speak to the council about his so-called dream of pure water, and after first insulting us he touched me with his insistence that all other systems were flawed and misguided if not unethically conceived. So strident he was when it came to his convictions. Feats of engineering would be required to access quantities of water to sustain our urban areas, and even then, who knew if these plans could ever be implemented correctly. Would the water remain pure when stored in reservoirs and piped though tunnels beneath the Delaware? When it emerged into 'every Philadelphian sink,' as Wharton liked to say, would it be better than what the population now drinks to its detriment? There is a considerable resource of fresh water beneath the pines and the city needs a potable source. Wharton's plan brings the water to the people. My plan brings the people to the water. Our charitable instincts are exact. Yet my plan is easier to initiate than even the filtration plans. Why is the city faced with sickness? Because it is overcrowded. And why overcrowded? Do the poor find communal living alluring? Or do they expose themselves to it out of necessity?

"The history of the world is the history of necessity. Colonists populated this land out of necessity, cities rose out of necessity, everything can be traced to need. Great need for pure resources and improved living spaces can now be fulfilled with one bold stroke. Knowing the poor would prefer to live in nature as God intended, closer to a paradise of the primeval garden, if we transfer their need to live near industry by transferring the location of industry to regions plentiful in open space and natural resources, all needs are met, with the added benefit of improving the city by depopulating it, which is another great and pressing need obvious to everyone. The city needs saving, not by pumping water from distant lands but by transferring its occupants elsewhere. In this way, and only in this way, all needs are met for the land, the people, the industry, and the city. All benefit, and none are left wanting. And with that we return to Olympus, to a young man left wanting, a sensation I understand too well, the ache of loving and losing and forever carrying that longing in one's heart. I am not bashful to admit that the degree to which I wanted that horse returned, my need for it, made me who I am today: someone who understands what it means to want, and who, in turn, provides for everyone in need."

As he was speaking, the stable walls gave way to a vision of my home territory transformed into a productive industrial paradise. Everywhere, the aquifer was tapped so pillars of fresh water spewed into the air, and on clear days the pinelands were lousy with rainbows. Beneath their arcs, laborers from the south and the southern countries of Europe who once devolved in a stew of unbecoming humanity now skipped through open spaces en route to work and home again, all around them the natural world joined in harmony with their presence, and all flourished, radiant, the whites of their eyes as clear as crescent moons. Oh to have been born into a paradise not conceived by *the poignant ache* (Stearns's phrase) of longing caused by a horse's possession by Wharton instead of a boy.

"Would it not," I began, "be easier to improve the current conditions in the city, leaving the pines as they are, not untapped and unoccupied but reserved space open to all for enjoyment if not settlement. The area is altogether prone to wildfire, engaged in a constant process of renewing itself by conflagration. Even if the water beneath the pines extinguished those fires, the damage would devastate workers displaced there, and then where would they go and what sort of work would they find if all they have according to your model is the industry they work for, with no real opportunity to develop their own concerns or buy land of their own unless you intend to sell acres of Wharton's tracts once you have manipulated them into your possession."

Stearns tried to look away from me and concentrate on my words, for it was clear he had not quite acclimated to their source.

December, too, seemed as though she sat not on a bale of hay in a stable on her property but floated on a cloud through dreams.

"The details," he said, "of our plans for the pines and the transportation of many of its people to work camps are more complicated than you present them. We would hope to allow workers a stake in their industry, but better would be if the companies provided land and homes. Instead of owning land and, with that, the liberty to defile it, the industries would oversee everything and the workers would populate it and take pleasure and rest and refresh themselves for their daily return to their labor. As it is now, they return to squalor, where their wages are extracted in exchange for shelter of the most questionable degree. It is absolutely corrupt, this system, and yet you seem to argue in favor of its perpetuation. Much needs to be done, but if the workers leave these unsuitable shelters, these owners will give them up to the city and the city will raze them and redesign slums as parks and promenades and attractions of international regard, so Philadelphia will be known as the Paris of the Atlantic Coast, an enlightened, civilized, smaller sister city of the infinitely sprawling New York. Every consequence of our actions has been addressed including wildfires and flood, but for now, after initial planning, we are in the implementation stage, which begins by debasing the land we wish to possess and develop into a true paradise.

"By emphasizing that the beast seen throughout the region and as far away as Philadelphia itself is the Leeds Devil, once the popular imagination ignites and the value of the land and all association with it plummets, we will convince everyone, particularly Wharton's inheritors and current executors of his will, to focus on his many other concerns and pass his *dream of pure water* to us, who wish only to maximize the water's good by bringing the people to it instead of it to the people."

"But the land will still be haunted, so why would anyone occupy it?"

"We intend, quite simply, to display the captured and slain beast and proclaim the land free of devilish menace. It will be far easier to fake the capture of such a beast than it has been to craft the live examples now being released throughout the pines and neighboring cities."

December had fallen for someone like her father, someone with an eye on only one prize. I was at the center of her father's attention, and Wharton was the center of her husband's attention. The latter obsessive seemed less mad, but remove his inherited wealth and transfer his upbringing so his primary early insult were not the loss of an otherworldly horse but the sight of his own father hanging dead, and their natures seemed similarly tweaked. It was a monstrous idea to parade some simulation of me through the streets, a false corpse, once Stearns and Daley and their associates claimed possession of Wharton's land. After stamping down its value until all Wharton's people understood his dream as squashed, they would roll through the streets a glass casket inhabited by a carefully rendered composite of real dead animal and plaster casts, signaling that the pines once haunted by Wharton and the Leeds Devil were ready to participate in the march of human progress.

Such an idea required an obsessive like Stearns to conceive and execute, a creative instinct unconcerned with distinctions between life and art. Why restrict oneself to painting or sculpture when the world at large could be one's medium? Art itself was imitative, a repositioning of senses stored in memory and inaccessible areas of mind, all placed in imitation of other works and impressions of the world. But for one's work to reposition the world, not imitating anything other than visions and expectations and hopes for what life could be, what could you call such an artist? He was more than a politician if he could do it. If he could modify reality to benefit everyone he was a genius. But unlike a traditional art form, when working in the medium of life, the natural world reacts. Legislative transformation rarely arrives unaccompanied by horror. Natural order resists imposition.

The arrogance of the plan angered me as Stearns carried on, with December attending to his performance as she may have once admired a magic trick. She seemed more swayed by Stearns than he seemed susceptible to her. This perception angered me more, such possession of a natural resource of the pines. He twisted reality but if one listened and remained upright, Stearns's head revolved on an all-too-human neck.

I was a supernatural beast attempting to be human. Stearns was a human attempting to be supernatural. The former was a natural desire, albeit a difficult one. The latter has always received the harshest judgments from gods and men.

"You cannot force the people to the pines or even attempt to convince them," I said. "If it is a feasible, attractive option, perhaps they will go there themselves, but not if forced. Force them and your plans will fail."

I pictured Stearns and a dozen councilmen pushing huddled masses into ferry boats to Camden and carriages that hauled them into the woods. Who would ever trust Stearns that on the other side of the river to New Jersey eternal damnation did not await?

How long would we have finessed one another out of standstill, the loggerheads of what we thought was right? We could agree to disagree, and like well-developed humans I could wish him well and then return to Braddock and Vermeule ashamed that Stearns had not converted to reason, that his delusion was engrained in his every aspect, that I'd have had better luck transforming him into a beast like me than convincing him that the dream of pure water was necessary for all.

He kept on, now saying that one did not *own* these horses or lands but had *dominion* over them, cared for them. He clearly had no belief other than his goal, and all argument was malleable as long as it served his purpose. He agreed with me, always, but then twisted our agreement to mean something other than seeing eye to eye.

No nets dropped from the rafters. Barn cats entered and froze and then slinked along the walls. Why had I wanted to help Wharton? Was it an instinct to once again expose myself to more than the same circles of flight? Which of Franklin's virtues were now in play? Which had I internalized well enough to know that Stearns was the enemy? Despite eloquent and impassioned arguments in favor of the poor, I began to reconsider industry and resolution and justice. I would perform what I ought, what I had resolved to do, I would lose no more time doing it. I would maybe "wrong one by doing injuries" as Franklin had put it but I would do so to ensure that so many others were disturbed by nothing more than falling snow.

"December," I said. "It has been such a pleasure to see you again after so much time. I hope one day you will share with me your thoughts. For now, I ask you to allow us a moment alone."

I didn't want her to see any more horror, but then I thought of her children, and I could not allow myself this indulgence. Animal urge and human restraint battled it out as Stearns insisted that December need not leave us alone, that we three now had a bond that required her presence. I sensed that December had sensed that Stearns had sensed that the hunter was now the game. Stearns's arguments were knots I could undo the moment he tied them, but the only way to end his artful tangles was to cut right through them. The tighter and more convoluted the knot, the more it needed definitive intervention.

I showed Stearns an extended finger of horn.

December recognized the gesture. Stearns stared at it and his voice, whatever he was saying then about his vision for the water, lost track.

Even the horses now were silent, their best eye trained on the stable entrance and my outstretched finger. My eyes, my mind, my heart were certainly human, but my larynx made me capable of language, and now by devolving into a silent creature, observing Franklin's ninth commandment to avoid trifling conversation and honor Silence, I did my best impersonation of the ceiling of an Italian church Larner had shown me long ago. The outstretched fingers, the tips separated by an inch, of God and man, the gift of life, like an electric charge shot down from heaven into one of Franklin's lightning rods.

Stearns focused on my fingertip. He had heard the story of December's father's troubles, how my unusual fingers had triggered Branley's obsession. He may not have been familiar with the Michelangelo fresco, but December certainly was—an education of the sort Wharton had provided would have included a tour of the Sistine Chapel. And when she saw that famous covenant, that nearly unified arc of human flesh, her thoughts must have traveled to images conjured by her father's contact with Larner and that mysterious Mr. Merriweather. At the time, I had thought nothing of extending a finger through assorted fabrics, had no notion that a generation later I would be confronted by that man's daughter, eyes pink, rimmed with tears as she bridged the distance between us with her own finger. Pressed to the tip of my horned nail, that tiny, innocent pad absorbed the fury of the storm above them.

It was remarkably human to personify storm clouds as gods of thunder, but did Zeus or Thor ever feel humbled when their most impressive jagged streaks were channeled from their destructive goal by a simple rod of iron? There's always been a popular saying about how behind every great man there's a greater woman. If Stearns were a bachelor alone on his faux-English estate, a mad political scientist concocting nightmares to spring on an unsuspecting, impoverished populace, an evil entity without potential for ever making good, he would have been no more. Such a man would have needed to protect against assassination by numerous enemies, and so my task would be so much simpler, duller, and bloodier than it was. Instead, confronted by this mollifying touch of humanity, a woman I had protected as a girl now saved another's life, whether she knew so or not.

She may have only been possessed by the memory of her father's encounter with the same finger that made her rise and come near enough to me so that when her fingertip touched mine, she whispered her father's final words, said them so not even Stearns heard, said them with an earnestness that forced all human organs within me to sink as though soaring wings had given out.

"I am the Leeds Devil," she said.

The proliferation of false devils rampant through the pines and Philadelphia, all those false devils were smote by a single true one standing before me when she pressed that bit of flesh to the rough edge of mine.

A small change in attitude, a charge to my eyes worked wonders, bloodlessly. My most human element keyed a lock in Stearns that opened him to notions regarding the importance of survival.

Meanwhile, the legend would soon be so widely dispersed that I would be forced to relinquish all claim to self possession.

So much in motion, the widespread act uncontrollable once unleashed. Falconers strapped horns and tails to their birds. Animals were slaughtered, so many necks of innocent livestock punctured as though by vampire. Eventually it would end but there was no way to end it. I added to it, considered another element of the infestation of devils throughout the snow-blanketed region, a trick of consistent snowfall perhaps, midwinter fantasy and mesmerized delusion, something people wanted to see—*needed* to see—to make it to the turn of the season.

Nothing unites like a common enemy: I improved the common good by flying through populated regions at dusk as the falling snow assumed a life of its own.

If such flights helped or hindered was not my concern. Acceptance of self, regardless of the degree of one's peculiarity, seemed a dream of pure water as well.

I released myself from all alliances. All arguments were illusions, no water on the surface was pure, the only thing that mattered was that subterranean ocean within. From the first moments of life on, everything corrupted and pulled you out of it.

I was not the only one of my kind: all men were devils. As humans evolved from clusters of cells to fish to their current form, by some celestial or terrestrial spark that slowly yet ceaselessly modified the dominant hominid, I became the first step toward the species' future. All the rest were bizarre archaic forms, throwbacks to days we would soon prefer to forget. Yet exposure to them compelled our progress, as well as my will to propagate this new human form should ever I find a suitable partner—a willing one, more so. In short, I was Adam updated for the 20th century—and it was time to find an Eve.

III

Streaks of phosphorus, a rabbit with wings and a rat tail, antlers on animals that should not have antlers, a week of oddities, sightings, declarations, prayers, shuttered windows, absenteeism, closed factories, children escorted to school by armed parents. Never was the area so charged with terror. Cryptozoological infestation, if not a sign of the apocalypse, never signaled the best of times. The pines, as though mourning its primary owner, released its spirits into view, some even traveled as far as Philadelphia, attracted to the bustle, the pestilence, the byproducts of common plight.

A week-long storm of sightings began late Saturday with streaking white phosphorus shot into the treetops, the sound of hissing, infant wails, a Victrola needle dropped on a disc of scratched steel. Dogs growled at a winged creature hopping and screaming—they chased the beast, never to return. An enormous glowing crane took flight off the Delaware. Footprints everywhere early Sunday. Muskrat trappers stalked a winged, bipedal cow. Monday: the first awake discovered tracks circling their homes and trash scattered as though by cyclone. Word spread. Doors were latched and barricaded, areas cordoned off. Prints on rooftops. Armed men prowled streets, seeking rewards. Tuesday: a woman watched the beast on her shed and told it to shoo—it barked at her then flew off. Elsewhere, a girl fainted when she saw an odd print in the snow and her sister encountered a retriever-sized rat, with wings and a chirping bark. An unusual antlered creature appeared outside a public library. Three-toed footprints were found.

Wednesday: in Burlington, a policeman saw what he called "a Jabberwock with eyes like blazing coals." In Pemberton, a reverend saw the devil. In Haddonfield, armed men found cow tracks that suddenly left no trail. In Moorestown, a man chased a beast with "arms and hands like a monkey, face like a dog, split hooves, and tail a foot long." Elsewhere, a trolley driver saw a winged kangaroo cross the tracks. A puppy was found dead: odd tracks surrounded the body.

Thursday: in Camden, a beast peeked in the window of the Black Hawk Social Club. It turned tail when members screamed. Not much later, a trolley conductor saw a devilish kangaroo. In Trenton, a horse in a barn panicked and its owner saw a beast covered in fur and feathers, approximately the size of a canine mutt but with the facial traits of a purebred German Shepherd, its eyes emitting unmistakable anger. That same night, a city councilman heard wings flapping and discovered cloven prints on the roof—the same prints were everywhere in the city. Armed guards protected the trolleys of New Brunswick and Trenton. In Atlantic City, a telegraph worker reported that linemen saw "The Terror" on a pole. In Philadelphia, a woman saw a six-foot-tall creature covered in scaly skin. When flames spurted from its mouth, she screamed, her husband threw a rake at it, the creature flew off, and a carriage driver swerved to avoid it as it crossed Pine Street. Across the Delaware River in Camden, the beast attacked a woman's spaniel and she beat it with a broomstick, but it lingered on a fence post. Police fired and it flew off.

Panic throughout the state. Schools closed, offices shut down, workers called out sick. The mayor of Philadelphia asked the Governor to send troops to protect against the beast, and also against armed posses roaming streets ready to fire on anything odd. Was this the first instance of government protection against popular delusion in America? Had the snow falling for a week released this beast from captivity in the ground? Had an archaeopteryx risen from extinction? Was it a sign of the apocalypse, a plague of glowing eyes and wings and tails and hooves?

Casts of prints were made, none varying much, and nothing was captured or confirmed killed. A threat to the collective sanity: news rippled through nights brightened by snowfall until a raccoon or squirrel, any sort of animal, any movement half-seen, conformed to reports. The reaction was not courageous and communal but locked doors. All human endeavor (armed posse formation notwithstanding) was suspended until the storm of psychosis passed. And in its wake, there was commerce: commemorative figurines, pewter dishes, my likeness burned into a yard of linen, woodcuts, specious rubbings of gravestones depicting similar beasts, and even a sideshow at Ninth and Arch Street in Philadelphia.

Stearns had made me want to walk the city's streets with the riffraff of Europe and the Southern states, all these newcomers coaxing their voices to speak a common tongue. Wharton had acquired the pinelands for them. Stearns had had them in mind when he thought to transfer the whole shambled concatenation of woodboards and bricks, all of it always liable to collapse, east to the pines once he acquired the land and proved it empty of beasts like me. I would have liked to have seen my funeral procession: a lifeless rendition in some glass casket, the expressions of all those drawn to witness the empty shell of what once had been a phenomenal creature.

If the pines were my Eden, I wandered the city once expelled from paradise. I walked in my wedding dress, which made me seem less like a hideous beast composed of thirteen animal elements and more like a healthy young man trying to maintain an even affect, disregarding comments from all angles. So conspicuous I was in the dress, I might as well have displayed my horns and wings. The dress was not my Eve. I imagined someone else might be out there not quite as disembodied, whose physical form I could see and touch and who didn't transform my unconventional shape into something more common when I slipped her on.

Jeers meant little to me, far less than gritty slush beneath my feet. The dress worked miracles, totally transformative wonders, yes, sure, but it was neither warm nor a socially acceptable garment for a man. In human form, I was susceptible to the cold, having only a vestige of anything one might call fur. In shop windows, in the odd expanse of mirrored glass outside a merchant's, I saw soft hair atop my head, somewhat overlong in front, almost to my eyes. I recognized those eyes, sensed the familiar mechanizations of my internal organs, but all else seemed to belong to someone else.

I was impervious to everything assaultive around me, that is, until I came upon a freckled man in a green velvet suit, like some overgrown elf, his orange sideburns ablaze.

"The Leeds Devil," he said. "Alive on stage. See it for a dime."

I stopped and stared at him.

"You in the dress, blushing bride to be, any desire to see a monster more ferocious than the marriage you're bound to endure?"

Staring at him still, not reacting, he continued: "Oh pretty young wifey, come see a diversion more exciting than any likely on your honeymoon."

I winked at him. "Let me in for free," I said.

"Why's that, lassie?"

"Because I ask you," I said.

"A lovely young lady who believes she deserves all she wants, as always."

"Because I am the Leeds Devil," I said, and now I stared at him deeply, my face drained of expression.

I stepped closer as I said it. The unexpected aggression left the barker speechless for a moment until he muttered something like "All the better the more freaks inside" as I entered the darkness to glimpse myself.

On stage, no longer a torment, now the prize possession of an Arch Street theater, this poor stable renovated and outfitted with benches, a platform, a makeshift curtain stitched from strips of common fabric. The walls were black, maybe charred or painted to resemble something more rustic and decrepit than it was. A few torches lit the room. I was comparatively clean, in permanently bleached white wedding dress, preternaturally shaven, a bright horizon after an interminable night.

"In need of a groom, dearie?" said a man who followed me in from the shadows. He was ogreish and aged, rumpled, covered in dermatologic lichen.

"All set," I said.

He didn't persist, but as I settled into the third of ten rows, center stage, it seemed that everyone who entered commented as though I were the show itself.

The barker emerged, quieting a crowd that seethed as though promised boiled meat after years of scavenged roughage.

My association with some of the area's wealthiest men made all those around seem all the more different. Other than their scent and unclean fingernails—so distant from godliness, per the saying, they seemed insectile, like the obsidian shells of cockroaches, liable to scatter with the slightest movement—what differentiated the crowd was their apparent unpredictability. Wharton, Stearns, Braddock, Vermeule, even Larner before his latter years: wealth engendered self-possession, self-control, a steadiness restraining flailing movements. I do not refer only to grace, composure, posture, but everyone who had paid a dime to see some impersonation of me seemed constantly on the move, blurred, likely to twist with unexpected violence in any direction, or stand and flail, possessed of urges that released within them a moment of bliss when they gave into them.

I sat as still as I could, trying to convince my neighbors that I was a wax figure the theater displayed as complimentary amusement. My fellow theatergoers seemed engaged in a struggle with their patience, physically present in the room in a way I never could be. We were less a crowd than a coven gathered to attend a fire sermon of some notorious half-human, half-goat warlock. Presence at such an event screwed one's features toward the animalistic, everything sharpened and exaggerated and shadowed until cheeks streaked with coal and the irises of everyone's eyes contracted into serpentine slits. Whatever sun had once existed within the crowd was now eclipsed. This ragged theater elevated and exaggerated basest elements in each occupant. I'm sure each in attendance was born perfectly cherubic.

The churning, unpredictable scrum of impatience seemed set to overcome the curtain and become the show itself. The crowd was now the Leeds Devil, waiting for an up-close sight of a captured beast, heart-rending simulacra of the new Adam, and yet the oversized elfish barker did not phrase his introduction in such terms. The past he mentioned more than the future. Satan he referred to often. Adam not once. Something else he said struck me and rallied the crowd's fervor: this was the last show, the final rising curtain for this beast. The significance of this statement was understood at once. Neighbors jostled me, nudged me, streaked my garment with their filth. One even presented his cracked, unwholesome palm, seemingly indicating that I should slap my hand to his in a gesture of complicit appreciation of what we might soon witness.

The barker stepped on stage, pitchfork in hand, tiptoeing as though hunting rare game. He turned to us and held an outstretched finger to his lips, a gesture others replicated with shushes. He extended the points of the pitchfork low to the ground, as though to prick with it the curly tail of a piglet. He pretended to scan the horizon, a pantomime of the hunt. Hecklers suggested he might improve his view if the curtain were raised.

"Silence!" shouted the barker. This entrance into the room's sonic territory struck us so forcefully that even the scariest in the audience (my suitor, for example) giggled in response. "This hunt is no matter for fools. Your voices scare off the beast, the one and only Leeds Devil that has invaded our city and its outskirts and caused so many lovely young ladies to fall into our arms in fear."

He now cradled his pitchfork like a beloved. He mooned over its spears.

"Yes, my darling," he said, addressing the pitchfork in his arms, "a most unpleasant week. Every movement, every sound, a sign of impending doom."

He spun the pitchfork out so it assumed the form of a dancing partner. He held it upright in his outstretched hand. "But now you are safe for we have captured the beast. We risked our lives, coming close to losing many a limb. My associate here, in fact, lost half his arm to the jaws of the beast. Forever damn its insatiable demand for human flesh!"

A dwarfish fellow waddled on stage to gasps as he rolled up a sleeve to reveal a stump where elbow should have continued to forearm and hand. The little fellow waved with his good hand and wiggled the stump as though its ghost were visible, and then he turned offstage as quickly as he had appeared, a prop no less than the pitchfork.

"Ladies and gentleman," began the barker, "swallow all capacities to shriek, for the sight forthcoming shall do more than haunt pleasant dreams. Your most pleasing noontime reveries will roil with gales of nightmare. What you are about to witness will burn across your vision when least expected. I raise expectations, knowing all hopes you have will be exceeded, for tonight we shall impress upon your memory and soul an everlasting image of horror. All those who now look toward the exit, doubting their capacity to withstand what follows, I suggest you stay in your seat or else pay an exit fee levied to discourage you from suffering regret. Yes, you heard it right, you must pay to leave before the show is over, so assured we are you will find the proceedings, if not entertaining, at least so peculiar you will never be the same. I did not coax you inside with promises of anything more than a look at the captured Leeds Devil, but we offer tonight, for only a dime admission, something unexpected. It was never our intention for the show to end as it will tonight, but it must, and other than proceeding as we have the last few nights, we herein close the most remarkable run at this theater with an unforgettable final act, one to triumph over all others and secure our names among the immortals of the stage. And without further preamble I present the beast that unleashed itself upon us for an entire week, slaughtering livestock, terrifying schoolchildren, charging every element of the world with threat, some hundred and seventy-five years after its purported birth. I present to you not only the Leeds Devil, but also its execution and death."

In my name, some poor animal would be slaughtered for entertainment's sake. I could neither watch as the curtain rose nor avert my eyes. I faced the decision to throw off the dress and save the beast or else forever regret. Only the real thing could save the replica. If wearing a wedding dress, who would heed my calls to rationality? Within every one of them was a capacity to choose mercy if others first were swayed. They seemed to want one voice with which to pass unanimous judgment. Yet I feared their blood-lust could only be expunged by serious threat.

The curtain rose. Instead of awestruck gasps, all I heard was laughter. It was a setup, a joke. Yet the barker didn't give in. He quaked, mortally afraid of an enchained kangaroo covered in green paint. Quaker-buckle boots adorned its paws, makeshift leathery wings, a sorry rack of antlers. So pathetic was the sight that the laughter turned sympathetic for this out-of-place animal. It also seemed unwell, not just nervous or sick but poisoned by its coat of paint.

It was untenable to see yourself represented as an exotic animal slathered like this, a noble marsupial made to look like a lizard with antlers and wings. The wings were no better than the curtain, a hodgepodge of leather hanging off long sticks, nothing like the comparatively glorious imposters commissioned by Stearns.

My possessions were limited to the dress I wore, and even that was less owned than bequeathed, betrothed, beholden, and therefore every one in the audience was my social better. Not only was I a monster—famous apparently, imitated definitely—but compared with most, I was an ascetic, a monk wandering the city for alms, outside the system of exchange of funds for services rendered, or even theft. I distinguished myself from my fellows by cleanliness, basic civility, silence, a show of Franklin's commandments, but each one surely thought himself my superior, not only because of the dress I wore but because the dress was all I had. Yet I laughed with them for a moment before the tenor changed as we worried for the beast. That moment of laughter was a wave above our heads that broke and submerged us in frothy soup heading for shore. I had never before laughed in a group. What other animal did that? The crow? Pigeons? Fish? Deer? Nor did they have any possessions. Birds had their nests, wolves their lairs, but none had baubles, ornaments, objects conferring status in the flock.

Forget Franklin's thirteen commandments for moral perfection, tracking the serpentine switchbacks of consciousness, registering the existential arrhythmia of the heart, the restlessness of the soul. Perhaps seeming human only required two things: acquire possessions and lose oneself among other people. Can other people become a sort of heaven? Maybe even devils become angels when they laugh together.

Voices tangled in shouts, insults, curses:

"That's your monster, eh fatty? Stolen from the zoo?"

"The only thing to fear is it keels before we get our money's worth!"

"You should be the one in chains, nadscatter!"

The show was worth a dime for the rise it provoked. The barker and his half-armed dwarfish associate and two other teenagers now on stage mimed expressions of horror and desperation. They crossed themselves, kneeling, praying. All the while an animal struggled that none had ever seen up close. It was covered in paint with off-kilter antlers on its head, its wings like crusty wash left out to dry, a vicious choker of spikes around its neck attached to the deck by cords and a leash at the barker's feet. The cords holding the animal in place made it seem like a balloon strapped to the earth—if cut, the health of the animal would return, it would elevate, and once in the air take its revenge.

The barker and his pitchfork now came behind the beast on stage as his associates got its attention with celery stalks and carrots. He held his finger to his lips again, asking for silence, and instead received a mixed reaction of encouragement and complaint. Pitchfork held with two hands like a shovel, he crouched and stalked the beast from behind on tip toes. He thrust the spears of the pitchfork into the rump of the beast, which reared forward, activating the spikes in the choke chain. Traces of blood muddied the paint as the animal hollered in protest, a sound that struck me as almost human. The barker's associates jumped back as though struck in the sternum by the shout. Had hidden voices screamed in unison to make it sound more like a human groan, a weary guttural sigh mixed with query and complaint, a sense that the kangaroo, obviously sick, enchained, bleeding now about the neck, were a sort of Job, pleading with higher powers to respond to questions he could only articulate in a way everyone in attendance understood at once, in the universal language of suffering?

So often I had imagined myself in this position, captured and tortured and flayed, my head on the wall of someone like Stearns. No more than a trophy. Eyes replaced with multifaceted circles of glass. How much had they milked out of this poor beast, a dime per person for how many shows? Was it worth it? Did the barker not have a sick heart? Did his associates? The half-armed dwarf surely harbored some sympathy, though they all played their part, urging the crowd to provide the soundtrack, a score as violent and pathetic and guttural as the action on stage.

I had only once seen a sacrifice. Had December told Stearns about the Umbrian girls? I remembered them as innocents, but they were murderers, too young to know what they did, released into the river to bring about eternal paradise, and in a way, it had worked: order was restored and Umbria was now an overgrown archeological site awaiting excavation in the pines. But animal sacrifice was something I had never seen. Voices all around me called for it as though it were commonplace. More than ending the animal's misery, they wanted to see it butchered. By some abstract equivalency, the more brutal the sacrifice, the more completely they would be released from their miseries. How such a sight could help them I did not understand. Maybe I was too sensitive, too weak, too concerned, too able to position myself within the animal's body and anticipate the next blow?

They had promised horror, and after a moment of comedy, they now seemed ready to deliver something only seen in nightmares. For some of my compatriots in the audience, expectation of slaughter sent them through unbalanced states of agony and ecstasy, as though such soaring and descending were punishment for attendance.

The set was minimal, a black velvet backdrop in front of which stalagmites and stalactites of shards of wood were painted to resemble fleshy wet cave rock. Orange-red flames of fabric jumped in response to disturbances in the theater's atmosphere, providing an appropriately flickering setting for a devil, like the mouth of hell. Now as the beast lost blood around its neck and rump from punctures, should I intervene, hesitate, vacillate until it's too late?

Wharton would ride in on Olympus, mesmerize the audience, ensure abeyance of their madness. Imagine that horse on stage itself, painted, outfitted in wings, antlers, and clogs, chained, bleeding, sentenced to die for whose sins? Olympus would snort flames as it reared and all humanity would bow in apology.

"Rear up, beast!" My shout was lost among riotous voices.

Each in the audience improvised the show's script, each in their mind an emperor. The animal's fate rode on their thumb: salvation (up) or slaughter (down). In that uproar, only a sideways verdict could be heard, split fifty-fifty, each unworried of the other half.

"Rear up and save yourself," I said. Did it look at me then? Did an eye turn in my direction? Was some element of my voice recognized as an animal register, familiar yet not quite uncommon enough to overcome resignation to its sickness and the sense that the most merciful act would be to butcher the animal into take-home steaks for everyone?

The barker and his merry helpers made more confident by the crowd strutted like gladiators awaiting final say. Armed with pistols and axes and the long, curving swords of a sultan, their weapons served if they chose sections of the animal to open or if the crowd rebelled to thwart them. But the crowd seemed passive, the barrier too intact between audience and stage for anyone to rush them, disarm them, overwhelm them, mortally wound them, unchain the beast, cast off its accoutrement, and slip unseen into alley and early-evening mist with this sickly green kangaroo hopping behind him.

"Silence," the barker said. "Silence or else we shall stay here all night!"

The crowd settled as persistent hecklers were stifled.

"What stands before you is the Leeds Devil, brought into this world when our country was a federation of subjugated colonies, with no notion of what was in store, independence after victory over the Crown, the wrenching war with the Confederacy that decimated a generation. The beast, according to legend, emerged into the world and devoured its family. Ever since it has been reclusive, yet commonly before the arrival of fearsome nor'easters or first shots of war it appears to murder and traumatize, as though the evil in the land releases this beast from far below to alert us of imminent calamity so we can prepare. Throughout time, throughout the region, despite so many accounts of this monster, it has never been captured or held responsible for all it has done. For devouring its family, it deserves to die. For so many grave acts and minor nuisances, attacks on livestock and related lost property, it deserves to die. For its recent appearance throughout the land, frightening children and full-grown men alike, consuming more than its share of canines and felines, interrupting the proceedings of industry, inciting panic and fury and charging all with wrath, it deserves to die. Further—why it now must meet the justice it deserves—it is guilty and accountable as a representative of evil in this world ... We are God-fearing people, peaceful, whether Quaker or Catholic, Episcopalian or Presbyterian, observant or not, we believe in the goodness of God. Why might He afflict us so often with miseries derived from His hand? Storms, floods, drought, pestilence, sickness, murder, war, death, the list of miseries is long and varied and none among us are exempt from suffering. Even if all has gone well, if you account yourself blessed in health and riches and family and occupation, miseries must come or else you have not lived a proper life. As those immortal men wrote when founding our country blocks from where we now stand, *we hold these truths to be self-evident.* And yet, despite these truths and the storehouse of evidence accumulated every year of each of our lives and every decade and century of our country's existence as a nation, some malevolent force must be accountable for sickness, murder, perversion, callowness, violence, aggression, madness, foul luck, sudden death, all the horrors visited upon the people of this city and region and country, each of us born innocent yet in time so misshapen by circumstances. Our original cherubic state, so like the angels of heaven, deforms until we are aged, bloated, broken, miserable, shuffling through this world of despair into death, our release from horrors into a better place. But why do these horrors exist? Why do we endure them, and if we had a chance to end them, or at least take vengeance and stand for justice and do what we must to uphold all we know is right, would we not take it upon ourselves to hold accountable a representative, an obviously hideous beast far more odious in appearance than any of us, if it meant the opportunity to limit suffering thereafter in this world and ease the spirits of all who have suffered in this country? I say it is our duty. Today we have an opportunity. Justice is in our hands. Do any disagree? If so, let your voices be heard so your better-headed neighbors might throttle some sense into you."

He made it seem less like sport or sensationalist entertainment than something altogether human and common throughout time from Abraham to tropical island shamans tossing virgins into steaming abysses to ensure the harvest. No other animal harbored a belief that such violence might please their gods and set things straight. No other animal believed an offer of death preserved life. No wolf pack sacrificed rabbits to wolf gods. No river trout sacrificed tadpoles so more eggs hatched this year than last. Imagine the noblest multipointed buck spearing chipmunks and maybe a badger with its antlers to appease the spirit its herd worshipped. This seemed more like vigilante justice. The barker had incited random passersby to pay a dime and now they gathered into a unified whole seated in pews by torchlight won over by an unexpected burst of elocution from someone who at first had seemed like a blockhead at best.

I tasted my tears, felt them thick and strong, and through tear-filtered eyes I saw that others also cried. What was this but imitation of Christ? Sacrifice a poor animal for our sins, chief among them our compulsion to turn poor animals—kangaroo or human—into scapegoats. My legs resembled those of the crane, my feet looked like donkey hooves, but I never blamed the heron or the donkey for my appearance. Each part was distinct and essential to the whole.

In tears, I was unsure if I could intervene without sacrificing all in attendance, even those moved by the *necessary* slaughter of an innocent burdened with the weight of a nation's sins. The green paint symbolized layers of corrosion, like oxidized copper superficially corrupted by the forces of nature. To intervene might be unnatural.

The barker once again asked for a dissenting opinion as his associates smiled with knives in hand. It would be so much easier if someone told me what to do. Or if there were guidelines beyond those ten from Moses and thirteen from Franklin. Predetermined, failsafe directions for every situation including those as uncommon as the current one: a man in a wedding dress, a unique beast, watches on stage a kangaroo in danger of being murdered for everyone's sins, a beast that is not the beast as advertised but good enough to stand in and bear the brunt of whatever unbearable burden must be placed on its bewinged back. What ought a man/beast do?

It is always the same question, to act or not, to watch or be watched, to enter into life in such a way after which there is no return and no guarantee of success.

"Should we save it?"

A voice whispered in my ear, a young man about the age my body now seemed, someone able to act, morally obligated to set what he saw was right, with adequate strength and endurance to possibly achieve it. He seemed to be gathering a counter force. I looked at him but did not speak. Something was startled about him, aghast, as though this night had truly revealed a devil. His face reflected it, all goodness in him keeping the evil on the surface of his skin, disallowing further entry.

"What can we do?" I said.

He began to rise, as did half the crowd, those whose legs and spirits responded to the backstroke of scimitars on stage. Larner once told me that before God had said let there be light, a breath had been taken before the words that brought about creation. Before that spark, an influx of air was needed to make the first sound. And now as those on stage hauled back curved swords, the beast did not think of the moment of creation. It turned its head to the side, exposing more of its neck, brave martyr with chest expanded in defiance of the firing squad. All protest came then but not soon enough. Surrounding the animal, they made deep cuts. Swathes opened in the paint to reveal striated flesh now exposed to a torch-lit, theatrical, cruel atmosphere, exhilarating but more sin than sacrifice forgiving all transgression.

The hacked animal held its eyes open toward the audience, as though it were the intention of an unseen director, some sadist interested in silencing the crowd, transferring the animal's guilt for everything personal and political to everyone in the crowd. Each hack of the long curving blades opened spaces in those watching, whole segments of midsection exposed. What impatience! A sort of purely human mode of thinking, the only species that believed in magic words. *Alakazaam! Open sesame!* All the world's an oyster if the right words open the shell. The original scapegoat outcasted, the Roman practice of stoning and heckling and driving a select poor soul out of the city into the wilderness to bring about good luck. And now the one meant to bear the burden was gone, the burden dispersed onto all shoulders, or just mine, though I believed that the silenced crowd understood what had happened.

The show was over, and once returned to urban wilderness, all guilt transferred from its temporary position in a green kangaroo to everyone who was there. Not bad for a dime. I looked the animal in the eye as the crowd trailed out, overcome, assured that infinite space inside itself was all the beast could see.

IV

A slushy night, early February 1909. The air seemed thick as though there would soon be sleet. A little thicker, everyone would be blinded by it. Thicker still, it would suffocate, like airborne cotton. Cobblestones were slick. Shops were shuttered. The prevalent scent was horseshit.

A chill entered my body. My feet bare, hands and head exposed except for the light veil, I needed to wear a fur, a cape, or maybe even a rug, some burlap.

I wandered east past Independence Hall and toward the river until, on Second Street, I came upon a tavern, lit with electricity, radiating human warmth. The separation between myself and those inside could not be more clear. Frosty extremities and clouds of breath emphasized the difference in temperature. Those in there only wore shirt sleeves. Stearns's people no doubt, or those who aspired to his state, enjoying themselves as though Misery, Starvation, Infirmity, and Death pursued no one nearby.

An alley led around the tavern, a freestanding structure, a meeting house more than a hole in the wall, a place restricted by price and an air of solidity that might scare off anyone without the means or ability to affect them. All structures offered some architectural deviance to exploit. In narrow spaces concealed by shadows, this was the natural habitat of thieves, and with nothing more than all worldly sin upon my cold human shoulders, I might as well steal some clothes.

The kitchen entrance was unlocked. Potatoes, garlic, onions, carrots, turnips, cloves, a storeroom for stock ingredients. How easy when hungry to find what's necessary. Foxes take advantage of the open coop. But tonight was different, the target was disguise and warmth. Hat and coat should not be a trouble, gloves and shoes that fit would be more difficult. There was spirited music on guitar, flute, tambourine, plus some singing, not the worst way to pass an evening sheltered from the elements.

I made my way toward the merriment. I told myself I am not a beast. I am a burglar, a man in need. Someone pushed past me, a teen moving too fast to worry if the wedding-dress wearer were woman or not. I heard him muttering in the storeroom as he chopped vegetables and tossed them in a tin bowl. The cold in my extremities was now replaced by nerves. Just a swinging door between where I stood and what must be the main room. No way around it. The same boy pushed by with a tin of whatever he'd needed. I followed him through the door, riding the slipstream of his movements. I was either invisible or thought a peculiar element of the evening's help.

This was the room I had seen from the street. Nothing ostentatious about it. Electric candelabra emitted an even, odorless light. Gathered around a table a group played and sang, as others leaned close at other tables, chatting, arguing, reveling. All that could be seen in the windows was the reflection of the room. All that happened here was all there was in the world.

I followed the boy down another hallway to what must be the kitchen. I explored a staircase. At the top of the stairs was another room much like the one below, with large round tables, bare except for linen napkins, a room for private groups on busier nights, and along a wall of this room were a few doors. Like my first adventure through the endless passageways of Larner's home, every step seemed fraught. As in Stearns's house, or Daniel Leeds's, to ever find comfort in such a shelter would be trickier than proving I was a man.

Doors led to rooms, some with beds, others spare, their uses unknown, but no coats, no closets filled with what I needed. Sound from below filled the second level with an unseen presence. It's what the room below will look like when all those there were gone, only pervading the tavern for those sensitive enough to see them.

In a corner by the windows looking over the street, there was a black, formal top hat, tipped on its side as though to trap mice. I tried it on and concealed the veil beneath it, plus it made me seem a foot taller. Not what I had in mind but it worked. Its brim was wide and came down more than it should over eyebrows and ears, but it trapped some heat when stuffed with the veil.

I descended toward a song that ended as I entered. Across the room, those doors must store all their coats, but how to get there? If I sat among them, maybe I'd blend in. The table was large and round, the conversations spirited enough. Sober women refreshed drinks. The men always wanted more, the lights too bright, squinting from glare and smoke. Here I was, seated at a table with reveling instrumentalists.

The flute player whistled for me to inch closer. "Big day?"

"Wearing this to pay a bet," I said. "The chance of winning was worth the derision."

It was my stock excuse, something Larner had instructed me to say, but he never said what to say if asked what the bet was about, as the flutist now did.

"Nothing special," I said. "Fortune can be unfortunate, though I make the most of it."

The flutist relayed to the others what I'd said. "Lost a bet, but not a loser in love. Whatever money lost can be made up on the wedding night."

I did not quite catch the wave of humor that washed over them, some suggestion of salaciousness, but I smiled and bowed my head in embarrassment.

"He blushes," said another across the table. "A blushing bride."

Drink transformed their every utterance into a burst of cheer. Laughter spilled from them as though they were brimming vessels themselves.

Was this what it meant to be a man? Someone who sat at a table and shared a laugh, exhaled humor with every breath, merry and easy, unaware of or at least uncaring about assorted seriousness that forever arose around them. I was pulled toward the door, sensing this was not my place, but first I needed warmth.

"The hat is an excellent touch, my friend," said the guitarist. "Bride and groom in one. How much easier it would have been had I married myself, my first true love."

More laughs. All then aired their marital woes. It seemed a hell, the way they described it, their wives more beastly than anything I'd ever been.

"Something scratches at the windows behind the house, so she investigates and whatever's there perches on the fence out back and she runs into the snow in the middle of the night, no more than a rolling pin in hand, ready to engage in unholy combat with, at least how she described it, *this devil with wings and horns*, not so large, but not a raccoon either, she insisted, and she insisted so much I was sure it was a raccoon yet there was a thrill to her retelling, an insistence, that made me wonder."

"Better than a watchdog," said one of the men at the table.

Speech and sounds and nips from glasses all seemed orchestrated, synchronized, harmonious. For a time they compared their wives to dogs, and then wolves, and then incomparable beasts, each outdoing the last until each woman became an abstraction only meant to amuse. This was what they did: sang and drank and smoked and demeaned the mothers of their children. Idealized Eve of mine, should I ever find her, I would never talk like that. So many years an abstraction I would respect her reality should she ever appear.

"What do you lack, my love?"

I had been aware of her presence. Now that she stood before me the room blurred.

A waitress. Smiling. Able to look into eyes and play tricks on a soul.

"I lack," I said, "a coat, and if possible gloves and shoes." I held a bare foot out from under the table.

Everyone had an extraordinary laugh, as though I only existed to amuse.

"Come with me," she said, and I followed as the others at the table catcalled and whistled before serenading us with some bawdy song.

She took me past the kitchen to where all the coats and hats were arranged as orderly as the tables now covered in ash and mess.

"The hat I recognized but the dress was not familiar—and not unbecoming, I might add." She spoke as she bustled through boxes of clothing, examining some and rejecting them as unworthy, extracting others and dropping them in a pile of possibles. "I could ask about the wedding but any man flushed from the honeymoon and forced to wear his new wife's dress, unable to locate his own clothes, must be in desperate need. Something about you says you're a fugitive, but not running from anyone apt to chase you down. If your wife sent you into the night, I doubt she'll give chase."

Every once in a while she looked at me, measuring my size. "These'll do. Try them," she said.

"I don't know how to thank you."

"You won't be the first I've helped who helps me long after I forget him."

"I hope not to forget your kindness, Madame."

"*Madame* is too formal from a man in a wedding dress. Call me Renner. And you?"

I stuttered and coughed. "Yes, my name … It is …" But she held her fingers lightly to my lips.

"No name is necessary to receive clothes on a cold night. I can help you faster than you can select a false name. Your real one must relate to the trouble that sent you here."

"I wish no inconvenience."

She leaned over the box and found spats, dusted and creased by the weight of shoes that might fit me. Her chest was exposed and freckled. I admired the slope of her breasts. She shook her head to scold me for stealing a look. I blushed even more.

"Shoes, coat, undershirt, ties if necessary, and here's a less formal hat. Try this and if it's not right we'll see what else we have," she said. "Shall I turn my head as you remove the dress?"

"I need to keep her on to protect against the cold."

"Her?"

"Excuse me?"

"Do you expect to stay out all night?" she said.

"I have no expectations."

At first when I wore the dress, I could feel my wings as though they were there. But then I would flex my shoulders and roll them forward, thinking I was missing something essential. If I removed the dress as Renner suggested and returned to original form, I feared I would be wingless.

Had I mutated as a reflection of my changing mind, the kangaroo sacrifice a blow to it? If I removed the dress now, would I just be a naked man? Wharton had dreamed of pure water. Was my dream to stand naked as a man?

"Listen," said Renner. "Stick around until we close and then escort me home. I've room enough to keep you off the streets."

Here I was, wearing a stylish bowler now instead of a top hat, pants bunched at the waist and buttocks and thighs with the dress beneath it, all concealed by a navy blue coat with wide shoulders and golden buttons decorated with eagles, a sort of ceremonial military garment.

"It would be an insult to refuse."

"I like how you say it," she said. "Now let's get back to it."

We returned and the room filled with catcalls, approving nods, knowing winks. In the improvised theater of the tavern, I was the sacrificial beast, the unexpected guest making the evening's proceedings all the more memorable. Rarely was anyone new there, I imagined. Their circle seemed rounded and reinforced with time and drink, the repeated processes of revelry, suffering, recovery, et cetera, forever.

In the long window glass I saw myself and yet someone else was standing there. In the pines, without knowledge of how I had looked, unaware of anything other than what I experienced, one with the elements, here in this city now, separation from one's surroundings seemed required to cast a reflection.

I sat down at the table, in the same seat next to the flutist. Renner brought me a glass of golden liquid wheat topped with what resembled ocean foam. I dipped my lips into it and drank. It tasted the way straw smells, unexpectedly sweet and enticing, knowing its effects on others. I swallowed and everyone laughed again.

"Dear friend, you've grown old so suddenly, just a sip and you're elderly."

I had no idea what they meant until one made a show of wiping his lip.

"Excuse me," I said. "My first."

They seemed to have a storehouse of whoops at hand. As I began to speak they prepared to release them no matter what I said, for now I was guest of honor, priceless comedian, though I also wanted to say something humorless to test their reaction. I did not say, "I am the Leeds Devil" or anything of the sort, though the more I thought about it, the more it seemed impossible to state anything that might wipe the smiles from their faces like the mustache of foam across my upper lip.

"You claim it's your first beer," one said, "and yet you lost a bet that required you enter this tavern in a wearing dress. Hardly sounds like someone who's never had a beer."

I tipped my hat and smiled as, aglow, they awaited my response. All faces turned toward me, all flushed and beaming with many more sips than too many. I made the mistake of thinking before I spoke. Thoughts stalled the animal reaction needed to please.

"Yes, my first beer, never much of a drinker, lost the bet, can't explain it," I said, or something like that, my words trailing off. Seamlessness between thoughts and tongue was disturbed. A polite chuckle nevertheless escaped, a generous response as though my flailing were a kind of sophisticated humor. Another blush warmed my cheeks. Whatever wave of embarrassment went through me deepened with another long sip, and no matter how strong its pull, the undertow inside me was far too weak to draw from their good time.

"Another song," said the guitarist, clearing the air. The rhythm he began removed our need to speak.

The finest balm is music, and they seemed to play as though to forgive me. With each strum and rattle and effortless arpeggio, they restored my spirit with these repeated figures. Music to the rescue, everyone united, bewinged. The lights flickered and dimmed and extinguished, and just like that, lanterns and candles were lit. We glowed mysteriously, golden, the lights turned off so we either looked less flushed or to signal the late hour. By candlelight and lantern, men sang and stomped and spun as though with ideal partners, sometimes arm in arm with their neighbors or kicking like offended mules. Nothing needed to be sacrificed. There were no sins. The more I drank the more I was sure Renner herself, overseer of this unexpected paradise, was my one true Eve.

V

"Come on now, wake up."

I opened my eyes to see her beaming over me, hand on my shoulder, squeezing it like a melon at the market. Finding me sufficiently fresh, she helped me to my feet and led me out the door, which she locked behind her. My mouth dry, my head heavy, my eyes aflame, my nerves registered every distant clatter. She had asked me to escort her home but here I was being helped along uneven cobblestone streets. It smelled of smoke and hay and as we neared the river, a general fishiness unlike around the Mullica, more like a muddy reek, a riverbank exposed, pollutants best left underwater aired for all to smell. I hoped at first she'd pause along the way but as we moved into shanty areas so disordered they seemed somehow tangled, I hoped she'd keep moving. Some slept wrapped in coarse blankets surely stolen from horse stables or stood around fires, warming themselves, rehashing arguments they believed winnable if a perfect mix of repetition and volume were attained, the greater the emphasis the lower the chance of rebuttal, perhaps they thought, though it seemed likely no one thought much. They stood and moved their mouths, destined to recover their senses only after sleep.

She set the scene in advance of our arrival at her home, not knowing that I had slept so many nights in trees and caves, and on beaches. I admit to not being the best listener, remembering only that she had lowered expectations so when we crossed the threshold whatever appeared would seem miraculous or at least a relief.

How she made this walk alone each night I did not know, or maybe she knew everyone in town. No matter my natural abilities, there was something askew about these dense quarters, especially at night. Steam escaped from unseen sources. Shadows fell across potential assailants. The sky seemed fractured, starless, as thick, milky, winter clouds streamed low like the breath of Death. These narrow streets forced me to hunch shoulders and press tighter to my escort—the one I escorted—the one with whom I made my solitary way, arm in arm, maybe my Eve.

"Here it is," she said. "Not what you may have expected."

"I have no expectations other than spending continued time in your presence."

She touched my cheek and smiled.

She pushed the door open with her rump. It led to a private alley, passing other gloomy doors before we came to hers. She keyed it open and led me into complete darkness. A sulfurous burst and the world returned around a match in her hand. She lit a wide candle scented with honey.

"My sister and child are asleep, so we must control our voices."

Her child or her sister's? Where did it say anything about Eve having a child?

"They live with you?"

"I said so as we walked."

What else had I not heard?

"When I come in late, I sleep here. We do not have much, but it is warm, and you seem a willing guest."

She lit a lantern that filled out the contours of the place. A small bed in the corner, chairs, a Franklin stove, nothing more than what was needed.

"It is not much but it is better than some, especially in this city."

"Could you not live elsewhere?"

"We don't choose to live here, and yet living here so long, beauties emerge, wonders within those rooms, or at least the remains of my youth. Every step releases memories."

All that Stearns had said about wiping these slates clean, about moving them to beautiful new compounds in the pines, how could all these streets transform into boulevards and parks? An American Paris, he had said. So tightly compressed the lives were here, the city would need to extract them by force.

"If granted the opportunity to leave for a paradise nearer the sea," I said, "a river community in the middle of the pines where the cleanest water were everywhere and conditions were serene and sanitary, would you consider it, especially considering the child?"

"How do you know of this?" she whispered, closer to me, guiding me to the edge of her bed.

"Know what?" I said. "Only I hear you speak of the conditions here and despite sentimental connections I wonder if another habitat may be preferred."

"But," she started, and then conflicted thoughts forced chin and cheeks in alternate directions. "What you said makes me believe you have heard what's been said about this."

"Is it so uncommon, to move somewhere more natural, if granted a wish?"

"You refer to something else. I see it in your face. Your eyes turn inward as though to have nothing more to do with what you speak."

My dear Eve, let us not argue, lie down beside me, let me feel your warmth on this cold night. Your eyes are alight. Use that heat otherwise.

"Then perhaps I should ask what you know?" I said.

"Who sent you, what sort of spy, on whose side?"

"I am baffled, my dear."

"What do you know about the recent bit of open-air theater?"

"Who does not know of it? But I cannot begin to retell the horror I saw tonight."

As soon as the words escaped I knew I was in trouble. But still I told her about the sacrificed kangaroo. My story, whatever it had been, was assailable now from all sides.

"And so what of the wedding?"

"At most I attended the marriage of an innocent animal to the infinite," I said, fearing she might open the door, indicating steps I should take through it.

"*Who are you?*" she said. "I thought you were someone in need, yet now I feel you are part of some larger plan. I hear so much. Every night I am told one confession and overhear another. Those musicians are more than they seem. Those men enjoying themselves were not drunks."

"There is more to my story than a wedding that did or did not occur, a stream of stories in fact that have brought me to this spot, and I am therefore thankful for each. I have heard stories too but I am not much of an actor in them, and the dress I can explain perfectly well, but perhaps not at first."

"For now can you fit beside me?"

We lay with hands at sides, as far as we could from each other. She did not ask me to remove clothes or shoes. The long coat I kept on. She lay beside me also fully clothed. We were models for a study of doomed lovers about to be entombed. The tension between us ran back and forth, related either to her suspicion or my attraction. We lay there, my chest rising and falling in time with hers, as the flame of a candle beside the bed made its way toward its own pooled wax.

"Stearns?" I said. "Do you know him?"

"Daley, his associate, is a regular patron. He questioned your bet."

Daley, henchman of Stearns, second in command, enjoyed himself in a city he wished to conquer. Young and old at once. His cheeks and eyes, his hair and build, suggested an incomplete possession of maturity but there was weight to him, jowls, a sagging lower lip, a slumpedness to how he sat that had doubled his age. Now some emanation of him occupied the space between us.

"How well do you know him?"

"They know me better than I know them. They treat me like a cousin with whom familial propriety doesn't always apply."

"If you have a child, then you have a husband?"

"*Had* a husband, but long ago, he went missing ... It was on a hunt across the river. His friends claim to have encountered the Leeds Devil."

"The same that infested the city this past week?"

"It is not so simple," she said.

"How so?"

"Rampant fakery, of course. Plus, I've overheard and intercepted so many words and glances, exaggerated surprise about the appearances and overacted worry for everyone's safety, each of them either mocking the general sentiment or congratulating themselves for playing some role in it. So often they forget their servers are sober."

"Might you ever sell your knowledge?"

"Drink loosens lips but what so often emerges is spew."

I might have to repay her hospitality with a visit from Braddock and Vermeule or one of their friends. "Did you know Wharton?"

"I served him once or twice, but he stopped coming once we harbored enemies."

"So you know his plans?"

"I should ask: whose side are you on?"

"My own," I said.

"The same," she said.

I tried to steer the conversation more personally and ask about her parents, her child (son), her sister, her hopes, dreams, desires. No matter how well she responded to my interest I would have to reciprocate when she felt obligated to learn more about me. I would need to either respond with truth or fiction, and then I would need to arrange the fiction as it arose, wary of inconsistencies and suspicious of her suspecting me again. Expecting the inevitability of difficulty, I rolled on my side and said, "There is something you should know."

"Yes?" She mirrored my posture, head propped on hand.

"The Leeds Devil did not kill your husband. He has not killed anyone—not for many years, at least—though recently he came very close to ending Stearns's life."

"How can you know this? Or even that it exists?"

"I know he flew over the city and some may have seen him but he was only investigating the costumed beasts meant to devalue his home."

"And you know all this how?"

"Because I am him, of course."

"The Leeds Devil?"

"The one and only."

She would ignore my shape in favor of heart and soul. I would protect her sister and son and live the rest of my time as a man.

I had anticipated neither the volume nor the duration of her laugh. It was a joke, she thought, a commonplace play for her affections, like every interaction at the tavern. I felt not quite gutted. *Conflicted* perhaps? My words entered her body and transformed her into someone momentarily possessed with good cheer. She reflected my attraction for her and gave me a playful little slap to the head, as though to say *you devil you!*

I was the Leeds Devil, none other, and yet ... I tunneled through passages in the hills of the future, weaving my way, rooting out her reactions and my reactions to those reactions, but then I forgot to attend to the fact of belief.

"I have questioned my own existence, as well," I said. "Whether I am only a legend as some have said, whether any of this exists—"

"At most you're a fugitive from a home for the deranged."

"You really must understand that—"

What a strange sensation when someone covers your soft human mouth with their soft human mouth and sucks at your lips, opening them, probing tongue to tongue, exchanging breath, holding you closer. My eyes were open and my body stiffened as though the spell would break and I would come to my senses if I moved, still asleep at the tavern, dreaming of a first kiss between Eve and her Adam. I looked forward to the future of man: shorter wings and thicker legs, no tail or not much of one, face much flatter than mine, but the same eyes, the same heart.

Solid Face

LET HER HELP ME remove the dress. Her face rivaled the first I had ever seen. It took a lot not to end her horror. She beat me with a broom as I failed to clothe myself in the dress and jacket and shoes. Her sister and son entered and looked on as I burst outside, every brick wishing me harm.

I stored the dress and whatever clothes I might need, and tried to stay away from humanity. Livestock became less common over the years. But pets flourished. Mistakes were made. I wished them no harm, especially kittens and puppies, each so difficult to work up the gusto to devour, despite their scrumptious, tender flesh. Yet often enough when I encountered a lost pet in the woods ... I am not proud of myself.

The dreams of Wharton or Stearns were never realized. Maybe December had dissuaded her husband at every turn. For a time, I spied on her as she strolled with her children along the grounds, but she no longer seemed like the same person I had watched so often when young. Most of her life, she stayed on that estate. She did not, as far as I know, hang herself by the wrists or in any other way prematurely end her life. She had said she was the Leeds Devil. Such a statement may have freed her from her family's curse. When she touched my fingertip, whatever life I had lived with her ended then.

Water works along the Schuylkill River established in 1815, deemed at first a wonder of the world, faltered and were overhauled and improved a hundred years later. Fresh resources flowed through the city. Society progressed at a slow and natural pace. More forces were at work than Stearns and Wharton's. Those who Stearns had wanted to relocate to the pines fought for the country overseas, returned victorious, and lived wherever they wanted. Even Stearns yielded to the ambitions of the world to conclude dispute in bloodbath and ruin. All those arguments and strategies and power plays … and then most of the pines were sold to the state to preserve as a national forest while the federal government acquired the north end for the military base, Fort Dix.

The spread of the human virus across the surface of the earth was not in danger of being slowed by anything other than an impulse to self-destruct. As the century proceeded and human beings flirted with extinction at their own hands, I imitated Christ and Socrates, practiced humility, did what I could to fulfill Franklin's thirteenth commandment. By which I mean I did nothing at all. Any footprint or hoof print or claw or tooth mark would be unbecoming of the entity I wished to become. An angel? Something almost nonexistent, but earthly, breathing, with the blood in my wrists and desire in my loins restrained.

Humans underwent cataclysms of energy come adolescence. Perhaps I was on a longer timescale than usual, only recently entering an awkward hormonal era? I liked that thought: in *Leeds Devil years*, I was only thirteen, the equivalent of more than two hundred rotations of the earth around the sun. If I lived to be seventy in Leeds Devil years, my life would not end until roughly 2800 or later—let's say 3000—long enough for anyone. There would be time enough to breed. Plus who knew how humans would mutate or customize themselves to adapt to environmental change? It was possible that breeding would no longer involve a sexual act by the time I was twenty five in Leeds Devil years. It would be more like shopping, based on best possible genetic union. In which case, if sex were only atavistic urge and intimate pleasure, I might be in luck if ever I encountered a woman who didn't mind if I forever wore a white wedding dress to bed.

Other worries arose during my weird extended adolescence: the air felt different. It seemed less capable of sustaining my flight, as though changes had occurred at the molecular level. The ultra-sensitive undersides of my wings noticed minute fluctuations that neither eased my flight nor encouraged the gulping of streaming air as I glided. Areas northeast of the pines released the foulest muck imaginable—perhaps this caused what I had sensed. I could neither say for sure nor share my perception with others. I never discussed the matter with vultures who had also noticed a change.

In most parts of the pines, it was the same inane bird chatter and insectile chirps, the same fluctuation of sunlight and susurration of wind, the same projection of clouds across the earth in the form of shadows. Newborns arrived as cute and cuddly as ever, seedlings transformed into mischievous saplings that solidified into elms and oaks before they lost their leaves and fell, along the way experiencing every pleasure, every stress. Life hadn't changed too much because work now required a computer instead of a shovel. For the most part, day after night and day again, year after year, was marked by an inability to understand the nature of humility, the foremost human virtue, according to the country's most creative founder. What would Jesus do? Socrates? Franklin would have rendered in memorable language what he *ought to do* and then commit to the opposite: he achieved humility by discerning how far he had fallen from approaching an imitation of those he admired. To always try as hard as you can and always fall short, what better goal can there be? I tried to be human, I entered the fray, I fell short of immersion and realized it wasn't for me, yet neither was isolation nor a ricocheting position between extremes.

If I could find a nice blind girl whose hands had no sense of touch, who heard my voice and loved its tones and the eloquent flow of my speech and the significance of cooing words relayed, perhaps we would do well together? A blind girl with no family or friends might never discover my commitment to a certain gown. The first thing we'd do when a child emerged would be to put it in a cage so preternatural aggression did not cost mother and obstetrician their lives. Home schooling would follow, and then what? How would we explain when our child saw others playing ball or doing anything normal kids might do? We would need to take care that inherent belligerence did not emerge—or channel it into athletics. We'd work with the kid on the books. Committed parents we'd be. Everything that comes with raising such a child. Or maybe my oddities might soften thanks to the traditional shape of another.

At mid-century, I had heard a call to engage with the world but how could I submit to regimentation, and how explain the dress to a drill sergeant? I could have acted as my own secret weapon. Had things gone otherwise and Axis outposts were established in North America, I would have undermined their efforts. But I only knew obliquely at the time what had been at stake, sensing it along my underbelly and beneath the wings, some trouble, some disturbance that agitated the stream of cognition. On still days, when not wearing the dress, I had been like a radio receiver, tuning into hundreds of thousands of broadcast thoughts. It was something I'd become better able to do—something that was easier as people seemed to have more time for thinking, time in their cars, thoughts streaming perhaps from their radio antennae, the cars themselves conveying thought into the air where it mixed with radar, television, and then cellular waves. Endless streams of unseen chatter actively transmitted by those ever-clever humans.

Through the 1920s, '30s, '40s, even the '50s and early 1960s, I imagined visiting far-flung cities and wildernesses but never roamed far from home. In the late 1970s, when the weather was warm, I sometimes considered spending days in the dress roller-skating around Washington Square in New York City's Greenwich Village, around the fountain, through the arch there, skating in circles, slapping hands with happy strangers, moving in perfect rhythmic sync with everyone else. It would be like the best days in the pines when the oscillation of birds, weasels, insects, and the elements seemed to elevate into a well-tempered music. Washington Square would seem conducted, a music to which my movements would be sensitive, the beast in me most definitely soothed. I wondered what it would be like to become a downtown fixture, a man in a wedding dress and sparkly blue roller boots, dancing and twirling and grinning to whatever music I heard. Tourists would photograph me, journalists would interview me (I'd never give a straight answer, if only for my own amusement, though once I'd tell the truth, knowing of course the journalist would think I'm nuts), but mostly I'd celebrate what had taken me so long to achieve. But it could never last forever, of course. Whenever something essential seems grasped, you wake the next morning to empty hands. And, hence, humility.

And then one fine day in my natural form, obeying the command of instinct, I left the pines for a paradise of graceful boredoms, somewhere I might live in peace, make some friends, get to know some people, blend in among the populace, and like Christ and Socrates, release myself into legend.

A wondrous invention appeared around this time. Velcro let me evenly strap down the dress so I could wear light khaki pants and a button-down shirt and not seem out of place among shoppers at the grocery store where I worked. Bagging groceries was my first job. It was an excellent if admittedly inauspicious start, with room to grow.

Thanks to steady employment, I saved money, worked well with a positive attitude, and achieved inconspicuousness. The trouble I faced was how to meet people, make friends, and do more than absorb music, movies, books. Every day, stabilized by work, seemed mature, purposeful. Each bag was a puzzle of shape and weight, adjusted for perceived customer strength. In place of Larner or Wharton, an old man named Buxton paid me in cash at the end of every week, and otherwise left me alone if I gave him no reason to know anything more about me than my name.

I am not sure what accounted for it, whether it was nature or nurture, but something within me started to change around this time. Triggered by daily industriousness or some insidious stirring in the environment, I was afflicted in such a way that, whenever I removed the dress beneath my grocery clerk getup, I seemed to have noticeably aged. Out for an evening soar, remaining airborne seemed more difficult, as though my natural buoyancy suffered from some idiopathic weakness. I could not visit a physician and explain the problem, or consult a friendly veterinarian I'd gotten to know in the checkout aisle, or complain when talking with friends over a beer: *yeah, I hear you about getting older—by the way, a weird thing, but lately I've had some difficulty flying—ever get that? Flying used to be easier than walking, but now every takeoff feels like it could be my last.*

If ever I were to divulge this newfound ability to age, my friend Riv would be the most sympathetic and intense listener, never questioning my sanity as I revealed the particular peculiarities of my life. His eyes would brighten as he slapped the table and said *I knew it, I knew it, I knew it all along!* Such was Riv's way. Short for *Rivkin*. We referred to our friends by their surnames, like professional athletes or Army grunts. My surname they sometimes shortened to *Merry*, though they never called me Adam, which I went by at the supermarket.

Not very long ago I obtained a cheap digital camera and began one of those photograph experiments every precocious student undertakes at one point, taking a selfie every morning for a year. I wanted to create an online slideshow and send the link to the Environmental Protection Agency. If I were a rare American beast, I needed to be declared an endangered species. The photos would provide undeniable evidence of an accelerating aging rate.

My friend Kirsch might be able to connect me with someone who knew someone who knew someone with influence at the EPA. He seemed to know everyone. His online profiles were linked to thousands. He'd lived everywhere, or almost everywhere, my source of insight about what it might be like in California, Texas, Chicago, Boston, even places that rarely crossed my mind like Austin, Missoula, Louisville, Oxford (Mississippi). He was like a journeyman infielder, playing forever at the university level, more apt to take another assistant professorship or a one-year contract on an emergency basis at a new school than settle down for long-time security. There would be time for long-term security. He taught composition classes, rhetoric classes, basic college-level literacy classes. The light infantry of the university system, he took on work no one really wanted. Recently, Kirsch returned to his hometown, having had enough of travels, and also to help ease his parents into old age.

People say that towns like ours are perfect for raising children. There's room to grow, excellent schools, peace and quiet, long-established summer recreation leagues, a well-educated citizenry thanks to the university, and it's less than an hour to New York and Philadelphia, and not much longer to beaches. But safety comes first. Young parents move from cities to communities like this one if they can afford it, or they scrimp to purchase stability and security. And yet, a certain percentage of a community anywhere, no matter how small, will be naturally cruel, and if they are a charismatic percentage of an elementary or junior high population, that number can double as they sway less willful members to attend to their business.

The day I met my friend Moss, a member of this cruel few had lured him to the woods with an invitation to smoke. Once letting him have more than his share of a joint, nefarious elements of the local youth population emerged. From behind thick bushes and the stray boulder from a long-retreated glacier, some played out-of-tune violins and others beat drums. It was an improvised funeral dirge, impassioned and slow, and to young David Moss's ears, it was terrifying once it became clear that he was the focal point.

In the last twenty or so years of the 20th century, particularly in that area of New Jersey, the concept of *woods* meant more than it had fifty years before or now with all land accounted for, either developed or set aside as park or nature preserve. But for a while every wooded area seemed a perishable conduit to the past. Moss, much later on, told me about how he had grown up playing in a thin strip of woods between his housing development and a cornfield that became what's now a well-established housing development of semi-expensive homes. At the time, Moss said, you could feel the housing development coming, like it was stirring alive, the ruins of some great society that needed to be excavated and restored. Everywhere you looked it was like this extraordinary archeological dig in central New Jersey. Instead of digging up and restoring a lost civilization, when the heavy machinery arrived, they excavated the future.

Moss admitted to spending a lot of time stoned in that strip of woods, sensing its possibilities, its perishable beauty. There was always a sense, like childhood, that all this must end. Now that he was more than twice the age he had been when I first met him, Moss associated any sort of wooded area with his youth. A walk in the woods let him remember when his imagination and perception were wide open to the world. A semblance of childhood returned in such places. It was not as sentimental as it was essential, knowing which vehicles carried one back through time.

For Moss, there was the moment when that paradise of youth was lost, and it was then, perhaps the lowest point in his life, that I met him: I had been walking through those woods, exploring the territory, not many years after I had relocated to the area. When not at the supermarket where I bagged groceries, I liked to walk, especially since I had spent so much time in flight, hovering, soaring, always at a remove from the dense particularity of the ground. Walking was a revelation, the streaming detail of feet over earth. There was so much territory to explore. All the sidewalks led into one another, ball fields, parks with paths through woods, and areas where it was easy to stray from those paths and cross streams and skirt the extensive backyards of estates on the outskirts of town. I sometimes found myself lost and by nightfall considered undressing to cover the remaining ground before midnight. Especially for the first few years, I tried to live a sane, socialized, domestic life as a young man. At times I was tempted to return to my bestial past and tour the areas I'd walked at high velocity, feasting here and there whenever able, but mostly I restrained myself. I changed my thinking so walking seemed more real, more natural, than flight.

On one of these walks, I came to a clearing in a strip of woods. Something unusual jutted from the earth. Some sort of hairy plant? A strange melon-shaped bonsai tree?

I approached from behind what could only be a human head. The dirt was loosely packed. It seemed that if a body were attached, all it needed was a quick shake of the limbs to free itself. Maybe the head had no body attached except a bit of neck and, for sport, buried itself as deeply as it could and waited for animals to approach before shouting them away when they came too close. Bones of deer and birds were not uncommonly found, broken egg shells, all mixed in with the illicit detritus of teenage hangouts. Deer and delinquents, both needed a place to go.

I stood in front of the head. The eyes opened. A voice played it cool.

"Wassup?"

"How's it going?"

"Just hanging," said the head.

A dun-haired boy, with clear pale skin and a long nose slanting to the left at the end, looked up at me. The angle made his eyes seem excessively white.

Late October. The scent and crunch of fallen leaves at early-evening dusk always made me want to attend a harvest ritual come the new moon. Addled by unprecedented amounts of high fructose corn syrup and progressively effective marijuana at the time, the approach of Halloween maybe was to blame for what had happened to the head.

"So what's the plan?" I said.

"Haven't thought much about it."

Something was obviously not quite right with this head. Its eyes were no more than rosy red slits accentuated by an underlying puffiness and an expressive arch to the eyebrows, as though those woolly carets across his forehead were responsible for all his charms. Whoever had buried him surely possessed damning evidence against the head, numerous infractions of unofficial high school law. Or maybe this was an honor, an autumnal sacrifice among high-schoolers, a dedication to their gods who, if appeased, feted them with every imaginable intoxicant.

"Does this happen often?" I asked.

"Once a year. This year's me."

"A ritual?"

"A bitch when it's you."

I asked if he'd ever helped bury anyone. He said no but he'd heard of these burials.

I went to work on the poor boy's self-esteem. "It's an honor when they pick you," I said. "Means you're special."

"Some honor," he said. "A badge of dorkdom."

"You want out?"

"Maybe in a minute."

Moss wasn't too difficult to get talking. I sat cross-legged and interviewed him. His responses were delivered in staccato phrases, as though he could only manage five words before losing his breath. Maybe the earth constricted his chest.

He told me about Marshall, the ringleader responsible for his current state. Years later when Moss suggested a Jersey Devil hunt in the Pine Barrens, his description of the area's chief delinquent came to mind. Maybe our hunt for the Jersey Devil was a severely late attempt at revenge.

According to Moss, his teenage antagonist was evil incarnate, a puffy white face atop a wraith-like frame, equal parts pirate, warrior, and rock star. Some said Marshall's cousin was the singer for a glam rock band on MTV. The association lent him more than his share of notoriety. He always wore slack black jeans and rock shirts emblazoned with Black Sabbath record covers. The rumor was that Marshall once ate a downed bat in imitation of Ozzy Osborne. He was suspected of igniting the map of the world on fire in a high school history classroom. It was widely suggested that he would never earn his driver's license, either because he would never pass the test or the community would band together to deny him the privilege. As Moss excavated stray images in staccato phases, Marshall rose as the reincarnation of Branley Jukes, a late-1980s update of the cursed lineage. Branley, as far as I knew, had never been captured, but this Marshall fit the description of a Jukes, that same wide-open disrespect for everything.

The shovels used to bury him were nearby, so it was easy enough to dig him out. Moss seemed incapable of humiliation. Maybe it was that nonplussed expression Marshall and associates had targeted to change. He seemed too often to breathe through his mouth, which accounted for over-taut cheeks. For Moss, the simple intake of air may have made it difficult for him to smile or frown or let someone's words affect the composure of his face.

He brushed himself off and thanked me as though it were a formality of rescue. Might as well get it over with, he seemed to think. Not that he was ungrateful, just that he knew Marshall's subordinates would return to exhume the body after nightfall. I understood why he was a target. As he brushed himself off, I considered smacking him with the shovel and crumpling him into a shape a little easier to bury completely.

Why do some people incite such reactions without ever doing anything really offensive? It's a type of negative charisma. Maybe there's a sense that if smacked hard enough something black and white inside him would reveal itself in color?

He didn't seem to recognize me when we met again ten or twelve years later. I rented a studio efficiency above a stand-alone garage, and he rented the third floor of the main house. I had a large room with breeze and light to spare. It was a comfortable, modest tree house of a place, ideal for what I needed. A bed, a bathroom, a desk, walls lined with built-in bookshelves. Each book was an emblem of everything I had achieved. Just spending hours in my humble apartment with a book spread beneath electric light, not mouthing the words as when Larner first taught me to read, I'd never anticipated such a simple, restful, civilized, meditative, sustainable, and uniquely human activity when I passed nights on beaches or in caves. Each book was an inhabitable world. Each page absorbed me deeper. I read as though my life depended on it. The words I read were as essential as air.

Not everyone needed to read to survive, however. Moss, for example, required no deepened perception, no instruction, no experience of wonder via the ocular intake of text. He was skeptical of artifice. His heart did not seem in conflict with itself or with anyone else. His essential conflict was, I think, his lack of conflict. He didn't even seem all that interested in his own self interest. His greatest hardship each day involved motivating himself not to hit the snooze button more than once, to feed himself, to make the five-minute walk to work, where he assisted a master architect. He had earned a graduate degree in landscape design, the two years in Providence endured with the urgency of a rainy weekend in bed.

Time had transformed my neighbor. The first time he invited me to his place to watch a Yankees playoff game, he engaged the event as though the television had challenged him to a duel. He'd needed a second and so he asked me over.

"My father and grandfather were Yanks fans," he said. "People hate the Yankees, but it's a family tradition. My mom loved them, too."

This suggestion of something beyond baseball came by the fourth inning, three Pilsners into the national broadcast. I half-understood the intricacies of the game, its rules and history, having read up on it once I determined that a grocery clerk in this part of New Jersey needs to know who's pitching for the Yankees, Mets, and Phils. Otherwise, when someone initiated an affable exchange about the national pastime, I would be useless, and my uselessness would suggest a failure in terms of becoming a cog in the machine. If this required studying the game's history and box scores, it was a duty I needed to fulfill for myself and society.

Did the aardvark ever make a similar decision? The antelope? The otter?

Moss's fourth-inning confession of being a grandfathered Yankee fan suggested there was more to his story. I waited to hear what happened to his mother, to hear anything at all during commercial breaks more than invitations to help myself to chips and beer. I was a welcome guest, mirroring my host's sensitivities to the game, as his heart recalibrated itself per out, per inning, per run.

He did not ask for, and I did not offer, information about my life. I suggested a long-lapsed allegiance to the Orioles, but offered nothing else. I was wary that at any minute he might say he recognized me from the woods.

Years later, when Moss introduced the idea of hunting the Jersey Devil, enthusiastic approval from our friend Riv indicated he needed something to take himself out of himself. He was just about where one began recovering from absolute bottom. He had turned to vodka stored in his freezer more than ever before, but drink was only a symptom of the underlying emotional stressor. He was like a gymnast who sent himself into a series of aerial convolutions only to wind up splayed, calling on every force within to scrape his crumpled humanity off the floor. Francesca, Francesca, it wasn't just a matter of forgiving her. Her crime against the state of their union was unforgivable, largely because she was neither repentant nor interested in forgiveness. She was overjoyed, by all accounts, despite Riv's obliteration.

Riv seemed like someone always in need of nicknames, especially shortened ones that matched his stature. He was sturdy, with such extraordinary calf muscles they seemed like separate entities, removable lobes of leg strength. Small round glasses, an undersized face, the features drawn in around an unobtrusive nose, curly hair placed on his skull like a helmet strapped down by overlong sideburns. If he didn't shave twice a day, a goatee appeared by evening.

Otherwise so stable, he had toppled and now thought a weekend night awake, walking through the Pine Barrens, would help him endure a stage of life he entered with reluctance.

The Jersey Devil, to Riv, meant betrayal. But it also rose in his imagination as the Soviet Union. His birthplace informed everything about him, even what seemed American on the surface. As a child, he was always teased about how he was a spy, relaying sensitive information to Moscow about the elementary school lunchroom.

His positive energy synched with equal yet opposite emanations from Moss. They brought the best out in each other, a rivalry built on arguments as small as the correct pronunciation of the surname of the drummer for Rush all the way up to how the United States should allocate its forces, if at all, in the Middle East.

Slowly, slowly, these strangers transformed into friends, and I learned to enjoy beer, finding it pleasurable in moderation and also necessary, as though the effect after the third downed pint, the looseness of talk, the immediate camaraderie and elevated urgency of everything, were an epoxy, a mortar, albeit liquid and always likely to end in dehydration, anxiety, headache, regret. None of which mattered much to our friend Kirsch, whose nationwide tour of college towns could just as well have been doctoral thesis research on the anthropologic variance/significance of taverns, dives, breweries, meat markets, sports bars, and beer gardens, with special emphasis on appreciation of subtleties distinguishing beverages available therein. At worst, it could be said that Kirsch was a beer bloke, which is sort of like a wine snob in the guise of an unshowered outdoorsman too lazy to hike. He had an air of the explorer to him, what with his not always well-kept beard and excess subcutaneous insulation secured by well more than the recommended daily intake of carbohydrates in the form of wheat, barley, and hops.

The Jersey Devil, to Kirsch, was *a hoot*, a story that nicely complemented his third Smuttynose Porter. If forced to excavate something more significant than an anecdote, Kirsch might say that the beast's composite parts accounted for each of his many stops on his college tour. Or, deeper, the beast was a manifestation of the superficiality that comes from thinking that a compendium of difference is any more interesting than the same thing in the same spot with the same people in the same setting. Or, further, the beast represented something he did not want to confront in himself, and he was happy to pursue it exactly because he knew it did not exist. He had read enough to admire such a quest. A hunt for anything other than a nonexistent beast, in fact, would have been out of the question.

That I could call these men *friends* seemed a fundamental victory. They invited me along without hesitation, although I was neither architect, chemist, nor educator. They often treated me as though I were a child prone to outbursts at the slightest change in routine. Maybe they noticed I was aging faster than they were. Maybe they suspected something about me, or wondered about my history. But they never let on.

The summer before we set off to hunt the Jersey Devil in the Pine Barrens, Moss had suggested a trip to Fenway Park to see the Yankees in enemy territory. I went along with Riv and Kirsch but it meant less to us than it did to Moss. The 37-foot-tall Green Monster, the left-field wall, was the best thing about it. Otherwise, seeing the game in its natural habitat, despite all its geometric beauty, the grace and power and slow-rising drama of a pitcher's duel, seemed overwhelmed by life in the stands, a communal instinct taken to a radical and mostly benign extent. I felt like the crowd might seethe and be used for a purpose other than saluting a blast off the Citgo sign or a ground-rule double around the Pesky Pole in right. In the Bronx, I vicariously fed off Moss's association with everyone else, and so in Boston, despite wearing neutral colors, I associated myself with the enemy. I exaggerated the rowdiness, the heathen indulgence in light beer and peanuts and tube steaks, the whooping for a strikeout of the famous Yankee shortstop, a roar simulating hatred, or maybe this was as real as it got. The stadium was a theater unaware of itself as such, the crowd on stage more than it realized, especially considering the television coverage. All of it was easy enough to spill out from the stands and into the streets, intoxicated, an unruly militia dressed as one.

Maybe such a crowd, with all its individual identities subsumed by the whole, was my Jersey Devil. But that was last year. This year I figured that Moss, Riv, and Kirsch were finally on to me when they asked, having first discussed it among themselves, if I would like to hunt the Jersey Devil on the longest night of the year.

We were at the Atlas in our favorite booth. Riv, Moss, and I shared a cheap pitcher of lager, while Kirsch savored whatever concoction of hops and licorice he'd ordered. It was early June and the Phillies and Yankees played in the new stadium in the Bronx, a simulation of the classic venue where the legends played, a billion-dollar mausoleum to the past century of the sport. The interleague matchup was of special interest in New Jersey. The high-def television screen offered clearer-than-reality broadcast. Moss seemed as animated as I had ever seen him.

"Sometime this winter," he said, pausing as though each pitch required a deeper breath, "I was watching the Devils against the Flyers. Hockey, not my favorite. But it got me thinking. We all heard about the Jersey Devil growing up. Something out in the woods, down in the Pine Barrens. It'd get ya if you got too restless when stuck in traffic on 539 going down to the shore. But I never really knew too much about it. I always pictured a red leprechaun sort of thing, probably because of the hockey mascot."

He lost track of himself as his attention drifted toward the television. Riv patted the table and said, "So then what?" His back was to the screen. The Atlas wasn't a sports bar. Only a single television was visible from where we sat.

"So I did some searching, educated myself about it, I'll send you the links, but the thing I learned is you can hunt it down."

"How can you hunt down something that doesn't exist?" I said.

"That's the beauty of it, right?" Kirsch chimed in. "Like Moby Dick."

"I'm pretty sure the white whale existed," said Riv. "But I really only remember chapters about rope and ambergris and that little black boy Pip bobbing in the ocean."

"Whatever it's like," Moss said, "it has a website, hunt the jersey devil dot com: an all-night tour of the pines, a sleepless night walking around, hunting it down."

"With guns?" I asked.

"Cameras," Moss said. "You in?"

"How much?"

"A hundred each. From dusk to dawn on the summer solstice. A Saturday. We'll drink so much coffee we'll start seeing things in the woods."

"We need this," Riv said, and the way he said it, so clear and earnest, I almost offered to pay his way. He needed it, definitely, to distance himself from recent events with Francesca.

I held my pint in the air. "We need this," I said, and the others said "here, here." From that moment on there was more to this trip than driving up to Boston last year. This trip would be like a tunnel we entered and afterwards emerged transformed, hearts turned in favor of our more courageous selves.

The rest of the session was spent conceiving glorious ways to catch the beast, what we'd do if we had the chance to encounter and overcome our quarry.

Moss described it according to what he had read online. It was mostly accurate except for my legs, which were not, as Moss said, like an ostrich's. Things would have been different with ostrich legs. Now that my capabilities for flight were getting shaky, I would rely on speed and power. And because he described the horns, wings, and kangaroo-like torso well enough, I didn't correct him when he said my feet were like talons.

Whatever Kirsch drank did a number on him. He was several steps beyond us in terms of inebriation. He talked about ensnaring the beast with a mind warp, using Jedi powers, singing some sweet song to soothe the savage beast.

"The only weapon I need." He held up his cell phone. "I'll mesmerize the monster with ringtones."

He fidgeted with the interface and managed to emit the tinny introduction to Beethoven's Fifth. All our phones were on the table.

It was clear we needed this hunt, now more than ever.

I thought it would be the four of us, old friends on a mission, but then Moss's girlfriend, Corrine, and Kirsch's girlfriend, Mack, piled into Moss's Cherokee. Corinne was a lapsed tomboy who erred these days on the side of femme. To see Moss and his mate together was to understand the notion of a perfect match. If "opposites attract" always applied, these two would live on either coast.

They'd met soon after I re-met Moss. Maybe as a consequence of the few times I'd accompanied him watching sports, he realized it was time to dig out of the ruins of a long-term relationship that had ended, I later found out, around the time his mother had fallen ill. All the women around him had disappeared within six months. His world had belonged to them, and then he belonged only to himself. His father had long ago left for south Florida, more interested in the sun than his son, or so it had seemed to Moss. He'd inherited all his father's characteristics, so perhaps the father understood he'd become redundant once the son returned home to settle and design constructions and maybe raise a Moss of his own.

I always assumed he knew I knew about the burial in the woods, knew I only looked a few years older, whereas he was now twice his age. Either his lack of curiosity or his restraint let us be friends. A more inquisitive, active, curious friend would have forced me into back-flipping lies. But he rarely asked about my history, content it seemed to have someone there who was reticent to the point of being almost neurotically unwilling to offer information about his past, allowing Moss thereby to fill in the blanks with anything at all, most likely nothing. Corinne only existed in our conversations as someone he'd do something with on weekends, a fixture of the perpetual near future. The more I knew of her, the more I hoped Moss didn't turn her away. He was not quite a complete person. Just the fact of Corinne made Moss twice the man he was. Without her, how might he survive? I pictured him naked, shivering, emaciated, gray, sharp vertebrae breaching the flesh of a hunched back.

It was strange to think that Moss and Kirsch undressed with these women—more so, that these women undressed with them. Kirsch's girlfriend made eye contact when talking with me in a way that made me question the strength and the boundaries of my friendship with Kirsch. Whatever deep beauty there was in him, she'd found it, I suppose. She must have, because otherwise life was deeply unfair. What I mean is: I found her incomparably attractive. Being in her presence was a treat. Her name was McClain, shortened to Mack since before she could remember. I never caught her first name or thought to ask. But Mack was perfect. She taught at Rutgers, same as Kirsch. Journalism. Like Kirsch, she'd lived elsewhere, mostly in the west, Portland, San Fran. And then Clinton Hill, Brooklyn, and then she settled for a semblance of tranquility in central New Jersey. She was a little older than Kirsch. It was hard to tell. Maybe a quarter Iranian. Or Italian. Dark, straight nosed, distractingly pale-eyed, dimpled when she smiled, with small, lovely, perpetually coffee-stained teeth. She wrote pieces about the end of the world, or at least the extinction of humanity. Kirsch must have sensed my interest, my bashfulness, my politeness, my inability to look at her. I did what I could to conceal it, unlike Riv, who, since the end with Francesca, had become overtly goofy in Mack's presence, all too sensitive to the irresistible qualities of her charms.

I sat in the back of the Cherokee, left cheek pressed to the window like a dog, the four of us squeezed in back for the ride to the Pine Barrens. Mack sat next to me. She leaned into me on curves, her elbow dug into my thigh like an armrest.

Not so many years had passed, really, since I'd left. A blip in the grand scheme of things. It looked the same, mostly. In some spots, swatches had been converted to retirement developments, or the land seemed freshly burned. We drove along the outskirts of Fort Dix. Military activities of some sort were underway on the other side of barbed wire fences. Some seemed to involve artificial sand dunes. It was deep into growing season: melons, berries, tomatoes, sweet corn. Vegetable stands along the highway. Elsewhere, we passed one-story businesses long ago ruined, their parking lots overgrown. After an hour, we came to the town of Leeds Point and entered the Jersey Devil Tavern, where we would meet our guide.

This establishment—a dank old roadhouse updated to quasi-gastropub status—was not here when I was younger, not to mention the T-shirts and bumper stickers it sold proclaiming someone had seen me. Jersey Devil burger was the chef's specialty. Eight dollars for a filet of medium-rare Jersey Devil served on a bun, a dollar more if you wanted caramelized onions and cheese. Five bucks for a bumper sticker proclaiming sight of the beast. Twenty dollars for a T-shirt decorated with something better suited for the back of a leather motorcycle vest. An industry was based on a legend I did nothing to promote.

We still had about an hour to wait for our guide, a guy named Christian Duven, another profiteer, exploiting a nonexistent natural resource. I made enough as a grocery clerk, but what if I managed to sue for five percent of all proceeds, could I quit my job and devote my time to philanthropy, dedicate a wing to a local library in the name of Larner or Titan Leeds? This could all be exploited for far greater profit. If we all pulled together. If I allowed myself to be seen, the tourist industry would explode.

Why have I spent the last few years so humbly in a provincial college town, hardly able to spend a dollar without worrying about its effect on my finances. I should dream big, live large, make the right associations and work them, start right now by demanding to speak with the manager: The Jersey Devil burger is perfectly fine for the price, I'll say, but the margins would be better if we went into business together, maybe with this Duven guy, our tour guide for the night. I'd make regular appearances but not too many to ever become commonplace. Just enough to charge the pines with the supernatural. We'd get Mack to write about it. Moss and Kirsch and Riv and even Corrine would sell souvenirs, work on a documentary and then a biopic. And, most importantly, I could once and for all forget about ever trying to be anything other than what I am.

But then I would be responsible for the livelihoods of so many, the children of all our employees, their mortgages and college tuitions, everything would rely on busloads of tourists, the Japanese, the French, and then what if I continued to age and one day found myself as an elderly monster unable to elude a teen hopped up on too much Mountain Dew? But even then, what a sensational end to the story, a centuries old legend, older by almost forty years than the United States of America itself, wrestled to the ground and strangled by an enraged kid who thereafter appears on the cover of every national newspaper. Autopsy reports follow. Biographies. Films. Then silence forever. Or maybe Leeds Point continues to prosper and the tourists continue to come to search for a beast they know is dead, believing rumors about apparitions, a proliferation nightly through the trees, a hoax involving lights and eerie sounds, whatever it takes so happy tourists recommend the experience to friends.

I dreamed of a theme park, then humbled myself, running through the list of Franklin's commandments as we waited for our food to arrive, a pint in front of me. Moss appreciated the most glaring, least attractive qualities of the décor, the nautical theme, the nets, the plastic marlin, as though the place had been a Red Lobster that closed, only to reopen in homage to me. All commandments converged in this case on *resolution*: "Resolve to perform what you ought, perform without fail what you resolve." To perform what you ought was key. But what was I *ought*?

So far, in so many years, I have done nothing truly honorable. I tried to maintain Franklin's commandments of silence and moderation, but what else? What could I do without fear of regret, what could I do that would animate me and propel my words as I spoke, possessed by the assuredness that what I did was what I ought—resolved and confident in my resolution?

I scarfed a Jersey Devil burger and fries, observed Franklin's second virtue of silence, and otherwise prepared for a long night ahead—the shortest of the year, really. Whatever was decided tonight would flourish this summer and bear fruit by October. Jersey Devil Land maybe would become a reality with the help of Mack, inspired by her, doing what I could to impress her, what I *ought to do* a function of what she wanted me to do. Her will, my command. My only desire and ambition was to please her. She seemed like she'd seen it all and emerged unflappable, assuming that all men were monsters once a layer or two of domestication were removed. I bet she'd shrug if I showed myself to her.

Looking at Riv, at Moss, at Kirsch, at all the other men at this tavern in shorts, sneakers, T-shirts, jeans, baseball caps, beards, it seemed like a step or two down the evolutionary ladder before they once again were cavemen, hooting, pillaging, their most affectionate moments coming when they picked beetles from the hair of their mates. Could it be so hard to profit off them? Imagine all the good we could do with the money. What if the Jersey Devil Adventure Pinelands Experience were intended as a preservationist non-profit or an organization that directed its profits to rebuilding areas of cities devastated by chronic neglect. I've lived in holes in the sand, caves, orchards, and now a studio apartment above a garage. What did I need a house for, a car I can't drive? All profits from the biopic and documentary and even my life story I'd donate so others lived a better life.

What did this Jersey Devil hunt mean to us? Clearly, as we'd toasted a few weeks ago, this was something we needed, something I needed, too. At first for obvious reasons I'd found the trip to the Pine Barrens and the hunt for the legendary beast not much more than amusing, at most a rare experience with friends, at worst an ambush as they unleashed their knowledge about everything I am, taking me into the woods, netting me, subduing me with an injection, disrobing me, flaying me, displaying my skin for all to see, using tonight as a launch pad for the rest of their lifework, profiting from their association with the infernal monster of the New Jersey Pine Barrens.

A man burst into the tavern. He was tall and thin and perpetually tanned as though for breakfast every morning he ate egg whites and motor oil. Moss stood to meet him. It was Christian Duven, our guide for the night. He pumped our hands and pulled a chair from an empty table, sat on it backward, crossed his dully tattooed arms along the top of the backrest, his soiled trucker's hat turned catcher's style to better bask in our light. He was Pastor Dade and Branley Jukes reincarnated in the 21st century as a carnie tour guide, almost militaristic—paramilitaristic, that is—but also there was something sweet there, like he had a secret soft spot for the films of Nora Ephron, which revealed to him the presence of so-called heartstrings in a lean and narrow chest. He wore a black wife beater and cut-off denim jeans, a pair of heavy black boots and white athletic socks pulled over nonexistent calves. He was unshaven and the mustache area seemed to have a head start on the rest of his face. His eyes seemed black, without a hint of iris. He paid special attention to the ladies of the group. The way he leered at Mack incited in me a protective instinct. Kirsch, I felt, suspected my attraction but registered no real threat, perhaps thinking I was asexual, too ashamed of what I had said was my burned skin to ever open up to another person that way. (A problem I had in summertime was that I always needed to wear long sleeves and pants, and the solution of course was to concoct a story about being terribly burned as a child. Suggestion of fire damage preempted further questions.)

"Ladies and gentleman, my friends, oh boy are we in for a night tonight, okay. The summer solstice, best night for it. I start taking groups in January. Now that's rough. It's night by six, but now we got hours till we need headlamps or night-vision goggles."

Mention of night-vision goggles activated a gender-specific reaction. The women seemed deaf to the prospect, but night-vision goggles accessed every nascent commando reverie in the men. What would it matter what we saw, the world would be transformed and the concealed would be revealed.

Duven noticed and smiled. He had a movie star smile, and his smile also seemed to have a gender-specific response. Corrine especially mirrored it, responding to something clever relayed beyond speech.

"My friends," Duven said, "this entire area, everything you're standing on, dry as it is, it's like a camel or a cactus. That's right, filled with water. Beneath these trees and sand, there's more than enough, turn any city into Atlantis. You think you're walking on dry land but beneath your feet, not that far down, it's water. Some say that's where the Jersey Devil lives, a dinosaur throwback that's survived because he's been underground feeding off whatever's down there. But he spends a lot of time up here, too. There's more room to spread his wings and I figure the food choices might be a little more various up here."

"Does he eat humans?" Kirsch asked.

I imagined eating Kirsch's beer-battered flesh. His arms roasted in garlic.

"That's a good question, my friend. He's no vegetarian, but historically I'd say you're in much more trouble if you're a rabbit or small game like that. Us big game, there really hasn't been evidence to say he did it or not when parts of a body are found in a peat bog. He comes in handy, sometimes, sure, when we need to blame something, okay, but I don't want to tell you we're not endangering ourselves tonight. We are most definitely endangering ourselves more than, y'know, safe at home. People disappear in these pines, a few a year. They find an entrance into that underground aquifer maybe and are still exploring it now, or maybe the Jersey Devil finds 'em and swallows 'em whole or captures 'em. Lots of people say he's more vampire than anything else, happy to live off the blood of livestock until he comes across a fine human example." Duven leered now in the direction of Mack and Corinne, and it seemed clear to me—maybe to all of us then—that the only devil we had to fear that night was our guide.

A vampire? How commonplace, though I suppose we both suffer from immortality-related sadness. Or perhaps I should say I *once* had sympathized with the vampire, for something had changed in the atmosphere—or at the very least, something had changed in me. I could soon find myself transformed into an elderly man, though it seemed that all was proceeding at a slow pace. Still, each day was marked by an urgency otherwise absent from my first few centuries.

Moss was blissfully oblivious to this, of course. He set his face to serious mode: we paid for this, we're gonna get our money's worth, we'll catch the thing, definitely. Be the first to bring back more than sketchy evidence. Moss alone would domesticate the monster with a stern word and finger snap. Thereafter, his pet would vanquish whatever devils persisted from the days of Marshall, or since his mother's death.

Through my native territory at dusk, our guide drove in circles, loop-de-loops, until we left the world we knew. We fishtailed through pools of hourglass-grade sand as Kirsch and Riv exaggerated the jostling, rammed shoulders in the backseat like boys on a school bus. Duven took us to an area not far from where the ferryman had long ago helped travelers cross the river, where December and her brother ran when we first met. So much still looked the same.

Each summer, fires reduced thousands of acres to charred spikes. You could smell the burn beneath the scent of evergreen and ocean. It will all be underwater once the ice caps melt, but for now the sea seemed distant. Supernatural territory. Older pines armored in thick gray scales. Some evergreens looked like cheerleaders radically deformed by environmental tragedy: stunted limbs, crooked spines, spiky pompoms.

Moss wanted to try the night-vision goggles. "Rejects from Fort Dix? Can't wait."

Duven took us deeper into the pines. "I got a special deal worked out with a cousin works up there. Outdated technology, okay, but they come in handy."

"Reuse, recycle, et cetera," said Corinne.

"That's the motto, my dear," Duven said. They laughed though no one else did.

Riv frowned. Like someone emerged from a traumatic accident, he'd developed extrasensory perception: the ability to tune into and exaggerate the volume of what's obvious yet insignificant to others.

Riv asked why the Army didn't sweep the area and catch the beast once and for all.

"They've got bigger fish," Duven said. "But maybe we'll see the Kid tonight." He tapped a camera bag strapped to his waist like a holster. "Long as ya don't scare him off."

Silence had overtaken me. It felt like wet concrete drying in my chest after it had been poured down my throat. I had to force it from me before it set. I muttered something about how I liked thinking of a shy monster in the woods, ashamed of itself, wings demure, its ten-foot tail coiled between weird crane legs. "The poor fellow, I feel for him," I said more clearly. "Last of an endangered species, a reluctant freak of nature."

We walked deeper into the pines.

Duven was about 6'1", but seemed taller when he stood next to the stocky-short Riv. About the same age as his clients, he seemed older, as though he had lived his life with his body in such a way that showed in his face. He had spent his time in the pines, whereas my friends had floated through a college town that had become progressively touristy and expensive. A change, too, that could be seen in their faces.

"Every time I seen the Kid I knew he was there before I turned," Duven said. "Gotta turn quick to see him."

Moss jerked to the left and pointed, a spastic gesture we all expected.

Kirsch had known Moss since before they knew how to speak. Now Kirsch stared Moss down.

"I swear I saw nothing special," Moss said. He pointed again into the distance and smiled.

Duven said we'll come to a fence twenty yards down the path. We'll crawl through a hole and then there'll be water. "I've got a boat waiting," he said. The fence was five feet taller than anything we'd like to climb. As Kirsch shimmied beneath it, a twist of metal snagged his jacket. Corrine and Mack made it through just fine, helped to their feet with some show of civility by our guide. On the other side, we saw the boat.

Duven let us drift after every few paddles. Mist blurred the separation between water and sky. Moss primed his finger on the trigger of his digital camera. He once said he wished he'd somehow taken a photo of the coma that enveloped his mother.

"Reminds me of the River Styx," Riv said. "Can't wait until a three-headed dog greets us at the gates of Hell."

Duven and Riv seemed amused by each other, though the words "fuzzy foreigner" and "redneck dirtbag" also seemed about to slip from their lips. But who would ever insult the bushy-eyebrowed, bearded Rivkin? "A very *compact* man" was how, after his divorce, Kirsch told me he would describe Riv to women he knew. "So much power in his calves," he'd say. "Strongest calves in America."

Francesca was half-Cuban, with halting eyes and almost-Asian hair dyed red. Soon after Riv introduced Francesca to his friends, she went to the beach with us on a perfect August Sunday. Moss watched her walk into the shorebreak in a bikini. "She's got big plans," he said, and Kirsch said, "How do you mean?" and Moss said, "I mean she plans on being *big*." But she fought off those plans at the gym, where she met a trainer who worked her over, inside and out. Poor Rivkin, who would have thought it would all work out like this?

Black water coasted beneath us. Stars, the mist, the erratic silhouette of pines and cedars, hypnotized, dazed, coaxed into a pleasurable stupor. The whole state looked like this before they selected the extraordinary out of existence. I could emerge sans dress, walk across the water, and they'd wave.

"Hear that," Duven said. It was a command, not a question.

Our eyes followed every sound. Water against the boat. Riv's breath. Spearmint gum snapping in Moss's mouth. Kirsch ironically knocking his knees together. An oddly rhythmic distant whistle.

"A whippoorwill," Duven said. "No worries."

We drifted and listened. Mack held her breath. Duven turned an ear across the water ahead.

"See," Duven said, "folks hear *a blue jay* get real scared. But I tell you what, you hear the Kid, you'll feel it first. You'll feel it. Hear it once, your bones'll know. Trust me."

Riv opened his eyes wide as though to better absorb the atmosphere. "So great if the Jersey Devil were a lonely lady," he said. "I'd one up Francesca."

Riv had been made to feel so small when the trainer at the gym who his wife had left him for demanded the picnic basket Riv and Francesca had bought to celebrate their fifth anniversary: a picnic out at Battlefield Park under a gnarled old tree from the Revolution. That basket had meant zilch to Riv. An overpriced wicker box with latches and leather handles, bought on sale at Williams Sonoma. But once the trainer wanted it, that sentimental nothing became Priceless Symbol of What Had Been, something Riv would have fought to protect if the trainer hadn't been twice his size and ripped. Oh but once he and his mythological sweetie shot across the skies and alighted on the roof of the trainer's condo. Or maybe Riv's eyes opened wide when Duven conjured these screams because he too wanted to wail but never permitted himself such an expression of grief.

Some boating, hiking, communion with the woods, we even heard a whippoorwill.

Moss said he had thought we would only see pines and sand, pines and sand.

We floated on. Duven smoked cigarettes and doused them in a puddle at his feet. Peaceful now. Legs numb. Not ready when Duven yanked the oars for a decent pace. The boat seemed lighter the more momentum it built. The trees were larger on this side of the water: oaks more than pitch pines, or what Duven called "Jersey Bulls." He pulled the oars into the boat and let the hull slide ashore. He jumped from the boat and tied a rope around the nearest pine. We all managed to get out too without anyone falling on their faces.

"Welcome to Kalikak Beach, my friends. Named after Boney Kalikak, a recluse who stayed out here for years, eating fish and squirrels and turtles and whatnot ... Speaking of turtles, who's hungry?"

He pulled from his backpack a plastic Cool Whip container. In it were sandwiches on small dark squares of spongy wheat.

Corrine whispered to me that Duven seemed more like a Wonder Bread guy.

"Snappers pull ducks to the bottom of the river and eat them," Duven said, "then I catch the turtles. Makes for real good, greasy meat. Try some."

Riv didn't hesitate. He must have been starving. Moss muttered and took one.

Corrine asked Mack how long ago she thought Duven had caught the turtle, how long it had been unrefrigerated, how much bacteria was on it, not to mention radioactive gunk from illegal dumping and run-off from Fort Dix.

"Those ducks, too," I said.

Riv made an exaggerated *mmm*. Moss feigned nausea. Kirsch said he'd think of it as a communion of sorts. "Cheers," he said.

I tried some. Fresh, flaky, moist. Duven had even put some sea salt on it.

"Sorry for the hesitation there," Corrine said through chews. "I'm never sure where *turtle* fits into my diet."

"Can't find it up where you guys live, huh?"

Duven told us there were more oaks here because this side of the lake hadn't burned in eighty years. Oaks give up after a few burns, he said, but not the bulls. They got this built-in mechanism that shoots new limbs out after a fire dies down, before things cool. Everything's still smoking when the pines start coming back.

He led us down a narrow trail through a patch of deciduous forest. These white cedars, he said, descended from the trees used to build the desk where Thomas Jefferson wrote *The Declaration of Independence.*

Kirsch smirked. "Really?"

"Verifiable fact you can search on your internet," Duven said. "They say it's mahogany but it's stained white cedar like right over here."

The oaks gave way to pines that gave way to an open expanse of smaller, fuller, conical evergreens, like a farm of perfect Christmas trees.

"Dwarves," Duven whispered.

Nothing out here but a sky filled with constellations and a horizon glowing with civilization. "As good a spot as any," he said as he led us into the field of dwarf pines. "Put the night-vision goggles on."

Kirsch faced the trail we'd made through the dwarves out from the woods. Moss had his back to him. Everyone else faced a horizon of weirdly perfect little pines in all directions.

"Remember to feel it first," Duven said. "Feel it before you see it. Once you feel the Kid coming you'll see him. No other way, unless he swoops on you."

A bird of prey soared from the woods. Through the goggles it looked like something in a video game, a blast from an Asteroids ship.

Kirsch whispered into Mack's ear: "If we see a winged kangaroo right now, it's one of Duven's buddies, right? Bet he works with some guy crawling out a pickup right now."

"Shit," Riv said. "No way." Our tight circle of surveillance broke. He pointed into the pines. "Something bounced across that line of trees."

"C'mon," Moss said. "What'd you see?"

Riv scrunched down. He spoke slowly, clearly, restraining himself: "It was like one of those Chinese new year dragons, but smaller, with wings."

Kirsch laughed to release the tension. He pulled off the goggles.

"There!" Riv pointed to the left of where he'd pointed before. "Just its head."

Kirsch seemed to feel it now. I almost felt it, too. It was infectious when someone like Riv saw it first.

"You serious about this?" Kirsch said.

Riv stumbled through the tiny trees, rearing from what he'd seen.

Duven grabbed him. "You need to chill, my friend."

Rivkin was not chill. He tried to look past Duven's shoulder.

"It was probably nothing," Duven said. "*Shit* what's that?"

The sound came from where we had been minutes ago, toward the water. No way it was a whippoorwill. A whippoorwill's like a model train compared to that locomotive. Riv squatted and wrapped his arms around his knees. Now that he'd heard the sound he needed to make, the night filled with so much grief it knocked him down.

Mack stood on her toes, waiting for something to move. "Seeing is believing," she said. "Here I am, Kid, a rock-solid potential believer."

"You set this up," Moss said. "You set it up, didn't you?"

"I swear to you, my friend," Duven said.

"Swear to me then," Moss said. "Put your hand in mine, look me in the eye, and swear to me no one's there." Moss nodded toward his hand.

Duven pulled a pistol from his camera bag. Moss stepped back with hands up. Duven pointed toward the woods and said, "If I had a friend out there would I do this?" He took long strides toward the place the wailing came from, and then he fired into the darkness. "Would I do that, huh? Would I shoot into the woods at a friend?"

"Please I can't stand it," Riv said.

Moss kept silent, an easier target than wailing in the woods. Mack and Corinne and I froze, all set to defend ourselves by running away.

Duven returned the gun to the holster. "Never fired it before," he said. "No one's ever doubted me. Not like that." He looked at Moss. Duven's skin barely covered striated muscle that clung like dark meat on a turkey bone. "Believe me," he said. "I'm not working with people. But maybe one of you are screwing around ... Tell you what, I'll walk twenty steps off. One by one, you guys come and let me in on it."

Duven stepped through the dwarves, head down.

He called back. "Who's first? How bout my little Russian buddy?"

Riv followed the path Duven had made through the dwarves. The two men seemed like different species.

Moss and Kirsch stood side by side, arms crossed, elbows almost touching, watching Duven's conference with Riv.

"Good thing he didn't shoot you," Kirsch whispered.

"You set this up?" Moss turned so Kirsch could see he was smiling.

"I'm just along for the ride," Kirsch said. "You?"

"Never crossed my mind."

"No reason to believe that," Kirsch said.

Riv trotted back and said, "He wants to talk to you." Moss jacked his hands in his pockets and slouched in Duven's direction.

"You're just joshing, right?" Kirsch said.

"I saw something," Riv said. "Saw it enough to know it wasn't right."

Kirsch turned to talk to us. "Ya gotta trust the Rivster," he said. "He never lies without revealing the truth."

Riv was straight and honest and clear, a life preserver in the wash of it all. But after Francesca, the trainer, the picnic basket, and everything else no one knew about, maybe Riv learned to lie like a Jersey native. This is the state, after all, haunted by a kangaroo crane with ram horns, donkey hooves, and pterodactyl wings. No simple Bigfoot.

Our guide wanted to talk to Kirsch and me together for some reason, so we trotted over and slapped hands with Moss as we passed. Duven offered a shot from his flask. I politely declined but faked a swig when Duven insisted. Kirsch didn't hesitate.

"They all say they're innocent," Duven said. He pulled off his cap and ran his forearm across his brow. He had a serious widow's peak, like a volcano set to erupt down his face. "Just tell me straight," he said, "these guys tell you anything they didn't tell me?"

"Whatever's up your sleeve tonight, as long as no one gets hurt, I'm down with it." Kirsch said this quickly and clearly, as respectfully and as forcefully as he could, like a catcher settling some rattled pitcher on the mound. "Lead us around. Scare the shit out of us. Get us home. But whatever you do, don't fire that gun again."

Duven seemed to appreciate the talk. "Keep it quiet but the gun shoots blanks. Still, your friend Moss better watch it."

"Six of us against one of you," Kirsch said.

Duven took a step back. "I've got the Pines and the Kid on my side, too."

I put my goggles down and scanned the perimeter for a sign of the supernatural.

Next few hours we hiked the trails. Kirsch armed himself with pinecones, one in each hand, ready to take out the Kid's eye with one and beam him in the nuts with the other. Each time we crossed a spot that reeked of sulfur, Moss said, "Jersey Devil farts."

We sat and sipped applejack whisky and talked and listened. Every nocturnal critter that rustled the underbrush made us jump as we waited for Duven to turn his trick, expecting one scary sight and sound after another.

We walked and rested. Riv bummed smokes from Duven and put them out in the sand. We'd been hitting a thermos of milky-sugary coffee. It was almost four AM.

Moss and Duven were serious Yankee fans. They complained about management's lack of concern for middle relief.

Cranberry bogs and wild blueberry bushes everywhere. Vines of thickets, dense like kudzu, choked whole acres. Recently burned parts of the woods seemed like scrubby sand dunes, only the pines coming back.

Duven indicated the remains of an old bonfire spot. On the vernal equinox, he said, about two dozen people come here to dance around a fire. Wearing face paint, some dancers seem like white folks, he said, but others look like real Indians. Drummers beat a staggered rhythm that enlivens the dancers before they establish a common rattle. A reenactment of an annual ceremony the Lenni Lenape called "The Missing."

"It's to protect the crops and children," he said, "plus there's a surprise guest."

Not fifty feet from where we are now, he said, something emerges from the woods and runs at the fire. Beneath its arms a stretchy fabric looks like wings. It wears an expressionless mask: eyes, nose, mouth, cheeks. Not diabolical at all. It's stoic. Flat. Like one of those Easter Island stones. The rest of the body is covered in furry animal hide. Woolly white boots around its feet, it runs at the others, dances with them, and then gets a good sprint going and dives through the fire with arms outstretched, landing in a graceful shoulder roll, popping up without missing a beat. It leaps over the shoulders of smaller dancers, stretching its arms while airborne. Chanting becomes more furious as the surprise guest flings itself through the fire, over the dancers, and through the fire again.

Duven couldn't remember the original Indian name for the masked beast, but translated to English it meant "Solid Face," the centerpiece of a ceremony European settlers thought was an evil spirit, when really it protected against everything. Groups now carried out the tradition each spring. Made no difference if the drop of native blood they claimed originated in legend. If they believed it, they believed it, and it sure seemed you needed to believe it to dance around a fire all night.

Once Duven finished conjuring the action around the bonfire a season ago, Mack said "Seems like we could all use some Solid Face about now."

I decided then I would make the trip worthwhile.

"The thing is, we really need to make a Jersey Devil theme park, like Six Flags," I said. "Maybe we could bring Solid Face into it and that stuff Duven pulled with his gun—and get the Jersey Devil on board, too, of course."

I'd hardly said anything all night, just going along, naturally gravitating toward Mack. I'd been quiet so long no one really seemed able to respond to me.

At this point, we were most interested in encountering dawn's early light. The major obstacle between seeing the beast and not seeing it was staying awake. Moss was more vigilant, but even Riv's energy had sapped. Kirsch looked like he would happily curl himself up in a pile of orange pine needles. Corinne attended to Moss and then chatted ahead with Duven. I trailed behind with Mack.

"You really think we could sell this to tourists?" she said. "Staying out in the woods all night with a guide is one thing, but we'd have to do a better haunting job. Shooting into the woods, that's not quite enough."

"I have some ideas I bet you'd like."

"Like what?"

I had learned not to announce who I was, so I suggested she record what she saw in the next hour and come back to the area every once in a while so I could see her. She seemed to hear what I said but kept walking, maybe thinking I suffered from sleep deprivation.

I slowed down, letting them walk toward what Duven said was a great spot to watch the sunrise, an overhang of rock I knew from my earliest days, where I peered into a pool of water and saw human eyes surrounded by so many animal elements.

They walked ahead. Mack now seemed to accelerate as though my gift to her journalism career were a stink bomb, an irrational come-on undercut by monster breath.

I had in mind a fireworks display at dawn. This hunt must end with my appearance and, after so much time, a transformation forever after into what I've always been. Cast off this mysterious vestment of domestication that's served me so well for so long, let her go now that her lost sailor has finally returned home.

I slipped from the path and into the brush. I removed shirt and pants and shoes and tore apart the Velcro clasps holding the dress in place. This wonderful dress, I must release her into the wilderness. I let it go, hoping it would move on its own toward the sea. But all the life in it seemed used up. It just lay there.

The sun was coming now, warming the ocean, lightening the sky, as thousands of birds commenced their morning tribute. For the last time I watched the transformation of my arms into wings, fingers into horns, feet into hooves, legs into delicate stilts. I crossed my eyes to watch the elongation of my face. Never again would I assume human form, everything united beneath a skin of human flesh, aware that within lurked my true, multiple, animal self, neither human nor man nor new Adam, neither beast, nor monster, nor vampire, nor dinosaur that survived mass extinction 65 million years ago.

I am the Jersey Devil, older than America itself, cursed at birth, damned to atone for an unfortunate reaction to my entrance into the world, perhaps doing what all infants would do if they could. Instead they wail about this wall-less world encountered beyond the womb.

The dress at my feet, used to its fullest and released to return to the earth or revive itself and do as it would like, I decided to hang for now from the limb of a suitable tree, thinking I might want to use it again, or need to, especially if my plan didn't go as hoped— my dream of a theme park, profit and philanthropy, everyone on board, all those who would soon notice I was gone, presumed devoured by what they would soon see.

I could feel the effort it would take. My legs as light as ever didn't provide much elevation when I pressed off the sand with my hooves. I tried to release myself into the air as I always did, just spread my wings and enter the aerial world.

A quick hop like a buzzard on a fence yet unable to fly.

Without flight, what would I do? What *could* I do? How spend my days in my natural state in my natural habitat if I couldn't release myself into flight? How would I feed myself? How anything?

I tried again, but it was like a switch had been turned off.

I limped ahead as fast as I could and tried to propel myself into the air but couldn't leave the ground.

I released a wail now that sounded so much like the sort I had made before I learned human speech. A wail I didn't intend to make.

They had to have heard it, the way it ran unimpeded through the pines like sunrays ablating the morning fuzz. I imagined them up ahead, realizing I was gone, hearing that pitiful shriek, and now either running away or maybe even toward me.

I stepped onto the path and expected to see Moss make the connection and realize I was the one buried in the woods now, a head above the surface filled with swarming thoughts, all else buried in my current flightless form.

Did they not hear me?

Would a louder wail bring them back?

I released a fearsome roar, more like a lion's than anything else, a jet engine, and as soon as silence restored itself, all birds quiet, I tried to scamper up the path, my legs so stiff. I ran slowly, like a mechanical animal, chasing after those I wanted to see again, at least speak to them in my own voice, the one they would recognize.

Was it possible I wore the dress too long and became degraded and devolved? All the time spent as a relatively normal human had cost me the benefits of my natural animal form? Or could it all be caused by that shift in the air I'd sensed?

I hobbled down the path, the sunrise behind me, my shadow cast far in front. Wide and bat-like, I spread my wings. Ahead, I saw my friends, huddled, discussing what to do, arming themselves with cameras.

Duven smiled the smile of the wholly impressed.

Corinne's eyes opened so wide they accounted for most of her face.

Mack took a step toward me, but only one.

Kirsch peeled off and ran.

Moss stepped toward me.

Riv fell to his knees as though I were his god.

I tried to tell them it's just their friend, Adam Merriweather, humble grocery clerk, but my words again came out all at once: every urgent sentiment and confessional phrase I mustered smeared in an inarticulate slurry, a percussive bark at most, something no one would understood pertained to plans to open a theme park, an irretrievable idea in my flightless state.

The sound of my attempt to placate had the opposite effect on my friends, even Duven. So many photographs they took, stumbling back and jogging away, expressions halted as though they watched a time bomb count down to zero. Even Riv crawled to his feet toward the car.

They must have thought that whatever beast they saw had consumed their friend. And, in a way, it did feel as though whoever I had been among them roiled in my gut.

What good were these wings if I could not fly? What next would I lose?

I'm being punished for every failure over endless decades to attend to anything other than the thirteen animal elements of my body. I've allowed an unruly democracy. Much better is a dictatorship of the mind, all lower organs subordinated.

The never-ending problem of the body. How to appease it, restrain it, and, in my case, conceal it.

I returned to the dress. Forever hadn't lasted long. I began the Velcro-strap process once more, securing myself in a sort of straitjacket. Dressed again as my socially acceptable self, my flesh unified, my form unimpressive, I traveled the sand trails toward the car. Footprints slowed from a sprint to a run to a fast walk before they disappeared into tire tracks.

Would they return for me? Did they suspect that the beast they saw and their friend were the same? And, if so, how might one introduce that opinion without being shouted down?

The logical conclusion was that the beast had devoured me—the beast now something I could speak of with some remove, something I might not survive if I took off the dress again. This garment of civilization felt like home, a safe and comfortable spot devoted to longing for acceptability, all that the dress—being outerwear—enabled. Time wearing it must have caused some deep transition within that made my original form, so unique and gifted in its way, now seem in need of a supernatural mechanic.

Rising sun on the back of my neck as I followed tire tracks I presumed were Duven's, walking west, I was sure I'd hit a river or a major artery of automotive traffic. I was in New Jersey, after all, not an inescapable labyrinth in the middle of the Sahara. Never to see Riv again, Kirsch, Moss, Corinne, Mack. But why return to see them?

The laces of my left sneaker had come undone. I stopped to tie them. On one knee, out of the corner of my eye, I saw it there behind me, open wings shading the rising sun. As I stumbled from it, it sensed something beyond fear in me, almost like a perception of the afterworld that scared even this beast but then it had mercy and wailed. It seemed to express every dissatisfaction and complaint and mystification at the incomprehensible tumble and undulation of days. The sound held something unexpected in its upper registers, a semblance of hilarity or maybe a joyful shudder, suggesting that the monster knew it was serving its purpose, wings spread, complaining at terrifying volume instead of whispering in a dignified accent "Please allow me to introduce myself." It seemed smaller than I ever was in my original form. Maybe it was a Lady Leeds Devil, my better half at last discovered? If I hadn't worn the dress all those years, we could have flown off and lived happily ever after. Whatever it was, its presence meant I wasn't unique, one of many humbling realizations I nevertheless welcomed at this point. The same forces that could compel my appearance during a ferocious nor'easter in late-October 1735 could come together to create another beast, perhaps a sign of calamity to come. It ran by me as though I were irrelevant, following Duven's tire tracks along the sand trail as I passed out. Hours later, parched, sunburned, like expecting to wake in your own bed when you're stranded on a desert island, I started to make my long way home.

I needed a break from all this, especially now that it seemed like my mysterious, fearsome presence in the Pine Barrens had been replaced. Let Mack tell the tale however she needed to tell it, let her reconstruct the evening's events, compile photographs and analyze them and return to the scene to search for my body, or pieces of it, and perhaps encounter my replacement. Would they call the police? The national guard? And what about Duven? Would he keep giving tours now that he knew there was something to see in the pines beyond illusions projected by his clients' will to see?

The reverence with which Riv had kneeled, the beatific horror, the splendor of his encounter with that beast, forever he would trip through life unconcerned about Francesca: life was precious and impossible to predict. There was more to it than picnic baskets. On sand trails in the Pine Barrens, he'd heard a wail pronounced with such force it purified him, or at least set thoughts churning around another more productive, ever-mystified axle: we wanted to know and we tried to know and we thought we could know but the beauty of it was our persistent ignorance.

Kirsch now had another anecdote. The way he ran, without remembering to soothe the savage beast with a ringtone salvo from Beethoven's Fifth, suggested he was quick to run from cities, obligations, confrontations, anything other than the easiest pleasures, always running from some core disappointment, uneasiness, underlying anxiety, or more generously, he wanted to live a long, simple, joyful life. He wanted to savor the coming season's concoctions from the local craft breweries, to use the newly improved ancient intoxicant as a vehicle to carry him away as he stayed in one place—not the worst way to spend one's days, especially when he spent his nights with Mack.

In a seriously prestigious national magazine, I would read Mack's piece on the loss of a mysterious friend upon encountering the Jersey Devil. Without the appearance of her article, I doubt I would have spent so much time composing this elaboration. She had written her piece in such a way that made me think that, at least in terms of natural-born humans, she may have been my one true Eve. I was too cowardly, too awkward, too unable to convince her of this, of course. Always better to regret and imagine what would have been if one were bolder. All the obstacles of my history and vestments and Velcro straps and now my flightlessness would have served to advance our love and whatever internal clock controlled my aging would synchronize with hers as we clicked in time for fifty years, like the world's most reliable metronomes, toward some golden coda. Instead, no happy ending other than acknowledgment of my muse.

Moss and Corinne would clench more tightly together after this night, united by it. Moss would tell her more. Corinne would respect him more. Their features would merge until husband and wife looked like brother and sister. Their children would look even more like both of them. The more Moss reproduced, the more difficult it would be to reduce the man to a head in the ground. Against all future embodiments of his teenage antagonist Marshall, Moss would protect his children, and by assuming the role of protector, rid himself of torments.

I made the long way back to my adopted home town in central New Jersey. In the middle of the night I reentered my apartment, packed a bag, recovered my savings in cash, touched the spines of my favorite books, and said goodbye to my life there, sacrificed for an uncertain afterlife. I hoped that everyone at the supermarket didn't mourn too long and then I set out in whatever direction seemed most promising at the time. I let myself drift, saw the country, lived off savings, made it to California, the Pacific Northwest, and then back across the northern territories and the Midwest, to the South and back to the East Coast, before I settled down for good.

I'm not sure how much longer I have. My limbs and digits swell and stiffen, and my mind seems unwilling or unable to describe these travels. Maybe it's better to say you may have seen me riding my bicycle, an old heavy cruiser complete with a little personalized license plate on the back, or reading on a park bench or on my lunch break at a café, maybe even handwriting in notebooks, trying to control the chaos of centuries alive.

I won't confess where I've settled but I will say that my new friends seem none the wiser. I do my best to imitate Christ and Socrates but it's not difficult: humility at this point comes naturally. Pursued by curses and the consequences of actions and reactions, I have escaped into reality. No more supernatural than anyone else, I devote what's left of my life to the most remarkable species of beast on earth.

Lee Klein's fiction, essays, reviews, and translations have appeared in *Harper's, The Best American Nonrequired Reading 2007,* and many other sites, journals, and anthologies. A graduate of Oberlin College and the Iowa Writers' Workshop, he is the author of *The Shimmering Go-Between, Thanks and Sorry and Good Luck: Rejection Letters from the Eyeshot Outbox,* and *Incidents of Egotourism in the Temporary World.* He also received a 2015 PEN/Heim Translation Fund Award for his translation of Horacio Castellanos Moya's *Revulsion: Thomas Bernhard in San Salvador.* He lives in South Philadelphia and can be found online at litfunforever.com.